ELLEN SUSSMAN is the author of the nationally best-selling novels *French Lessons* and *On a Night Like This*. She is the editor of two anthologies, *Bad Girls: 26 Writers Misbehave*, a *New York Times* Editors' Choice and a *San Francisco Chronicle* bestseller, and *Dirty Words: A Literary Encyclopedia of Sex*. She has published numerous essays and short stories. Ellen teaches creative writing both in private classes and through Stanford Continuing Studies. She has two daughters and lives with her husband in northern California.

www.EllenSussman.com

D0658576

ALSO BY ELLEN SUSSMAN

French Lessons

On a Night Like This

Bad Girls:
26 Writers Misbehave

Dirty Words:
A Literary Encyclopedia of Sex

The Paradise Guest House

A Novel

ELLEN SUSSMAN

Constable & Robinson Ltd
55–56 Russell Square
London WC1B 4HP
www.constablerobinson.com

First published in the USA by Ballantine Books, 2013

First published in the UK by Canvas,
an imprint of Constable & Robinson Ltd., 2013

A copy of the British Library Cataloguing in
Publication data is available from the British Library

ISBN 978-1-4721-0224-9 (paperback)
ISBN 978-1-4721-0226-3 (ebook)

Printed and bound in the UK

1 3 5 7 9 10 8 6 4 2

Dedicated to the memory of my parents,
Gil and Shirley Sussman,
who didn't get a chance
to travel the world

Part One

2003

"And you?" the man says. "What takes you to Bali?"

The plane breaks through the cloud and there it is—an island full of dense jungles, terraced rice paddies, and glorious beaches. Jamie flinches as if someone's laid a fist into her heart.

"Vacation?" her seatmate asks when she doesn't answer.

"Yes," she lies. "Vacation."

He's already told her about his silent meditation retreat, how he can't wait, how he needs to unwind, and she thinks: Start now. She curses herself for talking to him in the first place. It was the second scotch that loosened her tongue and made her break her rule: no chats on airplanes. You can't escape.

"All by yourself?" he asks.

Jamie turns toward him. "There's an event," she says. "I was invited to attend." She absentmindedly runs her finger against the long, thin scar at the side of her face and then buries her hand in her lap.

"A wedding?" he asks eagerly. He's already told her about his wonderful Australian fiancée who will meet him at the retreat in Ubud.

"No," Jamie says. Her mind's a muddle of thoughts now. There's no reason to tell him anything. And yet she's been telling the world: I'm going back to Bali. She's loved watching the astonished faces of her friends. How brave, they've said. How bold.

The plane shudders as it passes through a cloud, and Jamie grips the arms of her seat.

"What are you drawing?" her seatmate asks. "You're good."

Jamie looks at the pad in her lap. She's sketched the island from an aerial view. She uses a light hand and few strokes—she's self-taught, and it shows. Sometimes she gets it right and sometimes—like this time—the lines don't add up.

"Doodles," she says, covering the paper with her hand. The plane tilts to reveal the southern coast of Bali. "That's Kuta Beach."

The white-sand beach stretches for miles. The center of the island is all mountain and jungle. The color is astonishing—iridescent lizard green. Then it's gone and they're immersed in a thick cloud.

"You've been here before?" he asks.

"A year ago," she says. Her palms are slick with sweat.

"When my fiancée told me to meet her here, I said, No way, José. Hundreds of people were killed in the terrorist attack last year, right? Bombs at nightclubs? But she keeps promising me it's paradise."

How the hell will this guy survive a silent meditation retreat, Jamie thinks.

And like a man who doesn't know what to do with a momentary silence, he plunges on. "Why would terrorists target Bali? I get the World Trade Center—it was the core of the economic world. But kids dancing at a club on some remote Indonesian island?"

The plane bumps along the runway. Jamie releases her breath.

"You don't have to go," Larson, her boss and her best friend, had told her yesterday when he drove her to the airport from Berkeley. "You've been through enough."

"I have to do this," Jamie told him.

"Me, I avoid pain."

She watched a sly smile appear on his craggy fifty-seven-year-old face. He had been diagnosed with pancreatic cancer three months before. His life was pain.

"You'll be okay without me?" Jamie asked.

"Who needs you? I've got two dates this weekend."

Jamie put her hand on his bald head. She calls it her Wishing Dome. She'd rub it and make three wishes. Live longer. Live better. Live.

"Call me while I'm away and charge it to the business," Jamie had said. "Don't tell the boss."

"The boss never misses a thing," Larson told her. "I know what you're up to in Bali. And it's not all about the ceremony."

"It's all about the ceremony," she insisted.

"You're going to try to find that guy," Larson said. "Gabe."

"Wrong," Jamie told him. But her voice wobbled and she turned away from him.

Now loud static fills the air, and the pilot says something inaudible over the intercom. The man next to her pats her hand. She swings her head back toward him.

"You take care now," he says. He is already standing and gathering his things. The passengers fill the aisles. When did the plane come to a stop?

Jamie nods. She doesn't move. The man disappears down the aisle.

She looks at the drawing in her lap. A couple of the lines—palm trees, though she can't remember if there even *are* palm trees in Bali—look like monsters standing guard over the island. I'm back, she tells them. Don't mess with me.

Finally she pushes herself up and out of her seat. She's the only passenger left on the plane. She reaches for her bag in the overhead bin and then moves down the aisle, rolling the suitcase behind her. A flight attendant, her vest already unbuttoned, mutters, "*Sayonara* my ass," to herself. When she hears Jamie's bag knock against the leg of a seat, she looks back.

"Oh, sorry," the young woman says. "I thought everyone was gone."

"I'd fallen asleep," Jamie lies.

The flight attendant steps aside and finds her cheery smile. "Your first time in Bali?" she says sweetly.

Jamie hesitates, then nods.

"Spiritual journey?" the woman asks.

"God, no."

The woman laughs. "Good," she says. "So you won't be disappointed. I can't tell you how many of them get on the return flight and they're surprised that they've still got all the same miserable problems they came with. I don't know what they're looking for."

"The sun," Jamie says. "That's all I'm looking for."

"That you'll find," the woman assures her. "Happy tanning."

Jamie steps through the door of the plane and pauses before heading down the metal staircase to the tarmac. The heat wraps around her and stops her breath. She's blinded by the sun, and she remembers the moment after the club was washed in a hot white blankness as if it had been erased—sound, too, had stopped—and then it all came screaming in—color, noise, pain.

"Can I help you?" the flight attendant asks Jamie.

"No," Jamie says, and she takes a step forward, into Bali.

When the taxi jolts to a stop, Jamie's eyes fly open and for a startled second she catches a glimpse of Gabe in her dream—no, it's something more tactile than visual. His fingers drawing circles on her hip. The smell of the sea in his hair. She clears her mind with a shake.

"This is the street," the taxi driver says, patiently waiting for her.

Jamie had been wide awake at the start of the hour-long taxi ride to Ubud. She watched the hordes of motorbikes fill the streets, rolling down the windows to let in thick tropical air. And then sleep kicked in. Hours on international flights and she couldn't doze for a minute. Ten minutes in a beaten-up jalopy without air-conditioning and she was comatose.

"Lady," the taxi driver says. He is young and smells of ginger. On the dashboard are prayer offerings, probably to the gods of potholed roads with too many motorbikes.

"Thank you," Jamie says, paying the man and hauling her suitcase out of the car.

She stands on the sidewalk and looks around. She hadn't visited Ubud a year ago. She'd stayed in Seminyak for the first few days. And then she spent three days in a beach cottage somewhere until she could flee the country.

But Ubud is the home of Nyoman, her host for this trip down memory lane. The foundation that organized the one-year-memorial event sent her a packet with his name, his address, and an itinerary of events leading up to the ceremony on

Sunday. She'd also received a plane ticket, a gift from the government of Bali. She'd been promised a new Bali.

Jamie looks around. People swarm the streets, and she feels the immediate exhilaration that always marks her first day in a new country. But it's mixed with something else, something that chills her skin, despite the damp heat. I can do this, she tells herself, in the same way she has argued with her mother for weeks. I have to do this.

She reads the name of the inn on the piece of paper in her hand: *The Paradise Guest House*. She walks by a series of modest cottages, some of them with stone gates and elaborate carved entrances, none of them with names.

She feels someone's eyes on her and glances across the street. A young boy sits on the dusty curb with a dog. The boy is mangy; the dog is mangier. The boy boldly keeps his eyes on her, and, after a moment, his lips curl into a grin.

Jamie offers him a weak smile in return but thinks: Leave me alone.

The boy stands, and within a second the dog stands, too. The boy is probably twelve, Jamie guesses, and wily. He looks smart and vigilant, and she suspects that he's a street kid. Or maybe all kids in Bali look like this—she has no idea. She doesn't know this country. She doesn't want to know this country.

But isn't that why she's here?

"I help you!" he calls from across the street.

"No, thank you!" Jamie calls back. She hurries down the road, pulling her small suitcase behind her.

But in a quick moment, he's beside her, offering to take the suitcase, his hand on hers. She pulls away.

"I'm fine," Jamie insists.

"You want nice hotel?" he says.

Do kids speak English here? Is it possible that last time, in one whole week, she never saw a kid in Bali? She saw the inside of her hotel room, beachside bars, a mountain trail. She saw Gabe, standing in a garden, his feet lost in a sea of orchids and gardenias.

"I don't need help," Jamie tells him, her voice a little sharp.

"Everyone need help," the boy says, smiling. In fact, he has not stopped smiling. He is tall and he smells like earth and rain. His dog walks at his side like a shadow. It's a skinny pup, some handsome mix of black Lab and border collie.

Jamie sees a sign outside a gate: THE PARADISE GUEST HOUSE. The sign is painted gold with black letters. She turns abruptly down the path, hoping to lose the boy. But he's quick and again reaches for the suitcase. He must be looking for a tip.

"I've got it," she says testily. "Goodbye."

"You are tired," the boy says. "Tomorrow you will be nicer."

She nods, unsure how to answer him. He opens the gate for her and lets her pass through.

"I see you tomorrow, miss," he says.

As he closes the gate, she takes a deep breath. Jasmine. The gate shuts out the noise from the street, the boy and his dog, the hot sun, the dust. Her eyes adjust to the cool darkness, and a tropical garden emerges, thick with banana trees, ferns, and hibiscus. She follows a path through the dense foliage to a small stone cottage with a carved wooden door, where she lifts a knocker in the shape of a monkey and lets it fall. A hollow booming sound interrupts the silence. She waits. After a moment she knocks again, louder this time.

Finally, in slow motion, the door creaks open. A man stands

there, his hair tousled, his clothes rumpled. Did she wake him? He blinks at her and runs his hand over the front of his shirt.

"Can I help you?" he asks. His accent is better than the boy's. He adjusts his crooked glasses and peers at her.

"I'm looking for Nyoman."

"You have found him."

"I'm Jamie Hyde."

He stares at her.

"I received a letter from the organization that—" Jamie pulls open her small backpack and rummages in it to find the letter.

"Yes," he says even before she finds it. A smile breaks through the creases of his face. "Welcome."

"Were you expecting me?"

The man is silent for a moment. His hand goes to his head and he rubs it vigorously. When he's done, his hair swirls on his head, making him look a little crazy.

I should leave, Jamie thinks. But, oddly, she takes a step closer to him.

"Tomorrow you are coming," he finally says.

"I'm sorry. I thought it was—"

"You are welcome in my house. I am often confused." His smile transforms his face. He's probably around forty, Jamie guesses, and though he's badly in need of some grooming, he's a handsome man.

"I can find someplace else to stay tonight." Jamie unconsciously touches the scar on her face, and then she tucks her hand in her pocket.

Nyoman reaches for her suitcase. "Follow me."

He walks past her and out the door. But instead of passing through the gate and delivering her back onto the unfamiliar streets of Ubud, he walks around the house and toward a series of small cottages behind his own. Two young boys stand in front of one of the cottages, both with toy trucks in their hands. They stare at Jamie openmouthed and then turn and run, screeching as they disappear into the trees.

"Nephews," Nyoman says. "One is loud and the other is louder."

He is still walking, past one cottage and then another. A very old woman, her skin brown and wizened, sits on the ground in front of one door. She smiles a toothless grin at Jamie.

"Grandmother," Nyoman tells Jamie. He says some quick words in Balinese to the old woman, and she giggles like a young girl.

At the fourth cottage he stops. Wisteria spills over the front of the small house, its pale violet blossoms filling the air with a pungent scent. The ground in front of the wooden door is covered with petals from the flowers, a blanket of color as a welcome mat.

"Your home," he says.

Jamie feels something unwind inside her, something that had been knotted tight since she agreed to this trip. "Thank you," she tells him.

"Now you rest. The flights are very long. I come to get you when it is time for your dinner."

He pushes open the door and light pours into the single room. Jamie can see a four-poster bed with mosquito netting draped over the top. A wooden bureau with a mirror above it sits next to the wall. The room is simple and clean.

She takes a step inside. When she turns around, Nyoman is gone.

Standing in the doorway, she gazes out at the garden. There are lights in every cottage. His family, she assumes. She smells incense and she hears a rooster crowing. It is as if she stepped behind the wall of Ubud and found a different country. My home, she thinks. Her real home in Berkeley is a room in a ramshackle Victorian house that she shares with three other adventure guides, all of them usually somewhere else in the world. And her mother had just moved out of the Palo Alto home Jamie grew up in. "I don't want all those memories of life with your father," Rose said when Jamie begged her to keep the house.

"I was there, too," Jamie said, like a pouting child. She's thirty-two; it shouldn't matter where her mother lives. Maybe it's her homelessness that makes her pine for that childhood bedroom. Or maybe it's a yearning for all those dreams only a kid can have—parents who stay together for a lifetime, boyfriends who don't die, nightclubs that don't explode.

She hears the sound of someone singing. It's a woman's voice, high and sweet. The words must be Balinese or Indonesian—Jamie can't tell the difference between the two languages. But she hears something so haunting in the song that she feels herself back away from the door. The woman's heart is broken, she thinks.

She closes the door and the sound stops.

"I made it," she says, and her mother sighs dramatically. "I'm fine, Mom."

"I know you are."

"I'm in a mountain town. I haven't seen anything yet. I slept through the taxi ride."

"And the place you're staying?"

"It's a family compound. I've got my own little cottage. Very sweet."

"Is it safe?"

"As long as the chickens don't take up guns."

"Jamie."

"Bad joke."

"What happens next?"

"I sleep."

"When is the ceremony? Do you have to go *there*?"

There is the bomb site. Jamie's mother speaks in euphemisms. *Since Bali* means since the bombing. *Did you sleep okay?* means did you escape the nightmares that chase you.

"Not till Sunday. And, no, I don't have to go to the bomb site."

"Good. Lou thinks that would be good for you, but I don't think it's something you should have to go through."

Lou is Mom's soon-to-be-husband, a psychologist and apparently an authority on Jamie, though he barely knows her. Jamie ignores most of her mother's offerings of wisdom from Lou. She's not thrilled about the marriage—Lou is twelve years older than her mom and seems like an ancient ruin to Jamie, parts of him chipping and peeling away day by day. Everyone else's mom turned cougar and caught a hot young thing. Couldn't Rose ever follow a trend?

When Jamie asked her why they were getting married, Rose said, "He's very good to me." Which means: *Your father wasn't good to me.* Which means: *He'll never cheat on me. I'll never risk getting hurt like that again, even if it means I marry a relic.*

"Will you promise me you'll be safe?" Rose says.

"I'll be fine."

"That's always been your gift and your curse."

"What's that?" Jamie asks, suddenly impatient.

"You're invincible," Rose announces. Jamie has heard it all before. She knows what comes next. "No one's invincible."

"Good night, Mom."

"I love you."

"Love you, too."

Jamie hangs up the phone, bombarded by the complicated swirl of emotions that she feels every time she talks to her mother. She climbs onto her bed in the cottage, tucks in the mosquito netting, and leans back against the wooden head-board. If she puts her head down, she'll be sleeping in seconds. Her arm hurts, a deep ache at the elbow that was broken. The doctors have told her that it healed perfectly. The pain comes when she's tired.

She reaches for her sketch pad at the side of her bed, then turns the page and looks out the window. A wall of wisteria drapes over the cottage next door. She tries to sketch it with quick strokes, the flowers a rush of smudged pencil—and when she stops she takes a look at what she's done. Not bad. She's captured something primordial in the drawing—the flowers consume the cottage.

For Larson, she writes at the top of the page. She gives the drawing a title: *Nature Wins.*

She lifts her cellphone and clicks on his name.

"Out climbing mountains," his voice message tells her. "Leave a message."

She smiles. He recorded that voice message the day he started chemo. Larson's the one who sent her to Bali in the first place, to scout out a new tour. "You didn't tell me to scout out the damn nightclub," Jamie told him when he blamed himself for her trauma.

Now she leaves him a message. "I made it to Bali safe and sound. Why did I think this was such a hot idea? Listen, call me."

Larson won't tell anyone else he has pancreatic cancer and that he probably has about a year to live. His brother on the East Coast knows, but the guy is good for nothing but a weepy phone call every few days. Jamie has been Larson's best friend ever since he hired her ten years ago. She loves him dearly, but she's worried about what it means to be his only friend.

Jamie scooches down in bed and stares up at the ceiling. A gecko makes his way across the mosquito netting.

"Well, hello there," Jamie says to him.

He stops as if he hears her.

"Don't let me interrupt your travels," she tells him.

The gecko scurries on.

She picks up her cellphone one more time. She dials the number she has for Gabe in Bali, a number she has never called. After one ring the connection is lost and a recording in Indonesian follows.

She drops the phone beside her on the bed and turns on her side. She cradles her arm, pressing into her elbow to stop the pain. And then she sleeps.

Jamie's the only one at the table in the middle of the garden. It's a small wrought-iron table with a tiled mosaic top, large enough for a couple of people. She expected dinner with the family, but that doesn't seem to be the plan. Nearby, a stone elephant spills water from its trunk into a basin. Lotus lilies float at its feet.

A teenage girl walks up to Jamie, carrying a plate of food. She wears a black miniskirt and a torn T-shirt with the words CAN'T GET NO LOVE on it. She's got long shaggy hair, bleached blond, and thick black eyeliner; she wouldn't look out of place in San Francisco. Jamie's pretty sure this isn't the Balinese way.

The girl puts a plate of rice and vegetables on the table and turns to leave.

"Thanks," Jamie says. "Are you related to Nyoman?"

"Niece," the girl says. She stands for a moment, looking wary.

"I'm Jamie."

"Dewi."

"Pretty name."

"Where you from?"

"The United States."

The girl's eyes open wide. Her disgust and boredom evaporate. "I love America music!" she says with girlish enthusiasm.

"Yeah, what kind?"

"Heavy metal. America very cool."

"How old are you?"

The question seems to upset the girl. She says, "Sixteen," under her breath and then marches off toward the kitchen.

Nyoman walks toward Jamie from his cottage. He's combed his hair and changed his clothes, but his glasses still sit awry on his nose.

"My niece is rebellious girl," Nyoman mutters.

"I like her."

"In Bali, when a baby is born," he says, "the umbilical cord is buried in the ground in the courtyard of the family compound. As the child grows up, she might wander far from home. But in the end the umbilical cord draws her home. Dewi might wander, but she will come home."

Jamie feels a yearning for such a place.

"You like food?" he asks, smiling.

"I was hoping I could eat with the family," she says.

Nyoman laughs heartily, as if she has told a joke. "Bali family does not have dinner like on American television. We take food and eat by ourselves. No big deal like in your country."

"Are there other guest rooms here?"

"Just one. We rent out to tourist. Mostly empty now."

"Does Dewi live here?"

"Dewi is the daughter of my sister. She lives in the compound of her father, not far from here. In this compound lives my grandmother, my mother and father, my brother and his wife, and my nephews."

"And this is how Balinese families live? All together?"

"You do not live with your family?" Nyoman asks.

Jamie shakes her head. "I share a house with a bunch of friends. My mother lives about an hour away from me."

"All alone?"

"For the past eighteen years," Jamie says. "But now she's got a boyfriend. They'll get married soon."

"You have no father?" Nyoman asks. He looks bewildered.

"I've got one, all right. He ditched my mom and me and moved across the country with a pretty young thing. Now he's got a brand-spanking-new family, all little kids running around the farm." Her dad's place in Connecticut is more country manor than farm, and the little kids are now teenagers. But Jamie has been telling her father's story this way for so long that she hasn't learned how to tell the new version.

Hard to put all those people in a family compound, she thinks.

"You don't have to eat it," Dewi says. She's back at the table, and Jamie picks up her fork.

"I like it," Jamie tells her.

"Miss Jamie," Nyoman says, his voice loud.

She looks up at him. He squints at her as if he can't see her clearly. "You come alone to Bali. Do you have husband?"

Dewi giggles.

"No," Jamie says. "I'm single."

Nyoman rubs the bridge of his nose, pushing his glasses further askew. He looks baffled.

"In the States it's not so unusual for a thirty-two-year-old to be single."

"But you will have children?"

"I think so. Did my mother tell you to give me a hard time?" She smiles, but Nyoman just stares at her. "Only kidding," she says.

"I have many clients from the West. I know that the ways of the world are very different."

"What do you do?" Jamie asks.

"I am tourism guide. I take tourists to all the parts of Bali and show them our country. It has been a very bad time for my business. Since the bombing. But soon the tourists return."

"Uncle has no work for a year," Dewi says.

"And now my business begins to grow," he insists.

"I'm in tourism, too. I work for an adventure-travel company," Jamie says. "Since 9/11 we've had to develop a lot of trips in the United States and Canada. People don't want to leave the country."

"What does this mean—adventure travel?" he asks.

"Our clients want to be active while they travel. So we set up hikes and bike rides and river-rafting trips. They get to see the country in a more intimate way instead of driving through it on a tour bus."

"Is that reason you were here one year ago?" Nyoman asks. "With adventure travel tour?"

"I was setting up a new tour. I had been here only a couple of days."

"Which club were you in?" he asks.

"I was heading into Paddy's Pub."

"My wife, she was in Sari Club."

Jamie puts her fork down. The sound it makes against her plate reverberates in the quiet garden.

Dewi retreats a few steps, then turns and walks away.

A blackbird perches on the edge of the table, and Nyoman swats at it. It flies away, squawking.

"I am so sorry," Jamie says finally. Of course, that's why he's a host. There are so many of them. Widows. Widowers. Survivors.

She closes her eyes and sees the face of a blond Australian girl, her mouth open in an unending scream that still pierces Jamie's sleep. The girl's dress caught a lick of fire from a burning wall, and in an instant she was consumed by angry flames. Jamie pushes the image from her mind.

"My wife will come back to me another time," Nyoman says, his voice cheery. "Perhaps as my child."

"The Balinese believe in reincarnation?" Jamie asks. She should know. She should have learned about Bali. But she has kept herself busy, trekking in Chile, in Morocco, in Bhutan.

And then she remembers an evening on the beach when Gabe explained the Balinese belief in reincarnation. His voice was soft in her ear, and all around them candles flickered in the dark night. The moment fades as quickly as it appeared. Maybe that's why she can't trust her memory of Gabe. It's as hard to catch as a lightning bug. And yet she feels the weight of it, pressing on her.

Nyoman clears his throat. "Yes. Children are the reincarnation of their ancestors," he tells her.

"And that helps you in your loss?" Jamie asks.

"Yes," he says. "But there is still a small hole inside me that reminds me I am alone when once I was a man with a beautiful wife."

Jamie stands under the shower for a long time. Sleep will not come, and yet it's already two A.M. When the hot water runs out, she lets the cold water sting her skin. Then she towels off and lies naked on the bed.

There's a fan overhead and it clicks as it circles, as if it catches on something. Jamie's mind keeps getting caught on something, too. How did she escape memory for so long? She's an expert at her job, Queen of Constant Motion. Her tour guests ask for longer hikes, higher mountains, more-challenging rivers, and she says: *yes, yes, yes.* They're adrenaline junkies, and the minute the high wears off there's another adventure that beckons.

Now she lies still, like a dead woman. No, if she were dead, her mind wouldn't race like this. Her heart wouldn't drum in her chest.

Her skin is slick with sweat. Why doesn't the damn fan create a breeze in this room?

Miguel pushes his way into her consciousness. She can almost see that petulant scowl on his face. *Remember me.*

She had come to Bali with him a year ago, crazy in lust with the Chilean guide she had met in Torres del Paine six months before. She had convinced him to come along on her business trip—all the hotel rooms were paid for, and she had enough frequent-flier miles to get him a free flight.

She remembers sex in the large white bed in the large white villa at the luxury hotel in Seminyak. A swim in their private pool. A monkey leapt on the wall separating their villa from the one next door. He watched them making love on the futon, poolside. When they were done, he jumped up and down as if applauding. Somewhere there's a photo of that monkey, stashed deep inside a box that Jamie never opens.

She and Miguel hiked Mount Batur on their second day in Bali. A local guide picked them up at one in the morning to make the long drive to the volcano. The guide spoke little English—the three of them silently climbed the trail in a cool darkness that thrilled Jamie. Our tour guests will love this, she thought. They reached the top of the mountain at six in the morning, just as the sun broke the horizon. The vivid green landscape of forest and rice paddies brightened with the first rays of sunlight.

On the way down the mountain, Jamie and Miguel ditched the guide. When they came to a waterfall, they stripped off their clothes and swam in the cold basin at its base. Miguel led her behind the curtain of water and they found a cave there, sheltered from the spray. They ducked inside and watched the water tumble in torrents in front of them. The sound was astonishingly loud and urgent. And yet there was something so peaceful about their hideaway. When Miguel kissed her, she thought: Can I love this man?

Above her, the fan whirs and clicks. Whirs and clicks. Her mind catches on memories, halts, drags, and then moves on.

A noise wakes her. Someone's tapping on the door, a light, insistent sound. She feels the hot pressure of a headache coming on, the dull ache of pain in her arm. Even in her sleep, she cradles her arm as if it were still broken.

It must be late—the room is full of light. She lifts her cellphone—9:30 A.M. She slept for five hours.

Another knock at the door.

"Yes!" she calls out. "I'm coming."

She stumbles out of bed, wraps herself in a cotton robe, and opens the door.

Nyoman stands there, holding a tray of food.

"Breakfast," he says.

She's a mess in her robe, her hair scrambled from sweaty dreams, last night's makeup smeared on her face. She must look as crazy as he did yesterday. They're spiritual twins.

"Thank you," she says, and starts to reach for the tray.

"In the garden," he tells her, stepping back. He turns and walks toward the table in the middle of the garden.

"I'll be right out," she calls, shutting the door. She needs coffee.

She takes a quick shower and throws on linen pants and a T-shirt. She runs a comb through her long auburn hair, then brushes her teeth and looks in the mirror. Her eyes are bloodshot, her face pale. Her scar runs from her eyebrow to her jaw, a thin white line that curves like a comma. The doctor told her that she shouldn't spend time in the sun, that her scar will burn and change color. She's not sure she cares.

Again, a knock on her door.

Impatient, she throws it open.

"I'm coming," she says, and Nyoman turns around and leads her to the garden.

The table is set with a plate of unusual fruit, a bowl of yogurt, a glass of watermelon juice, a basket of rice cakes.

"Looks great," she says. "Coffee?"

"Tea," he tells her, and walks away. Where's his smile this morning?

The teapot perches proudly on the table.

She sits down and takes a deep breath. Now that he's gone, she's glad to be awake and sitting in the middle of her private paradise. She nods good morning to the elephant god in the fountain. He's got a bird sitting on his head, but he doesn't seem to mind.

There's no sign of any of the family—they must already be at school or at work. The sun is out, but Jamie sits in the shade of a banyan tree, and for once she hasn't started to sweat. She hears the trill of a bird, something she doesn't recognize, and looks up into the tree. She can't find the bird, but its call is answered by another bird, in the next tree, and suddenly it's a symphony up there. Her shoulders relax.

She eats her meal slowly. She doesn't want to leave.

"Barong in three hours," Nyoman tells her, reappearing at her side. He reaches for her empty breakfast plate.

She has no idea what he's talking about. Must be something on the itinerary.

"You want more tea?"

"I've had plenty. I'll go walk around town," she says. "Thank you for breakfast."

"I come with you," Nyoman tells her a little forcefully.

"I'll be fine on my own," she says. It's a line she says so often, but this time she's not sure that it's true.

The boy and his dog look up, both faces full of delight, when she walks through the gate. They stand at once and cross the street to greet her. One day in Bali and she's got a frigging family.

"Good morning, miss!"

"Morning," she says flatly. She needs to ditch him, and fast.

"I give tour?"

"I'm just taking a walk," she says. "I'm good on my own."

He's already following along, like an eager puppy, his own eager puppy like a persistent echo.

She stops mid-street.

"I'm taking a walk by myself," she says.

He offers a mischievous smile. "You did not sleep well? You still a little bit not nice?"

"I'm always a little bit not nice," she explains.

"But Bali is beautiful! Bali is paradise!"

"You work for the tourist bureau?"

"I work for you! You tell me what to do and I do it."

"I want you to walk in the other direction. I want you to do whatever young boys do in Bali. Go to school. Work in the rice paddy."

"I am fourteen. Done with school!"

The street is filled with Balinese men and women, most

headed toward the center of town. She feels a flash of fear, but she pushes it away. For a year now she's hated crowds. But Gabe taught school in Ubud. He might still be here. She'll join the morning stampede. She needs to lose the kid, somehow, and then plunge into the heart of town.

In the distance, a neon light flashes BALI BALI CAFÉ

She thinks: coffee.

"I do have a job for you," she says, turning toward the boy. His eyes open wide—this kid is desperate for either money or attention. Both, perhaps.

"You want marijuana? You want a man?"

"No!" And then she laughs. "Is that what most women want?"

"Western women funny," he says, smiling. "Western women want many things."

"I want—" He is suddenly her genie. Three wishes. I want to sleep without nightmares. I want a medical miracle to cure Larson. I want to go back in time and, when Larson tells me to travel to Bali, I tell him that I'm allergic to paradise.

"Yes, miss?"

"I want coffee. Can you find instant coffee for me?"

"Coffee." He looks disappointed.

"Is there a store somewhere? I'll give you money."

"Sure, miss," he says, the smile gone from his face.

She takes her wallet out of her pack, pulls out some rupiah, and gives them to him. It is worth ten dollars to get rid of him. She's sure she'll never see him again.

"Meet me here at noon. Okay?"

"I am Bambang," the boy says.

"Bam-bam?"

"Bam-*bang*! It is my name. What your name, miss?"

"Jamie."

He bows. "It is very great pleasure to meet Jamie."

She bows back, smiling at his well-practiced English.

He tucks the money into his pocket and runs down the street. The dog keeps pace at his side.

Jamie finds herself still smiling when he is gone. Bambang.

She looks around—there are throngs of people on the main street in front of her. Ahead, she sees the central market, a teeming mass of color and noise. She takes a deep breath and then slips into the tide of people, as if catching a wave.

As she passes a store, she sees a rack of straw hats, some with wide floppy brims, and realizes she could use one. Already the sun is beating on her head, and her headache is making a fast return. She steps into the store, which smells of incense and oranges. A short heavyset woman greets her with a loud voice. "Hello, hello. I help you."

"Can I try on a hat?" Jamie asks.

"Yes, yes," the woman says eagerly. "Very good price. Only one hundred thousand rupiah."

Jamie steps up to the rack and chooses a hat with a yellow bandanna tied around the crown. It fits her perfectly.

"I give you better price," the woman says, as if Jamie had been bargaining with her. "Morning price. Only seventy-five thousand."

"Yes. That's good."

Jamie reaches into her backpack and realizes in a panic-fueled second that her wallet is gone. She scrambles through the contents of the pack, finally emptying everything onto the counter in the shop. Passport. Cellphone. Camera. Notebook. Eyewitness Travel Bali guide. Sunglasses case. Lip gloss.

No wallet.

She slaps her pockets—all of them are empty.

The damn kid. How could he have gotten it? The pack was on her shoulder the whole time.

Except when she pulled it out to give him money.

"You have problem, miss?" the woman asks, watching Jamie stuff everything back into her pack.

"I have big problem," Jamie says.

She heads for the door.

"Hat!" the woman shouts.

Jamie's still wearing it. She takes it off and puts it on the head of a giant bronze Buddha that sits happily at the front door. The hat fits him, too.

It's noon and she's waiting. She already combed the streets of Ubud, looking everywhere for the kid. He won't show up with her coffee, asking to be caught, but she can't think of anything else to do. She'll wait for fifteen minutes, then—well, she doesn't know what she'll do next.

What an idiot. A smart traveler hides money in different places and keeps a credit card tucked somewhere apart from her cash. She has always been that smart traveler in the past and has always advised her clients to do just that. She must be more rattled by this trip than she realized. When she changed money at the airport yesterday, she put it all in her damn wallet without thinking. At least her passport is here—in fact, she's surprised the boy didn't take that, too.

"You lucky, miss," a voice says, and she spins around.

Bambang stands there, a mile-wide grin on his face, holding out a jar of instant coffee.

"Where is it?" she asks, her voice loud.

"Here," he says, waving the coffee. He reads from the jar. "Folgers instant coffee."

"My wallet," Jamie says.

"You gave me one hundred thousand rupiah. I have change," he says proudly, waving the bills in the air. He's standing too close to her, and she wants to pummel his sweet face with her fists.

"You swiped my wallet."

The boy takes a step backward, as if already struck by her words.

"No," he says, his smile fading. "I take money you give me."

The dog whines, feeling Bambang's fear.

Jamie eyes him. Why would the kid show up again? Another scam?

"Listen," she says, softening her tone. "You give it back. I'll pay you well."

"I no have wallet," he says, his voice pleading.

"Twenty dollars," she tells him. "Give me the wallet and I won't go to the police. I'll give you twenty bucks and my promise. You go free."

"I no have wallet," he repeats. His face droops in sadness.

The kid is a good liar, she thinks. And she can't figure out his scam—why is he back here? What can he possibly get out of this?

Is it possible he's innocent?

"I have no money," she says, trying for a heartfelt appeal. "I have no way to get any money."

"No, miss. You wrong. I buy your coffee. I have your change!" Again, he waves her money hopefully, like a flag of surrender.

She turns and starts to walk away.

"Stop, miss! Take coffee! Take change! I no have wallet!"

She keeps walking. The dog's pitiful whine follows her down the street.

Jamie calls her boss but again gets his voice mail. She tries to remember if Larson is traveling somewhere out of cell reach. He went to Houston last week to consult with a new specialist. No, this week he's got chemo again. He's supposed to answer his damn phone.

She calls her mother and leaves a message for her, too.

Then she lies down on the bed in her cottage, watching the errant ceiling fan. When her cellphone rings a few minutes later, she leaps at it.

"Mom!"

"Are you all right? Did you get hurt?"

Jamie sits up. "I'm fine. I didn't get mugged, but someone stole my money and my credit card. I don't even know how they got it."

"Come home, sweetheart."

"No," she says calmly. "I'm going to stay. I just need you to wire money."

"All you have to do is change your return ticket. I'll pay for the penalty."

Jamie lies back on the bed, the phone at her ear. Jamie loves her mother's love and flees from her mother's love. She stayed with her mom in Palo Alto after returning from Bali the year before, seeing doctors at Stanford to reset her broken arm, to remove the stitches on her face. Rose made a list of all the friends who called Jamie, all the good people who tried to visit and send gifts. But Jamie turned them all away. She took the list and ripped it into tiny pieces, and when she dropped them into the trash can, she saw parts of the names swirl through the air, as if they, too, had been blown apart and were no longer recognizable.

She left Rose's house a month after the bombing, pushing herself back to Berkeley, to work, to the next Global Adventures trip. She was terrified of spending every evening of the rest of her life watching a romantic comedy on the blue couch in her mother's den, sharing a bowl of buttered popcorn.

Now, on the phone, they're both quiet, breathing into each other's ear.

"Tell me where to wire the money," Rose says wearily.

"Never mind," Jamie replies. "I'll figure this out."

"You don't have to stay," her mother says.

"Actually, I do," she tells her.

When Jamie was fourteen, she came home from school one day to find her mother baking dozens of brownies. Boxes covered the dining room table, the center island, the kitchen counter. Smoke curled from the edges of the oven—a batch was burning while Rose furiously beat eggs into brownie mix.

Jamie rushed to the oven to pull out the blackened pan. "Mom. What the hell?"

Rose continued to beat the batter into a frenzy.

"Stop. Talk to me."

"Put those in the garbage," Rose said, her head down. "I'm starting a new batch."

Jamie placed her hand on top of her mother's and held it still. She waited while Rose caught her breath.

"Your father," she finally said. "He's leaving."

"What?"

"He's tired of marriage. He's tired of me. I don't make him happy."

Her father loved brownies. Jamie turned off the oven. The smell of burned chocolate filled her lungs. Her stomach heaved.

"Come outside, Mom," she said.

"I can't. I have to get the next batch in."

"Now."

Jamie led her mother into the backyard. They sat down at the table on the patio in the rain.

"You're getting divorced?" she asked.

Rose looked at her for the first time. "You think it's my fault. You think everything your father does is right." Her eyes were burning bright, as if she had a fever.

"That's crazy," Jamie said. But already she was thinking: He'll take me. I'll go with him.

As it turned out, her father didn't take her. When he came home that night, he told Jamie that he was moving to Connecticut, that he would send her a plane ticket to come visit him on her school vacations. Already he looked changed somehow. He was wearing a sweater she had never seen before— a dark-green V-necked sweater without a shirt under it. It made him look like a movie star.

"When you visit, we'll hike the Appalachian Trail," Dad promised. "It takes months if you do the whole thing. Won't that be something?"

That night, Jamie rode her bike to the Stanford Park Hotel. Her father had told her that he'd be staying there for a few weeks, until they could "straighten out this mess." While locking her bike, she glanced through the window and saw him in the hotel lobby. He walked across the room, took a woman in his arms, and kissed her. Jamie felt a gut punch of fury. As Dad stepped back, the woman looked in Jamie's direction. Miss Pauline. Months earlier, her father had tried to get Jamie to study ballet, even though she hated all things girly. "Why would I want to take a ballet class?" she'd snapped at her father, who made a deal with her: Take one class and they'd go camping that weekend.

Miss Pauline, tall and skinny with blond hair pulled into a tight bun, made all the girls walk around the room as if they were floating. She told them to imagine a string that pulled them up from the crown of their heads. "Grace," Miss Pauline had promised them. "Grace and beauty." Jamie had walked out before the class was over. "Why would you want me to do that?" she asked her father later, finding herself close to tears without understanding why. He didn't have an answer for her, and, in the end, they didn't go camping that weekend.

When Miss Pauline pointed at the window, Jamie told herself to run, to get back on her bike and ride as far away from the Stanford Park Hotel as she could possibly get. But she was still standing there when her father walked outside and put his hand on her shoulder. She slapped it away.

"She's, like, twenty years old," Jamie said. She felt tears on her face and angrily swiped at them with the sleeve of her sweatshirt.

"She's twenty-six," her father said.

"You are such a liar," Jamie said.

"I haven't lied. I'm doing the right thing by leaving."

"You lie about everything," she told him. Her father had taken her on her first camping trip. They summited Mount Shasta together. He taught her to rock climb at Pinnacles. They rafted class-five rapids in Idaho the summer before. How could he fall in love with a ballerina?

Over the next years, Jamie visited her dad and Miss Pauline during Christmas break and for a week or two each summer. Pauline had baby after baby, losing both grace and beauty with each passing year. And though Jamie and her dad would take day hikes when they could escape, he never had time to trek the Appalachian Trail. Over the past ten years their relationship had cooled—now Jamie talked to him only a couple of times a year. He didn't even know she was in Bali last year until weeks after she returned.

Nyoman knocks on the door of the cottage, even though it's open.

"We leave for the Barong now," he says. He's smiling again, tourist guide at his best. He wears a colorful sarong, wrapped like a long skirt around his legs. It's tied at the waist with a green sash. His shirt is a simple white polo shirt, but he wears a bandanna of some sort around his forehead, wrapped in an elaborate bow.

"Do I need a sarong?" Jamie asks.

"You are fine," Nyoman tells her.

"I'm not so fine. Someone stole my wallet."

Nyoman's face darkens; he lowers his head. "For many years we have no crime in Bali, and now things change. I am sorry for this."

"I'll work it out. It happens everywhere."

"Not in Bali. My country is different." He looks up at her. Even his sad face makes her feel better.

"What is Barong?" Jamie asks.

"Dance performance. Very important in Bali."

"I didn't see it on my itinerary," she tells him.

"It is on my itinerary," he says proudly.

"Let's go, then." She sighs and then stands up, gathers her bag and her sunglasses, tucks her hair up with a clip.

When they pass through the gate of the compound, Jamie looks for Bambang and his dog. They're nowhere in sight.

Nyoman leads her to a small car parked down the street. They both climb in and he drives out of town.

"The dance of the Barong," he explains, "is the story of good and evil. The Barong is a magical lion. He has to fight against Rangda, the witch. We watch the story of the Barong many, many times."

Jamie doesn't care about the dance of the lion and the witch, but she likes driving with Nyoman. He's got air-conditioning in the car, and the view of the countryside is astonishing. They drive through long stretches of rice paddies that follow the land up hillsides and down toward the river. The brilliant blue sky bumps up against the green landscape, and the colors collide. Nyoman falls into a long silence, and Jamie stares out the window.

Several months ago, she sat on the porch of Larson's Berkeley house, riffling through a pile of catalogs and brochures about Bali, many of them filled with alluring photos of terraced hills like these.

Larson walked outside with two beers and handed her one.

"Put that crap away," he snapped. "We're not going to Bali."

"We?" she asked, as if she didn't know what he was talking about.

"Global Adventures. You're off that assignment, remember? There's not one American who will sign on for a trip to Bali right now."

"Later," she mumbled. "A year from now."

Larson leaned over and swiped all the catalogs off the table. They tumbled onto the floor at her feet.

"Hey!" she yelled.

"Jamie, listen to me." He squatted down at her side. "I don't think this is about Bali. You don't even want to go back to Bali."

"It's not for me," she said weakly. "It's for a tour."

"You haven't stopped thinking about Gabe. Not for one minute since you got back."

"Cram it, Larson." She tugged on his ponytail. Before he stood up, he kissed the top of her head.

"Let him go," he said softly.

Now she glances at Nyoman, who is lost in his own thoughts.

"We are here," he says finally.

At the edge of a small village, he pulls the car over to the side of a road. They walk into a park where rows of chairs face a makeshift stage. Most of the chairs are filled with children. There are a few old men sitting in the back row and a group of tourists who gather around a Balinese guide. Nyoman leads her to a couple of seats near the front, among the children. The day is hot, and the only shade comes from a large banyan tree.

Music fills the air. The musicians file in from somewhere behind the audience, and they take their seats on the grass at the side of the stage. Jamie can't identify many of the instruments—this must be a gamelan orchestra. There's a collection of bronze gongs, a xylophone, drums, flutes, cymbals. The music percolates and flutters.

Jamie would be happy just to listen to this for an hour or so. Already she feels better.

But soon the curtain that stretches behind the platform opens up and a lion scampers onto the stage. He's a two-man lion, with a shaggy coat made of something that looks like shredded leaves. His face is a spectacular mask, carved of leather, painted gold.

The audience cheers wildly.

"This is the Barong," Nyoman explains.

The four legs of the Barong, dressed in striped leggings and with bare feet, dance wildly, and somehow the huge head of the beast moves as if it's light as air. Jamie notices that Nyoman already wears a smile on his face.

"And this is Rangda," Nyoman whispers in her ear.

Rangda explodes onto the stage. She is more ferocious than the Barong, and more opulent. She has a gold-painted mask with bulging eyes. A long red tongue hangs from her open mouth, reaching almost to her knees.

Rangda looks out at the audience. Her gaze settles directly on Jamie. She cocks her head, as if thinking, and then she bellows. The monster stares at Jamie, and Jamie stares right back. I know you, she thinks.

For the next hour, the Barong and his followers try to kill Rangda, but she is too powerful. They finally turn the daggers on themselves.

When the show is over, and when the applause dies down, Jamie turns to Nyoman.

"Good doesn't win over evil?" she asks.

"No one wins," he tells her. "There is always a balance. That is the way of the world."

"My wife, she was a waitress at Sari Club," Nyoman says into the silence of the car. "She loved her job very much. She went to work that night—the night of the bombing—and she was very happy."

They are driving back through the rice fields. These are his first words since watching the performance.

"I'm so sorry," Jamie says.

"I was angry for a long time," he tells her.

"At the terrorists?"

"Yes. And I was angry at you. At Westerners. The bombs were meant for you. Not for my wife."

"You're no longer angry?"

"No. There is no reason for my anger. It does nothing. This has happened, so it was meant to happen. I accept my loss."

Nyoman is squinting into the sun, and it looks as if he's making an effort to believe what he says. Jamie doesn't know this man or this religion. Maybe acceptance is the easiest thing in the world.

"My wife, she died right away," he says.

For a year now, Jamie has been haunted by the bodies she saw in the nightclub after the bomb exploded. They hover like shadows in her mind; they whisper to her when she first awakens.

Her body trembles as if she's freezing. Tonight she will sketch the face of Rangda.

"My wife was the young sister of my friend," he says. "I knew her when we were children. I was a serious boy, and she was a spirited girl who laughed a great deal." He stares at the road ahead. "We lived in the same village and our parents knew one another well. I loved her the moment I saw her."

Jamie smiles and watches Nyoman's face soften with the memory.

"We married when I was twenty-four and she was sixteen. We should grow old together, but that will not happen."

He doesn't speak for a while, and Jamie wonders if his story is over. She cannot imagine his loss.

"She was pregnant with our first child," he tells her.

Jamie presses her fist to her stomach. Somehow this is worse than all the rest. She had imagined that Nyoman was much older—perhaps grief has aged him.

"She took my hand," he says, "and led me into the world. Now I go alone."

They are silent for the rest of the drive home.

Nyoman parks the car near the Paradise Guest House. Jamie gets out and sees the boy right away.

He's there at his spot on the curb across the street, the thief and his dog. She glares at him and marches toward the cottage gate.

"I have wallet!" he shouts, waving it in the air.

She spins around.

He's jubilant, running toward her, the dog at his heels.

"I found it. Man stole it. I got back for you this wallet!"

He's shouting these words as he leaps in the air, as if borne by his happiness. When he reaches her, still waving the wallet, she grabs it.

"God damn you, you little—"

"No! I found it!"

She looks around—Nyoman has disappeared inside his cottage.

She opens the wallet and looks at the wad of bills, the credit card, the driver's license. She'll count the money later; she's sure that a good percentage is missing. Right now she just wants to escape committing homicide. She's shaking with fury.

"Twenty dollar! Twenty dollar!"

She glares at him. "Scam artist. You steal the wallet, then produce it and expect me—"

"You said. Twenty dollar!"

She shoves the wallet into her backpack and storms across the street, toward the guest house.

Of course, he's at her side, as persistent as a mosquito.

"Thief is man who lives in cave. He steal wallet before, many times, always tourists. Especially pretty girl. I go find him and I find wallet. I swear is truth."

Jamie stops and stares at him. Could he be telling the truth?

"I'll give you twenty dollars. Then I want to never see you again. I want to come out of my guest house and there's no one on the curb across the street. There's not even a dog there. You're nowhere near me when I walk around town. You don't exist for me after this."

"I promise. Twenty dollar."

She pulls her wallet out of her pack and draws a twenty from her wad of bills. His hand snatches it from her fingers, then he's gone. Gone. The boy and his dog fly down the street, away from town, the dog yipping with delight.

She's an idiot.

But she's an idiot with a wallet and some money, her Visa, her driver's license. Her lifelines.

Inside her cottage, she drops everything on her bed. She rummages through her pack, takes bills and cards and tucks some in her pocket, some in her toiletry kit, some in her backpack.

Before she puts the wallet back in her pack, she pulls out one photograph. She and Miguel stand on the rocky summit of Fitz Roy in Argentina, their arms wrapped around each other, fierce smiles on their faces. She looks at herself as if looking at a stranger. The woman in the photo is beautiful. She has just climbed one mountain and wants to conquer another. Bring it on.

Jamie runs her finger along the scar on her face. Its edges are smooth. She's curiously numb around the scar, and she likes the sensation of feeling nothing.

In the photo, Miguel isn't looking at the camera; he's gazing at her. He doesn't care about vistas and summits—he cares about love.

A few months later she would leave him and lose him. That same night she would break into a million parts.

Jamie wanders the chaotic streets of Ubud. She had imagined the city as an artistic center—at least that's what her guidebook had boasted—but this feels as commercial as Seminyak. The tourists are older here than at the beach resorts an hour away, and the shops advertise healing potions rather than Gucci sunglasses. But there's noise, lots of noise. Some of the restaurants blast music out into the streets. Drivers honk their horns and gun their engines, scooting around the tourist buses.

She finds a small unpretentious restaurant in the center of Ubud and gazes in the window. It looks quiet and calm. A wooden Buddha sits on the bar, as if he had too much to drink and can't get up. Purple pillows cover the benches of the teak tables. Jamie enters through the open door.

A pretty young woman leads her to a table by the window, overlooking the street. She orders a Bintang beer right away.

The diners, mostly late middle age, speak so loudly that their voices bounce off one another. One table holds two couples, their guidebooks sprawled on the tabletop, their cameras hanging from their necks. At another table, three men argue about the election in Australia.

The waitress serves her an icy bottle of beer. "Your order?" she asks.

Jamie hasn't even glanced at the menu. She orders nasi goreng—the name of the dish she ate at Nyoman's house last night.

The waitress nods and disappears.

She sees another table in the corner of the restaurant. A white man and a Balinese woman, with two young kids, an obvious mix of races prettily displayed on their faces. The man must be an expat.

She thinks of Gabe, an expat in Ubud. Could he walk into this restaurant? She has pushed every memory of him far away from her, as if they're white-hot embers—touch them for too long and she'd burn.

She has no right to see him again.

The waitress brings her a steaming plate of vegetables and rice, and Jamie digs in.

A young couple enters the restaurant, and Jamie looks up from her food. The woman is white; the man looks Balinese, with his dark skin and his broad handsome features. The woman has long blond hair and a dancer's willowy body. The man is dressed in jeans and a pressed white shirt—his hair swoops down over his forehead and makes him look like a Balinese Elvis Presley. They sit at the table next to Jamie's.

The woman immediately smiles at her. "Lovely evening, isn't it?" She has a clipped British accent.

"It is," Jamie says. "If I get over jet lag, I might even stay up long enough to enjoy the night."

"You just arrived?" the woman asks.

She's probably Jamie's age, but the man looks younger.

"Yesterday," Jamie says. "Have you been here long?"

"Three years," the woman says, laughing. "Be careful. The Balinese men have a remarkable power to keep you here."

The man looks up from his menu and gazes at the woman.

"I'll remember that," Jamie says.

"Your first time here?" the woman asks.

"No."

The woman reaches out her hand across the space between the two tables. "I'm Isabel."

Jamie shakes her hand. "Jamie."

"You want to join us?"

"Please," the man says, smiling shyly.

She takes her plate and beer and slides over to a seat at their table.

"My name is Made," the man says. He pronounces it *Mah-day.*

"Do you know many Americans who live in Bali?" Jamie asks. The question is out of her mouth before she can stop herself.

The woman wrinkles her brow. "Some. Why?"

"I met a guy here a year ago. An expat."

"Sounds romantic," Isabel says.

"It's complicated," Jamie tells her.

"Did he live in Ubud?"

"He taught school here. I assume he lived here, but I'm not sure."

"Well, most of the expats are here in town," Isabel says. "Ubud attracts the folks who come for more than a spiritual retreat or a weeklong drunk. What's his name?"

"His first name is Gabe. I don't know his last name. He's around forty, I think."

"I'll ask around," Isabel says.

The waitress brings two beers and the couple orders their food. Then Isabel reaches out and touches Jamie's arm.

"Were you here during the bombing?" she asks quietly. Her eyes trace the long scar on Jamie's face. Made lowers his eyes.

Jamie nods.

"You came back."

"There's an anniversary ceremony—I was invited back. It's harder than I thought. To be back in Bali."

"Were you badly injured?" Isabel asks. Her voice is quieter now.

"A broken arm. Some cuts."

"Made lost a cousin," Isabel says.

"He was a cook at Sari Club," Made tells her. "He lived for a couple of months. Very bad. Good that he passed."

The waitress sets plates on the table.

"I have a girlfriend who teaches at the international school in Denpasar," Isabel says. "I'll ask her about your teacher. Give me your cell number."

"What do you do here?" Jamie asks once they've exchanged phone numbers.

"I teach yoga," Isabel says. "I have a studio in town. I came here to take a workshop and fell in love with my tour guide on a one-day trip to Mount Agung." She leans over and kisses Made on the cheek. He blushes.

"Maybe I'll come take a class," Jamie says. She stands and riffles through her wallet for some bills.

"It's my pleasure," Isabel says, pushing the money back toward her. Jamie notices a tattoo that circles Isabel's thin wrist. It's a vine of red and yellow flowers.

"Gabe had a tattoo on his forearm," Jamie says, suddenly remembering. "Of a bird."

She was lying on her side in the green bed. She opened her eyes and saw the bird, taking flight. She reached out and traced its wings with her finger. He stirred, waking up beside her. He kept his eyes on her.

"That's you," he said, his voice as gentle as a blessing. "You'll fly away soon. And I'll be left here."

Nyoman smiles. He smiles and smiles and Jamie chases his smile. He keeps a few strides ahead of her, and she moves as quickly as she can to keep up. But the heat of the midday sun and the heavy humidity make it feel as if she's pushing through sludge. She just can't walk fast enough.

"This way, this way," he says, endlessly cheery.

When she turns a corner, she sees an enormous parking lot on the edge of Kuta where hundreds of people are gathered.

"Nyoman!" she calls out, her voice ragged.

He spins around and waits for her. He's still smiling.

"We are here. No more running. I was told to be on time. I am never on time. And so I race too fast."

Jamie can hear herself panting, as if she has never walked a city street much less climbed a few mountains in the past weeks. "Why are there so many people?"

Nyoman turns and looks at the mass of people across the street.

"This is gathering for all survivors and widows," he says, confused. "Children will give wonderful performance of dance and song for us."

"There are hundreds of us?" Jamie asks.

She hasn't bothered to imagine this. Yes, she had said. I'll go to Bali. She remembers the list of reasons she gave her mother: I'll support the country, help build back tourism, show the world that terrorism doesn't win. But she never let a picture come into focus in her mind: a ceremony for people who were injured in the bombing. Her bombing. People she might have pulled from under the rubble. People she might have stepped over on the way out.

"Survivors. Widows. Widowers. There are many of us," Nyoman says gently. "There is an organization that has been helping us all year. The activities of this week are very important to us."

"I'm having a little trouble breathing. I don't know why," Jamie tells him. Her heart races as if it needs to escape her chest.

"I will be with you," Nyoman says. "At your side."

Jamie feels as if she might cry. She swallows.

They cross the street. There are many young people in the crowd—both Westerners and Balinese. A man on crutches stops and high-fives another guy, then they embrace. A red-headed girl with terrible burn scars on her face shouts, "Hey, Charlie!" and Charlie lifts her in the air and spins her around. Survivors.

A small group of Balinese stands to one side, watching a toddler with an oversize beach ball. Their smiles look strained. Widows. Widowers.

"We must check in," Nyoman says, his voice close to her ear. "We look for Miss Dolly. She is very fat."

So Jamie squints into the crowd, searching for the fat lady.

"Over there?" she asks.

"Yes."

They make their way to a middle-aged woman with very short hair and a Humpty Dumpty body.

"Miss Dolly," Nyoman says.

The woman throws up her arms. "Oh, Nyoman. I am so very glad to see you."

They hug, and Nyoman looks a little afraid.

"This is my American," he says.

She puts out her hand. "Jamie Hyde."

"Dolly Thompson. You're our only American."

"There were no other Americans?"

"Seven who died. The families could not come."

Dolly Thompson sounds Australian. The air is full of loud Australian voices.

"Thank you for coming," she says. "Many people didn't want to return so soon. We offered to pair the families of victims and the survivors with a host—like Nyoman—to make the stay a little easier."

"I'm very glad to be in Nyoman's home," Jamie tells her.

"Where do we go?" he asks.

"You're over there with the families of the deceased," Dolly says, pointing toward the bleachers at the far end of the parking lot. "And Miss Hyde is at this end. With the survivors."

Jamie looks at Nyoman. She clamps her mouth shut.

"I stay with her," he says.

"You can't," Dolly says. She's bossy, as if she's used to herding kindergarten kids.

"I can. It is children's performance. At ceremony I stand with widows."

Dolly shakes her head. "Everyone has to make this more difficult than it should be," and she walks away, pushing her large body through the crowd.

"Thank you," Jamie says to Nyoman.

"Ladies and gentlemen," a voice booms over a loudspeaker. "Welcome. We would like to thank you for coming to Bali for this very important occasion." Jamie closes her eyes while the same voice speaks in rapid-fire Indonesian.

The show, performed on a stage in the middle of the parking lot, is chaotic and long. One group of Balinese teenagers, dressed in elaborate costume, performs a traditional dance. A choir of young Australian children sings their national anthem. Jamie tries to focus on the entertainment, but she feels fidgety and unsettled.

In the middle of a solo performance—a boy plays an instrument that looks something like a flute and pierces Jamie's heart with its sad notes—she turns around and finds herself looking at a girl a row behind her, who stares back at her with penetrating blue eyes.

Just like that, Jamie smells fire. She hears screams. She tells herself: It's a memory. This feels like the beginning of one of her nightmares, but she's wide awake. It's broad daylight. There is no fire. There is no bomb. She blinks and the girl behind her tilts her head, as if searching for something in Jamie's face.

Jamie looks down. The girl wears yoga pants; a prosthetic foot emerges from the bottom of one of the legs.

"You—" the girl says, and then she puts her hand over her mouth.

Once again, Jamie hears screams. She's back in the night-club and the air is thick with smoke. A wooden beam has crushed the girl's leg. She tries to lift the beam but it's too heavy. The wood is hot, as if already on fire. But the fire is on the other side of the club, sizzling and popping. Jamie can smell burned flesh.

"Stay with us!" she yells, and the girl opens her eyes. Blue eyes. There was no color and then there is the shocking blue of the girl's eyes.

Now Jamie looks from the girl's prosthetic leg to her star-tling eyes. The girl nods her head with recognition, and Jamie turns back. She stands, then steps away from Nyoman, so fast that he never glances in her direction. She pushes through the row of people, bumping shoulders and knees, muttering words. *Sorry. Have to go.* At the end of the row, she turns and runs.

She runs until the crowd is far behind her. She runs until her breath is ragged and her body trembles with exhaustion.

Then she stops and leans over the curb and throws up.

She wipes her mouth and keeps on running.

"Marry me," Miguel said, leaning toward her over their plates of seafood curry.

It was her last dinner with him in Bali, almost a year ago to the day, at a restaurant in Kuta, the night windy and hot, the noise of so many young Australians lifting in the air like a con-stant cheer.

"You're crazy," she told him. "We barely know each other."

He was tall and lanky and his hands felt wonderful on her

skin. Somehow they had been together for six months, longer than she'd been with most of the men in her life. They had spent a couple of weeks in Patagonia when Jamie was between trips ("Bold Brazil," then "Wild Argentina"); he had taught her to ice climb at Fitz Roy and she was a natural on the gla- cier, so fearless it made her giddy.

"I'm not crazy," he said. He pushed a box toward her. Her gin and tonics lurched in her stomach as she reached for the gift.

She held it in her hand for a moment without looking at him. The gin slowed down her brain, and she scrambled through her thoughts to find words: No, thank you. I'm not ready. Not me.

She opened the unwrapped box and saw the glint of the dia- mond, then shut the box as if blinded. She eyed him, a worried look on her face.

His face glowed in the light of the tiki flame. He had a kind of fierce pride, this handsome boy from Santiago.

"Marry me," he said again.

She shook her head and pushed the box back toward him.

"We're just starting," she said weakly.

"Yes," he said, his voice insistent. "Look at what we've begun."

"I've never even been in a long-term relationship," she told him. She didn't say: I don't even know if I'm in love. "I can't marry you, Miguel. I'm not ready. And I can't pretend that I'll be ready in a week or a month. That's not what I want in my life right now."

Miguel flinched at her words. He looked stunned, as if he'd never imagined the possibility of her refusal. And why should he? For three days now, they'd played at love, like accomplished actors in the most romantic setting. They kissed in the backseat of their taxi, they held hands while hiking the mountain, they soaped each other's bodies in the hotel room's outdoor shower and then made love while the water cascaded over them.

Miguel stood up. His body swayed, and Jamie wondered if he had drunk too much. But he turned and walked toward the door without a word, steady on his feet, not looking back.

Jamie left some money on the table and ran after him.

She stood in front of the restaurant for a moment, frantically searching in both directions until she caught a glimpse of him through the crowd—his royal-blue shirt flashing in the glare of the streetlight. She ran toward him, calling his name.

He stopped but turned his face away from her.

"Miguel—"

"I do not want to be your adventure," Miguel told her. "I want to be your husband."

"Don't walk away from me."

"I need a drink."

"I'll come with you."

"I want to be alone, Jamie. Please."

He wouldn't look at her. She dropped his arm.

"Should we meet back at the hotel?"

"Right now I just want a drink."

He turned and walked toward a bar at the side of the road. Reggae music blasted from the open windows of the building.

"Miguel."

He shook his head and kept walking. Jamie stood on the sidewalk and watched him go. He walked through the doors of Paddy's Pub without ever looking back at her.

Jamie stood on the sidewalk, struggling with the urge to run after him. She could join him in the club, lure him onto the dance floor. Don't think about marriage, she could whisper in his ear. Think about this. Later she could take his hand and lead him to the hotel, where they could make love late into the night.

Or she could walk away. She could go back to her hotel and get some sleep.

Still, she stood there.

She could have told him that she loved him even though she didn't want to marry him.

But did she love him?

She loved to chase his well-toned legs up a mountain; she loved acrobatic sex with him. But she was hungry to see every corner of the world, to have every adrenaline-fueled adventure. Wasn't marriage the thing that stopped you?

A young man bumped into Jamie, almost knocking her over. Dazed, she looked around.

"Sorry, miss," the man said, slurring his words. "Buy you a drink?"

"My boyfriend's in there," Jamie said, and she started walking toward the club.

It was then the sky flashed white. Blinding white. The sound came a split second later, a series of small pops, like firecrackers, and then a deafening explosion. She felt herself lift into the air, into the white space above her, and, just like that, she was flying.

Jamie slides down the wall of a building until she is sitting on the street, her back pressed against the cool wood. The farther she ran from the children's performance, the more the memories chased her. She had to stop. She has found an alleyway that is almost abandoned—the rest of the streets in Kuta are flooded with people.

"Larson?" she says into her phone.

"Jamie—where are you?"

"I don't know. Lost in Kuta. Why haven't you answered my calls?"

"I met someone. We went to Point Reyes for a couple of days. No cell service."

"Christ, Larson."

"It's the middle of the night here."

"She in bed with you?"

"Jamie. What's going on? You sound awful."

"I can't do this. I thought it would be no big deal. But I'm losing it."

"Maybe you *need* to lose it a little bit."

"Fuck you."

"I'm going back to sleep now."

"No. Wait."

Larson doesn't say anything.

"Help me," she says quietly into the phone.

"Let me go into the other room." Larson sighs. She hears him walking through the hallway of his Berkeley house. She can imagine him: He's thrown on his ratty terry-cloth robe. It hangs on his too-skinny body. He will make his way to the leather chair by the fireplace, and, when he sits down, Rosalee, his old cat, will settle onto his lap.

Jamie has shown up at Larson's house in the middle of the night after a bad fight with a boyfriend; she has slept in his guest room for a week when she was between apartments. He understands her—they've shared so many trails in so many obscure parts of the world, it's as if each knows the landscape of the other's life.

Once Jamie told Larson that he was her replacement father—a better version of the man who'd walked out of her life. "Don't do that to me," he warned her. "Too big a burden." But he has never failed her. And now he's dying. Her damn father is alive and well in Connecticut, and this gift of a man in Berkeley is fading away.

"Talk to me, Legs," he finally says. He's been calling her Legs since their first marathon hike together, when she kept pace at his side for hours, to his great surprise.

"I'm going to come home tomorrow."

"The ceremony isn't until the weekend."

"I can't stay."

"Don't give up."

"I saw a girl from the bombing."

"So?"

"I don't want to go back. I want to move on."

"This is moving on."

"The guy I'm staying with believes that his wife will be reincarnated as his child."

"Maybe she will be."

Jamie begins to cry. She saves her tears for Larson. Her mother once yelled at her: "Maybe it would be easier if you weren't so damn tough." But Larson knows that she's not so damn tough after all.

"I'm here," he says quietly into her ear.

"Listen. Put me on the New Zealand trip. I can get there easily from here. I love that trip."

"Stay where you are."

"I'm sitting on the sidewalk like a beggar. I'm probably sitting in someone's pee."

"Then that's exactly where you're supposed to be."

"You sound like Nyoman."

"Who's Nyoman?"

"My host."

"His wife died?"

"In the bombing."

"Maybe it works. His philosophy."

"Not for me," Jamie says.

"Give it a chance, Legs," Larson says. His voice is low and serious.

"I didn't even ask how you're feeling," she says, wiping her nose on her sleeve.

"I'm doing fine," he says, too quickly. Jamie realizes that he's lying—there is no woman in his bed.

Even though she knew that pancreatic cancer was a death sentence the moment Larson told her about his diagnosis, she hasn't let herself think about the end. His end. She's the only one who can take care of him. She doesn't know if she's big enough for that job.

"I don't want to lose you," Jamie finally says.

"Oh, I'll be haunting you forever. That's my plan. I'll tuck myself into your backpack and follow you around the world."

A couple of Balinese kids race down the alleyway, chasing after a puppy. They pass by her as if she's invisible.

Jamie stands and looks at the sky—the setting sun sends out streaks of red across the cloudless blue.

"Go on back to sleep," Jamie tells Larson.

"Stay in Bali, Legs," he says, and hangs up.

Jamie puts her phone into her pocket and starts walking.

It takes her a long time to find the parking lot. Nyoman sits peacefully on a bench at the back of the now empty lot. All the bleachers have been put away and the stage has been taken down. He watches Jamie walk toward him.

"I'm sorry," she says when she reaches him.

"In my garden is a sculpture of Ganesh."

"The elephant?"

"Yes. The elephant. He protects us from the demons. I wait for you. I will be your Ganesh."

Jamie dreams about Bambang. He's on a bicycle, dog at his side, and Nyoman runs after him yelling, "Stop! Thief!" Bambang laughs, the dog yips, and Nyoman plunges a dagger into the boy.

Jamie sits up in bed, her heart jackhammering.

"Bambang," she says aloud, and she realizes that she needs his help.

She throws on clothes. She should shower, but she doesn't want to take the extra time.

She opens the door to her room and sees Nyoman setting the garden table for her breakfast.

"I'll be right back," she calls to him.

He looks up, surprised, as she races past.

She opens the gate to the street and, sure enough, Bambang is waiting for her, as if summoned. His dog waits, too, ears perked, tail wagging. If Bambang had a tail, it, too, would be wagging.

She hurries across the street. The boy looks worried.

"Bambang in trouble?" he asks.

"You're always in trouble," she says. "But I couldn't care less. I need your help."

His wide smile lights up his face.

"Twenty dollar," he says.

She pulls a twenty out of her back pocket. His eyes open wide.

"Find a man for me. You can do this. You probably know everyone in this country."

"Only this town."

"We'll start here. Ubud. A year ago he taught school in Ubud."

"Your boyfriend?" Bambang sings, taunting her.

"Not my boyfriend."

"Your baby daddy?" he asks, grinning wildly.

"How the hell do you know that expression?" she asks, laughing. "No, he's not my baby daddy."

"Yoga lady teach me that. Baby daddy."

"Isabel?"

"No. Lots of yoga ladies here. This one Lucy."

"I don't care about yoga ladies. You find this man."

"I promise you," Bambang says proudly. "What is his name?"

"Gabe. I don't know his last name. You gotta earn your twenty. Here's what I know. He's American. Schoolteacher. Green eyes. Dark hair and a beard. Tattoo of a bird on his forearm."

"What's forearm?"

"You know baby daddy and you don't know forearm?" Jamie asks. She shows him her forearm. "Here."

"He teach in Ubud now?"

"I don't know. You start here."

"This cost more than twenty," the boy says, crossing his bony arms across his chest.

"You got a list of services? It says somewhere: *Find missing man* . . . what—forty dollars?"

"Forty dollar," he tells her.

"You find him, you get the other twenty." The dog rubs against her leg, as if adding his own plea for more money. "What's the dog's name?"

"TukTuk." Bambang runs down the street, waving his twenty in the air, TukTuk bounding after him with paroxysms of joy.

"Boy is no good," Nyoman says when Jamie sits down for breakfast.

"He may be good for something," she tells him.

"Ubud does not want trouble."

"He's an orphan?" She puts her napkin on her lap and drops a tea bag into her teacup. Nyoman pours hot water into the cup. We're like an old married couple, she thinks.

"He came here one year ago. No one knows where he came from, who are his people. Bambang is Javanese name."

"Maybe he ran away from home."

Jamie eats her yogurt and fruit while Nyoman stands over her. Usually she waits until he disappears into his cottage, but she is starving this morning.

"This is not America. We do not have children who run away, who live on street, who play tricks on tourists. We have community. Boy does not have community."

Jamie feels an odd kinship with the outcast kid.

Nyoman walks back to his cottage with the empty tray and the teapot.

Jamie imagines a woman inside Nyoman's cottage, greeting him with a smile. Nyoman places his hand on his wife's round belly. She reaches up and straightens the glasses on his nose.

"They will be crooked again in another moment," he tells her.

"For now, you are perfect," she says, smoothing his hair on his head.

Jamie stands in front of Isabel's yoga studio in the center of Ubud, watching class through the window. The roomful of remarkably flexible people move gracefully through pretzel poses. She hopes they're close to the end of class—she's hot and impatient. She has walked through town, trying to figure out some way to find Gabe or to miraculously spot him on the street. She's a Nancy Drew failure. She doesn't have a plan; she doesn't have a hope of finding him. Why has she taken on this mission?

It's as if she has now turned those embers of memory into a raging fire. She can't put it out. She has to find him.

Finally the yogis settle onto their backs for corpse pose. Jamie is glad she didn't join the class. Her muscles are too tight from scrambling up mountains; her mind is too frantic for an hour and a half of focused breathing.

The yoga class ends with a series of oms. The yogis file out, many of them hugging one another as they part. Isabel is the last to leave the studio.

"Jamie!" she calls, and she kisses her on both cheeks.

"Looked like a good class," Jamie tells her.

"Join us next time."

"I'm curious—did you do this before you moved to Bali?"

"No, I was an accountant in London."

"Come on."

"Really. I needed Bali in a big way."

Jamie can't imagine this woman behind a desk in an office, a computer in front of her, her legs primly crossed, serious pumps dangling off her feet.

"Listen. I haven't made any progress finding that guy I told you about. Gabe. I was wondering if you talked to your friend at the international school."

"I did. I was going to call you." Isabel shakes her head. "She doesn't know anyone named Gabe."

"Damn."

Isabel puts her hand on Jamie's arm. "Don't be discouraged," she tells her.

They kiss goodbye, and Jamie heads down the street as if she has someplace to go.

She turns down a path between two buildings, and within minutes she's walking in the middle of a rice paddy. The city disappears and the rich green landscape surrounds her. She breathes more easily. The sun beats down on her, but she's wearing a broad-brimmed hat she bought earlier this morning.

There's a dirt path that runs along a ridge between the rice fields. A sea of green spreads before her. The trail leads her to a river and a thicket of trees, the only visible shade. She sits on a rock and takes off her shoes, letting the cool water stream over her feet, then pulls out her cellphone. Amazing—the middle of nowhere in the middle of Bali, and she's got full reception. She calls her mother.

"Jamie!" Rose shouts as if she's been lost for weeks.

"I got my wallet back," Jamie tells her.

"Really?"

"I was probably scammed, but most of my money was there. The thief is my new best friend."

"Jamie, don't get involved with bad characters over there."

"He's just a kid," she says. "And I'm not getting into trouble."

"How are you, sweetheart?"

"Not so great." Jamie's voice breaks. She doesn't want to cry.

"Oh." Rose's voice falters, too.

Jamie stands up and takes a step into the river. The cold water rises up her legs and soaks her shorts.

"I tried to find Gabe," she says.

"I wondered about that," Rose murmurs.

"Suddenly it seemed important to me."

She takes another step into the river. The water covers her stomach, her breasts. It's almost up to her chin. She feels off balance, and it's not just the rocky footing. It's the heat and the cold, the quiet and the noise.

"You might be disappointed if you find him," Rose says. "Sometimes you turn men into heroes when they're mere mortals."

Jamie knows that her mother's referring to her dad. Has she done the same thing with Gabe?

"Hang on," Jamie says.

She slogs her way out of the river. Water pours from her clothing.

"Where are you?" Rose asks.

"I have no idea," Jamie says. She walks back out from under the trees and stands at the edge of the rice field. The heat of the sun envelops her.

"Thanks, Mom," Jamie says.

"For what?" Rose asks.

I need to find him in order to let him go, Jamie thinks. But she doesn't say a thing.

Bambang is waiting for her in front of the Paradise Guest House. He leaps up from the curb and runs to meet her in the street.

She feels a momentary panic. What if he's found Gabe? What if she sees him again? Why has she failed to imagine the rest?

"I have name! I have name!" Bambang yells.

The dog leaps on Jamie and almost knocks her over. He licks her legs, her hands, her feet.

"Easy, TukTuk," Jamie says, petting his velvety fur.

"Mr. Gabe Winters!"

"Gabe Winters," she says, trying out the name. The words fit in her mouth as if they had been there, waiting for her. "Where is he?"

"Twenty dollar," Bambang says.

"You didn't find him," Jamie argues.

"I found name! Twenty dollar!"

"Where is he?"

"Twenty dollar."

"Damn you," she says, digging into her wallet. She pulls out a twenty. Bambang takes it and whoops with joy.

"I go to tattoo girl," Bambang says. "She paint bird on Mr. Gabe Winters three years ago. She remember every tattoo."

"Does she have an address for him?"

He shakes his head.

"How do I find him?"

"Twenty more dollar."

"You ever do anything out of the goodness of your heart?" Jamie asks.

"No understand."

"Of course you don't."

"You no happy? Have name now."

"Yes, I have his name. Find his address," she says. She pulls out another twenty and tucks it into his hand.

Jamie goes to an Internet café in the center of town. Almost everyone in the café looks like a first-generation hippie—she's in a Woodstock time warp. The waiter wears a ponytail and a Grateful Dead T-shirt; he's got a flying-high smile on his face. She orders an iced mint tea and hides behind a computer at a corner table.

She Googles *Gabe Winters* and finds nothing that relates to the man she met in Bali. Next she tries *international schools in Bali* and copies the list in her notepad. She finds phone numbers and starts calling. "No, there's no one here by that name," she's told, over and over again. The harder it is to find him, the more driven she becomes.

Gabe had a sister in Boston, she remembers, but when she Googles *Winters Boston* she gets reports on the weather. She tries *Gabe Winters Boston* and finds one article:

Boston Couple Creates Foundation
in Memory of Their Son

Gabe Winters and Heather Duckhorn have created the Ethan Winters Foundation to support research on childhood meningitis. Ethan Winters died of meningitis at the age of four.

Jamie remembers sitting with Gabe on the patio one morning. The pale-pink hue of the sunrise colored the mist over the lily pads. "When I woke up this morning," he told her, his eyes focused on the water, "I realized that I had dreamed about Ethan. That's the first time I saw him in a dream."

Jamie types *Ethan Winters Foundation* on the computer. She finds the website devoted to the foundation and scans the home page. It's a mess—there's too much info, all of it screaming for her attention. She races past words: *meningitis, donate, events, survivors' stories.* None of it leads her to Gabe.

"Will you be done soon?"

She looks up, completely disoriented. A skinny teenage boy stands at her side, impatiently hopping on his toes. He's amped up on something, or maybe it's the music blasting through his headphones.

"No," she snaps. "Maybe. I don't know."

"Chill, sister," the kid says, and moves on to the next occupied computer.

Jamie sets her eyes on the screen and tries to slow her thoughts. *Find him. He's here, somewhere.*

She clicks on the link for the board of directors. Gabe's name is last on the list. His short bio reads: "Gabe Winters lives in Bali and teaches at the Ubud Community School of Bali."

Jamie signs off the computer and races out of the café.

Bambang sits on the curb across from the Paradise Guest House. He waves cheerfully when Jamie walks toward him.

"You need me?" he calls.

"You know where the Ubud Community School is?"

"Yes," Bambang says proudly.

"Can you take me there?"

"Yes, yes," he says merrily. "Only two dollar."

"You're a taxi service now?"

"Bambang tourist guide."

Jamie pulls out two dollars and places it in his open palm.

"Right now?" he asks.

"Right now."

Bambang and TukTuk lead her up the road, away from the center of town.

Jamie remembers how one tourist she guided on a mountain hike in Chamonix described her fear of descending a knife-edged ridge that was exposed on both sides: thirst, a cold sweat, tingly arms. Jamie's got it all right now. And she's just walking on a street in Bali.

"Mr. Gabe there? He teach at school?" Bambang asks.

"I think so," she says.

"You fall in love with Mr. Gabe?"

"A tourist guide learns not to ask questions."

"You tourist guide?"

"Too many questions," Jamie says. "Let the tourist tell

you what she wants. You'd be surprised how much she'll tell you."

"You too quiet. You tell nothing."

"Give me time," she says.

They walk up the long road out of town. It's the end of the day—there's no reason Gabe would still be at school at this hour. But Jamie feels compelled to see the place, to know where he works.

"There is school." Bambang points to a small building set back from the street. Unlike the many stone structures in the area, this one's made of bamboo—it looks a little bit like a tree house. Jamie stops where she is, across the street, and Bambang comes to a quick halt.

"We go in?" he asks.

"No, I'll wait here. Your job is done."

"I wait with you."

"No. I'm good. Go on, Bambang. Go spend your money somewhere."

The boy looks disappointed; even TukTuk hangs his head.

Two women open the front door of the school and pass through. As they approach the street, Jamie hears one say, "I'd rather be home grading papers than sit through that again."

The other woman laughs and they kiss each other goodbye.

Jamie fishes two dollars out of her pocket. She hands it to Bambang. "Get lost," she says.

He and TukTuk race down the street, back toward the center of town.

Jamie leans against a tree. A man walks out of the front door of the school. He's Balinese. Not Gabe. She takes a deep breath.

She remembers a day, a year ago, in the beach cottage. She lay in bed, two days after the bombing, trying to push ugly images of the burning nightclubs out of her mind. Think of Miguel, not the bombing, she told herself. Remember how he sang Spanish ballads to you from the top of the mountain. Remember his wild roar when he jumped from a cliff into the Pacific. Remember his sweet breath on you as he slept with his face on the back of your neck. All of the memories collided with the last image, of his broken body in her arms. She felt a rising panic. She pulled herself out of bed and walked, groggy and unsettled, out of the house and into the garden.

Gabe sat on the patio, reading a book. He looked up and saw that her face was wet with tears. He stood and moved toward her.

"Miguel's gone," she said quietly.

She stepped into his arms. And then, before she let her body press against his, she wrenched herself away from him.

Even now, a year later, she feels the pull of that moment. Toward Gabe. Away from Miguel. She feels herself stepping back, away from the school, as if she can change what she did then and what she is about to do now.

Then the door of the Ubud Community School opens again and a small group walks out. One is an old man, hobbling with a cane. Not Gabe. One is a woman with a child in hand. And then, finally, a man stands alone in the doorway. He looks around and his eyes fall on Jamie.

Gabe.

In that moment it's as if her tough exterior falls away—skin and muscle and bone—and all that's left is her pulsing heart. Now she remembers each complicated day after the bombing.

All of it was absolutely true. So, too, are her unsteady legs and the sound of her heart filling all the space inside her.

He is tall, with black hair peppered with gray. His face is clean shaven; the beard is gone. He runs his hand through his hair, and she remembers the gesture just as she remembers what happens next—a lock of hair falls onto his forehead, untamed. He's wearing a black T-shirt and a pair of jeans and carries a messenger bag over one shoulder. She watches and waits: He doesn't smile, but he begins to walk toward her.

Breathe, she reminds herself. And, without thinking, she's counting backward, as if counting the steps between him and her. She takes a long deep breath between each number as he approaches.

He blinks his eyes and his face pinches with concentration. "Jamie," he says.

She can't speak. Her mouth feels dry and unfamiliar.

He reaches out and touches the scar on her face. She remembers how he would change her bandage, his fingers so gentle on her wound. Now, even though the skin is numb, a jolt of electricity runs through her. She trembles and he takes his hand away.

She watches his green eyes. She waits for him to speak. But he is silent.

"I came to say I'm sorry," she says finally. She hears the words in her head, and they reverberate, as if she's been saying them over and over again for months. In a way, she has.

"Jamie," he says. Then he shakes his head.

His hand reaches toward her face again. This time he touches her lips.

"Please," he says. "Go home."

Part Two

2002

"Do you think you'll come home?" Molly asked, pausing for a moment before she added, "Ever?"

"This is home," Gabe said gently.

He honked his horn and waited for the pigtailed girl on the motorbike to move over before he passed her. The oncoming herd of motorbikes swerved by, only inches from his window.

"I don't know how you drive here," Molly muttered.

Without looking at her, Gabe could envision his sister's face, tightening as if in pain, trying to hold back tears. He knew Molly better than he knew anyone—even his ex-wife.

"It's like you threw away a whole lifetime," she said, her voice small.

"I didn't throw anything away."

"I feel a little discarded. Yesterday's family. Too bad they don't have a recycling bin for things like that."

"Oh, come on," Gabe said. He reached out and flicked her arm with his finger.

"Ouch! What? I'm not supposed to say I miss you?"

He glanced over at her. She was watching the traffic, and he could see her outstretched foot press an imaginary brake. He smiled. They used to tease their mother about pumping the brake when she drove.

"I miss you, too," he said. "You know that."

She poked at buttons on the dashboard. "It's so damn hot. How can you stand it?"

He reached over and turned up the air-conditioning. The fan surged, then slowed, coolish air pushing out at them, making little difference in the temperature.

"You slow down," he told her. "That's what I've learned."

"I'm sitting here. That's slow, wouldn't you say? And I'm drenched."

He smiled. "You're in motion even when you're sitting still."

"God damn you," she said, and then she was crying, her head down, her face in her hands.

He reached out his hand and rubbed her back.

"Sometimes I just need you around," she said, her voice muffled behind her hands. "And you're a million miles away."

"I'll call more often," he told her.

"Maybe I'm crying for Mom. I'm forty-three years old and I feel like a fucking orphan."

When Gabe was eleven and Molly was fourteen, their mother died of a heart attack. Their father, an artist, holed up in his garage studio, creating tortured sculptures out of found objects. He rarely spoke to them; he rarely spoke to anyone after their mom's death. Molly's sympathy eventually turned to anger, and one night, after serving Gabe macaroni and cheese for dinner, she barged into their father's studio. Gabe tagged behind her. Their dad was sitting and staring at a sculpture of a woman twisted into some inhuman shape. "*We're* here," Molly said when he finally looked at them. "You still have *us*."

Gabe found out years later that his dad had told Molly where he kept all the financial papers—just in case something happened to him. But nothing did happen to him. He poured his grief into his art, turning his back on his kids.

Molly took care of Gabe, choosing to live at home while attending Harvard, so that the two of them could sit at the dining room table, doing their homework side by side, the sound of their dad's welding tools screeching through the night.

Their father died a year before Ethan was born, and though Gabe and Molly had reconciled with him, it was always their mother's death that they carried with them like a stone.

"You're not alone," Gabe said now, his hand drawing smooth circles on Molly's back.

"When Ethan died," Molly said, and Gabe flinched. He returned his hand to the steering wheel. "I felt like I mattered in your life."

"You do matter."

"You needed me. But what happens when I need you?"

"Molly, I can't move back. I don't want to move back. I'm still trying to make a new life for myself. And it's here."

"You're going to be alone for the rest of your life?"

"I don't know anything about the rest of my life," Gabe said. "This is what I want right now."

"I think you're just torturing yourself by teaching kids. It can't be good for you."

"It *is* good for me," he insisted. He remembered the first day Lena asked him to help out at the school in Ubud, when a teacher got sick. The kids were seven—the age Ethan would have been then. He'd walked through the classroom door as if entering a nightmare. Would Ethan have been loud and rambunctious like that kid? No. He would have waited for a while before he tugged on Gabe's shirt, the way a boy named Christopher did.

"What do you need?" Gabe had asked him, squatting to be at eye level with the boy, who had eyes like deep pools. He wouldn't say a word.

"Do you want me to help you pick out a book?"

Christopher nodded, and his curly hair bounced on his head. Ethan's hair had been lighter, straighter. His eyes were green; this boy's eyes were blue. Gabe smelled something familiar—did the kid use the same shampoo?

"Do you like books about animals?"

The boy nodded again.

Gabe walked to the shelf as if expecting to find all of Ethan's books lined up there. No, these were unfamiliar. The boy pulled one off the shelf. A red lion, mouth mid-roar, graced the cover.

Christopher took Gabe's hand and led him to the reading corner, tugged until Gabe settled on the floor, and then the boy sat, leaning his bony shoulder into him.

Gabe began to read and soon the other kids gathered around, trying to sit as close as possible.

A car honked, and Gabe swerved around a stalled truck in the middle of the road. He glanced at Molly, who had her eyes squeezed shut.

"It helps me remember him," he told her. He didn't tell her about the days that he couldn't speak because someone said something Ethan-like. Or the days when parents came to complain about their children because they weren't reading well enough or weren't making friends and Gabe found himself shaking with sudden anger. What he would give to have problems like that.

"I remember his voice," Molly said. "When I'm lying in bed at night I listen for him. If I could hear him say Mollipop again—just that would make me happy."

Gabe imagined Ethan at the beach on the Cape, shouting
for his aunt to come in the water. *Mollipop! Jump waves with
me!* He was brown from a summer in the sun, and his hair had
turned blond. He hopped around the edge of the surf, a boy
with too much energy. When Molly ran toward him, he leapt
into her arms and wrapped his body around her like a monkey.

A bus driver blasted his horn behind them, and Molly startled.

"They call this paradise?" she grumbled.

Molly had been single for two years, ever since the man she
loved moved to Germany and didn't ask her to join him. She
wanted a child, she wanted love in her life, she wanted to be-
long to someone else's family if she couldn't have her own.
Gabe worried about her, but he knew he couldn't save her.
Since Ethan's death, it took all his resources to save himself.

"We almost there?" she asked, looking up at the long stretch
of crowded Bali highway. In a quick second, she was a kid
again, nine years old, in the back of the car with him, while
their parents drove them to the Cape.

"We're almost there," he assured her.

At the airport, after hugging Molly and promising her that he'd
come visit in Boston sometime in the next year, Gabe sat in the
car for a moment, feeling her absence. She stirred up the air
around him, and even though he worked hard to keep his life
calm and measured, he already missed the intensity of his sister.
There was something about all that love emanating from her,
uncovering needs and desires that he was usually so good at
tucking away somewhere safe.

Was he lonely? She had asked him that in the middle of a

dance ceremony they watched last weekend. They were surrounded by colleagues from his school, friends with whom they had just spent a few busy hours. She knew him too well. All of those people, and still he ached with loneliness.

He pulled out his cellphone and scrolled through his contacts. Theo Huntley. A guy who could be counted on to fill up all the space. He called the number.

"Gabe Winters!" a deep voice boomed. "You still in Bali? Haven't heard from you in two years, mate."

"I'm in Ubud," Gabe said. "Teaching gig."

"No shit."

"You doing anything for dinner?"

"Tonight?"

"Yeah. I'm at the airport. Meet me in Kuta in an hour."

"Guess I better show up. Might be another long while until I hear from you again."

"Might be."

"Santo's?"

"Thanks, Theo."

He dropped the phone onto the seat next to him and pulled out of the airport. Theo had been his first contact in Bali, a friend of a friend at *The Boston Globe*. He, too, had been a journalist; he, too, had dropped out. Theo rented a villa near the beach in Seminyak to write the Great Australian Novel. From what Gabe understood during the two weeks he spent with Theo when he first arrived, the guy spent much more time surfing than writing. Bali was a mecca for young Australians— a short flight, cheap rooms, great waves. They partied hard. Gabe stayed in Theo's small, cluttered writing room, on a sofa bed, and Theo had promised him: "Oh, don't worry about wrecking my rhythm, man. I haven't written a word in a month." The desk was covered with surfing magazines.

Gabe turned in to traffic and headed to Kuta, his mood lighter. He didn't want to go back to Ubud just yet. Maybe for one night he could use a little party in his life. Ubud was the anti-Kuta. An hour away, up in the mountains, Ubud attracted the spiritual seekers, the thinkers, escapees from the frivolous life.

If he drank too much, maybe he'd crash on Theo's sofa bed, for old times' sake, and make the drive back to Ubud in the morning.

"It's not as if you didn't have a life before you moved here," Molly had said at the airport. "You were happy in Boston before Ethan died."

"I can't remember," Gabe told her.

But he could remember. One night Ethan woke up in the middle of the night from a nightmare. He climbed into bed with Gabe and Heather, squeezing between them. Heather sang to him, a soft lullaby that settled the boy into an easy sleep in minutes. She kept singing, though, and Gabe stroked her hair, his arm stretched over Ethan's shoulder. "Don't stop," he whispered, as if he knew that all of it—sleep, good dreams, a beautiful boy, a loving marriage—was minutes away from its last sweet note.

Now he turned on the radio and blasted the music—Bob Marley—then opened the windows and let the heat, the thrum of motorbikes, the blare of horns, course through him. So much for quiet. A visit from his sister and all he wanted was noise.

———

Gabe watched Theo maneuver through the crowded restaurant, forging a path back to his table. Even among Westerners, Theo stood out. He was tall, blond, and more arresting than some of the women in the crowd. Gabe wondered for a moment if Theo had ever been a serious journalist—hadn't he written about pop culture? Maybe he just went to social events and reported on the lives of the rich and famously depraved.

Christ, Gabe thought. Two years in über-serious Ubud and I've become a snob.

"You're a mountain man!" Theo roared, and threw a hearty arm around Gabe's back.

My beard, Gabe thought. He liked the surprise of seeing someone unfamiliar when he happened to look in the mirror.

"Good to see you, Theo."

They sat and Theo waved over a waitress, then called out for a large Bintang.

"So you're a schoolmarm?" Theo asked, turning his attention back to Gabe.

" 'Fraid so. Found my true calling."

"How the hell did that happen?"

"I met a woman who started a school and one of her teachers got dengue fever. I said I'd step in for a week. That was a year and a half ago."

"You must be rooting the woman. No other reason for something like that."

"Rooting?"

"Shagging, mate."

Gabe shook his head. He *had* slept with Lena a few times, but now they were friends. He wasn't about to explain any of it to Theo.

"Just a midlife crisis," Gabe said.

"Fuck that," Theo said, and the beer appeared before him. He looked up into the face of the pretty Balinese waitress and a smile spread across his face. "Cheers, my friend," he said to the grinning girl.

"Cheers," Gabe said, lifting his whiskey.

The waitress glided away.

"You writing?" Gabe asked.

Theo shrugged. "Don't ask."

Gabe laughed, then stopped. Theo's face was dark.

"Tell me about the waves, then."

Theo talked surfing for a while, and Gabe pretended to know about swells and bottom turns. Suddenly he couldn't remember why he'd wanted to come to Kuta in the first place, why he wanted to get drunk with Theo and sleep on the guy's scummy sofa bed. He thought of his small house in the hills outside Ubud. He could be sitting on his back deck right now, staring at a million stars.

The restaurant was humming with loud conversation, Tracy Chapman songs, and wooden fans circling noisily above their heads. Gabe saw a hefty man moving from table to table, shaking hands, kissing cheeks. Must be the owner, he thought. Santo's was a glitzier restaurant than most in Kuta, catering only to Westerners. It was sleek and modern, a little too cold for Gabe's taste.

"You gonna stay in Ubud?" Theo asked. Gabe had missed something—weren't they just talking about swells?

"For now," Gabe said. "I spent the last fifteen years planning my life. Now I'm trying to spend a few years without a plan."

"I talked to Devon a few weeks ago," Theo said. Devon was their mutual friend at the *Globe*.

Gabe lifted his whiskey glass and poured what was left into his mouth. He looked for the waitress, ready for a second one.

"He told me you were one of the best."

"Easy to say when I'm long gone," Gabe muttered. *Long gone.* The words echoed.

"Why'd you quit?" Theo asked. "I never asked you that."

Gabe lifted his glass to the waitress, who nodded her head. Then he turned to Theo.

"You know what I don't understand," he said, and immediately he could hear something nasty in his voice. Theo was staring at him too intently. He took a breath. "Everyone comes here to reinvent themselves. We're dropouts. We got sick of our lives back home or we failed or we got lost along the way. Bali beckons. We get here and discard our old selves like we toss those worn-out winter coats. But then what do we do? We talk about the past. Endlessly. Every fucking expat I know spends more time talking about his old life than whatever new one he might have found. Why is that?"

Theo didn't answer, but he looked amused.

"Ignore me," Gabe said, his head down. "I just took my sister to the airport after a weeklong visit. I'm a little crazed."

"It's good," Theo said.

"What's good?"

"Your anger. Ubud puts most people into a spiritual coma."

"It's got nothing to do with Ubud."

"No worries, mate. I don't give a fuck about your life in the States."

Gabe smiled. "Good man," he said.

"You need to get back tonight?" Theo asked.

Gabe shook his head.

"Then we'll head to the clubs after dinner. I'm going to meet a friend at Sari Club later."

The waitress brought Gabe's whiskey. "Here you go, sir," she said, while eyeing Theo.

"Another for me," he told her, lifting his beer.

She placed menus on the table and brushed Theo's shoulder as she walked by. Gabe didn't know why he felt a pang of jealousy. He was too old for these kinds of pickups. It was one of the reasons he'd left the party town of Seminyak and headed to quiet Ubud two years earlier.

"You living in town?" Theo asked.

"Found a place about twenty minutes outside Ubud. It's a joglo—one of those Javanese houses. It's made of old teak, and it overlooks the valley. Pretty damn nice."

"You live alone?"

Gabe nodded. "At the end of a day with seven-year-olds, I need a lot of quiet."

"Can't imagine any of it. The seven-year-olds. The mountain life. Give me my board, a six-pack, and a girl in my bed."

"Who pays the bills?"

"Hell, I can support myself here by selling a few pieces of jewelry each week."

"Jewelry?"

"Some chick I met strings beads and calls them Balinese art necklaces. We set up a website and I'm selling shit in Australia and Hong Kong and the United States." Theo leaned back in his chair and ran his hand through his hair. "I kept pretending I was going to write that fucking novel. And every time I sat down at my desk, my brain hurt. I get on my surfboard and I'm soaring. Easy choice, mate."

Gabe nodded. "I hear you."

"Those seven-year-olds making you happy?"

"In a way."

"How's that?"

"Maybe it's like surfing," Gabe explained. "For seven hours a day, I lose myself in the rush of noise and energy. It's bigger than I am. I just drop into the swell and ride it for all I'm worth."

"Man, I hope you have that six-pack at the end of the ride," Theo said, toasting him.

They clinked glasses, and the room rocked with a thunderous boom. There was a pause between the sound and the movement—first the roar, then the rumble. And moments later, while everyone seemed to hold their breath, glass broke—from windows and walls, cracking and splintering, smashing on the floor. After another split second of eerie silence, screams filled all the space of the room. Terrifying, earsplitting screams.

Gabe was standing, though he didn't remember getting up. He watched a blur of people run out of the restaurant. He looked for Theo: Where did he go? When did he leave? The cook stepped out from the kitchen, his mouth open in terror, his hands over his ears.

Earthquake? No. Somehow Gabe knew: It's a bomb.

And then came the second bomb—bigger, more forceful and violent. The ground under Gabe rocked, the walls sagged, and then, as if the earth were about to split open, the mezzanine of the restaurant buckled and crashed to the ground. The lights went out.

Gabe stumbled toward the door in the darkness. He fell over someone, then bent down and lifted the waitress to her feet.

"You okay?" he asked. His voice was lost in the noise of so many screams. "Can you walk?" he shouted.

In the dust-filled haze he could see her face, streaked with blood.

"Let's go!" he yelled.

She stared at him, as if she couldn't understand. He wrapped one arm around her waist and pulled her along with him, pushing over toppled chairs and tables, bumping into someone headed the opposite way.

The waitress buckled over, then pushed away from him.

"Leave me alone!" she shouted, and fled in the other direction, back toward the kitchen.

Should he go after her? Should he be leaving through a back door? Were there more bombs waiting for him on the street?

Go, he thought. Keep moving. The air was thick and putrid —he could smell something chemical and something burned. Skin, he thought. Burning skin.

He pushed through to the door, knocking a table out of his way. Someone behind him—the big guy who was the owner?— called out, "Everyone stay calm. Don't panic. Walk toward the door if you can. We'll get help for those of you who are trapped."

The cook wailed, drowning out the calm, measured tones of the owner.

Gabe stumbled over something—a part of the mezzanine, now crushed into planks of wood—and when he looked up, he saw that he was in the street. What happened to the front of the restaurant?

He felt a blast of heat. Across the road, Sari Club was swallowed by flames. Did the fire set off an explosion? No. A bomb set off the fire. He could feel his brain sluggishly trying to make sense of this, as if it, too, were shrouded in dust and darkness. Bombs in Bali? At nightclubs?

The scene in front of him made no sense. In the smoke and darkness he heard horrific screams—words called out in Balinese, Indonesian, English, and sounds that had no language. He could see a wall of fire at Sari's, and then, when he looked to the right, he saw more fire—was that Paddy's Pub?

The second bomb?

Someone slammed into him, running past. He felt heat on his arm: The man was shirtless, and his shoulder was as hot as an iron. People were moving in all directions but mostly away from the carnage. Cars in the middle of the street were flipped on their sides, burned-out shells, smoking.

Gabe felt the air go out of his lungs. He stopped and crouched, his hands on his knees. Still, his head spun. He leaned over and threw up.

Then he headed toward Paddy's.

He stepped over bodies—dead bodies, lying at broken angles in the street. With his hand over his mouth and nose, he tried not to breathe through the acrid stench. His stomach heaved again. He could feel his pulse pounding in his temples. Another bomb could go off. Another fire could start. A wall could tumble.

And yet he headed toward the carnage, not away from it. He pushed against the crowd of people fleeing the clubs.

A man with his clothes on fire, his mouth open in a silent scream, tore past him.

A woman shouted, "Pool! Get to the pool!"

Someone lying on the ground screamed words in another language—German? Dutch? Gabe heard a grunt, and when he reached the kid—a boy, a teenager—he was already dead, his body burned, his young face eerily untouched.

Without thinking, Gabe turned and ran into the open gaping hole of Paddy's Pub.

Fire lit up the place. Unlike Sari Club, which seemed to be a mass of flames, there were only patches of fire at Paddy's—the bar ablaze, one wooden wall on fire. He could see dead bodies, charred bodies. These are kids, he thought. Twenty-year-old kids. Who wants to kill kids?

He stopped for a moment. The chaos overwhelmed him—the screams, the noxious smell, his own icy fear. Move, he told himself. Do something.

A flash of fire lit up part of the room, and he could see someone dragging a man out from the rubble. He ran toward them.

"Can I help?"

"Take him," a woman yelled. An American accent. "I'm going back in."

Gabe reached under the man's arms and got a firm grip on his body. The woman ran toward the back of the building, shouting, "Miguel!"

"Hang in there," Gabe yelled to the man. It was a boy, not a man. His eyes fluttered open and then closed. His body was covered with blood, and one leg dangled from his hip at an odd angle.

Gabe hoisted the boy up to get a firmer hold and then carried him out to the street.

"Need help!" he shouted.

"Yes, yes!" someone yelled.

Gabe laid the boy on the ground and leaned over him. "Someone's coming. Help's coming."

He looked up and saw a Balinese man run toward him.

"Get him help!" Gabe yelled. "I'm going back in."

He ran back into Paddy's and scanned the thick haze. Again, the screams and the smells assaulted him. He could hear the American woman's voice over the din: "Don't you dare fucking die!"

He raced to her side in the back of the room, climbing over bodies as he went.

She was pumping the chest of a young man, her arms strained and taut. The man was covered with blood, his eyes closed.

"Leave him," Gabe said. "There are so many others."

He touched her arm and she pushed him off. "He was breathing. Breathe, Miguel. Breathe, God damn it!"

Gabe heard a muffled voice from somewhere close by. "Out! Get me out!"

He started pulling wood and plastic and boards from the wreckage beside him.

"Where are you?" he shouted.

"Here! My leg—"

Gabe hauled what felt like a boulder from the pile, and he could see the boy's head.

"Almost there," he shouted, but the boy passed out. "Stay awake! Stay with me!"

He looked over at the woman; she was crouching over the young man, her head down.

"I need help!" he yelled.

She glanced over at him, then back at the dead man.

He couldn't wait for her. He frantically pulled more debris while the boy's eyes fluttered open again.

"Let me get this side," the woman said—she was suddenly beside him—and together they lifted one last wooden plank from atop the boy's leg.

"I've got him," Gabe said. "There's someone else trapped behind him. Start over there and I'll come back."

The woman looked at him. He saw her face, wet with tears, and then he saw something else—a kind of fierce determination. She moved to the next mound of rubble. Gabe heard garbled words in another language from underneath the pile, and the woman began to scramble through the wreckage.

Gabe scooped the boy into his arms and ran back to the street. He found the Balinese man and the first boy in the same spot and laid the new boy beside them.

"Where the hell are the ambulances?" Gabe yelled.

"Need help," the Balinese man muttered. "Need more help." The man had tears running down his cheeks.

"I'm going back in. Watch them until the ambulances show up."

He turned and ran into the building. He heard a deafening crash; one portion of the wall had crumbled to the ground. More screams rose up. The fire raged, so close he could feel it and hear it, as if it were already licking his skin.

He found the American woman and helped her pull a man from under the mass of wood planks. They lifted him, but the man immediately fell to the ground.

"I've got him!" Gabe hoisted him over his shoulder. "Move away from the fire!" he yelled to the woman. "There are more people trapped on that side." He pointed toward the far corner. "This whole wall will fall!"

"I can't leave him!" she cried.

"We'll lose you, too!" Gabe shouted. "Get over on that side. Now!"

He turned and made his way out to the street. The man slowed him down—he was heavy, and Gabe couldn't lodge him securely on his back. He stumbled over a dead body and almost fell. When he regained his balance, he heard another part of the wall crash to the ground. A new roar of screams rose up from the bedlam.

Gabe got to the street and heard the distant siren of an ambulance.

"They're coming!" he called to the Balinese man. "Get them over here. These people need a hospital fast!"

He laid the big man next to the others and ran back into the burning building.

For a moment he couldn't find her. He scanned the side of the building that was on fire and wiped smoke from his eyes. She couldn't have stayed there. He looked toward the far side and tried to decide which way to move, which bodies to save. And then he heard her voice above the others.

"Help! Get me out!"

He ran toward the flames.

She was lying on top of a boy, her arm pinned by a ceiling beam that had fallen on her. Her forearm twisted away from her elbow at an awkward angle.

"I've got it!" Gabe yelled.

She focused on him, her face washed with terror. Blood soaked her shirt and dripped down her arm. The fire was close, the flames hot and heavy.

Gabe found the end of the rafter and tried to lift it; it was too heavy.

"I need help!" he screamed.

He glanced around. There was no one else nearby—no one except the dead and dying.

He heard a loud crash and felt the onslaught of dust from another fallen wall. And then a flame scorched his arm.

"Now!" He bent his knees and got under the rafter, and with all his strength he pulled it up. It moved only inches, and still the fire roared, close to his side. He pushed into the wood from the inside and got it to pull away from her arm; then he let it tumble back to the ground.

The woman started to get up but fell. Blood streamed down her face.

"I've got you!" He lifted her up and held her in his arms. She screamed with pain, cradling her arm.

"Leave me," she cried. "Get others!"

"No! I'm getting you out of here."

She struggled against him, but she was small and in pain. He made his way over the bodies and out to the street.

When he put her down, she swayed, as if ready to faint. He grabbed her and held on.

"Ambulances are coming. I've made a line of the injured. Go with them. They'll be the first to get out of here."

"No," she said, grimacing, her voice weak. "I can help."

"Please," he begged.

Finally, she nodded. He let her go and she turned from him, heading toward the line of injured bodies. He raced back into the building.

Half of the club was now engulfed in flames. The screams were louder, the smells more putrid. He covered his mouth and nose with his hand and ran to the other side of the club, avoiding the fire. He could hear more ambulances. Please. I need help, he thought.

A curtain caught fire, and a swoosh of flame shot up—more screams, a rush of searing heat, a wailing "No!"

He heard a woman's voice nearby, but there was too much rubble and not enough light.

"Where are you?" he shouted.

"She's over there!" The American woman was at his side again, a scarf wrapped around her arm as a sling, a bloody rag tied around her head.

They moved in the direction of the voice. "Help! I can't breathe!"

Gabe started to scrabble through the pile of debris, and the woman used one arm to lift broken boards. He glanced at her; her face was bleeding, and she kept swiping at it to keep the blood from running into her eye.

"You need help!" he told her.

"I'm okay," she muttered, as if to herself.

They moved the rubble, but the woman beneath it was already dead. The American woman gasped—a terrible sound without words.

Gabe put his hand on her back. "You have to stop," he said gently.

But the woman heard another scream and turned away from him. She headed toward the fire.

A man ran from the flames in the rear of the club, his arms on fire. The American woman pulled him to the ground and rolled him, and when the flames were out, Gabe lifted the man over his shoulder and made his way out of the club. The woman knows what she's doing, he thought. The heat from the man's arms burned Gabe's back, and he held his breath for a moment, thinking: Don't stop. Don't scream. Don't quit.

Outside, an ambulance had finally pulled up, and the Balinese man was yelling instructions about the injured people on the sidewalk. Gabe wearily set the burned man next to the others.

He turned to reenter the club, and a wave of exhaustion hit him. How many more bodies, how many more screams?

Back in the club, there were flames everywhere. Panic seized him. Where was she?

A new flame shot up near him and illuminated a corner of the room. Someone was standing there—he could see her face in the light of the fire—and then, a moment later, she toppled over.

He ran to her side. She was barely conscious. He lifted her, maneuvering so that her arm wasn't pressed into his body. Blood seeped through the bandage on her head.

She looked at him, her eyelids fluttering.

"I can't . . ." she said, and then her eyes closed.

"No more," he said to her, and ran from the club with her in his arms.

When he reached the road, he slowed. "Can you walk?"

"I think so."

He put her down and wrapped an arm behind her back, securing his hand on her waist. They started to walk slowly, and she leaned into him for support.

He searched for a new ambulance. He didn't want to add her to the long line of waiting bodies, all of them urgently needing help. The litany of screams seemed to have moved outside with them—more people screamed for help, screamed in pain, screamed as if the nightmare had just begun.

A strong voice shouted, "Get the burning bodies to the pool! Everyone who can—please help! Follow me!"

An Aussie. A tall flagpole of a man, maybe thirty, his shirt off, his body covered in soot. He was carrying a wailing child in his arms.

The man ran and two people followed him, each one help-ing an injured person to hobble along. One girl's dress was still on fire, sparks of flame, like glitter, shooting off her.

Move, Gabe thought. Get help. He didn't need the pool; the woman wasn't burned. She needed medical assistance, fast.

"I'll get you to my car," he said to her. "We'll get to the hospital. Stay with me."

For a moment he couldn't remember where he had parked his car. And then, when he did, he couldn't imagine how he'd find the street. Nothing looked familiar. This was a war zone— where the hell was anything recognizable?

They headed up the street toward Santo's, stepping over bodies. He muttered to the injured, "I'll get help. I'll be back. Hang in there."

Off in the distance, he heard the sound of more sirens. Soon, he thought. They'll get help. I need to take care of this woman.

They turned down a side street and he was back in the world he recognized. A Kuta street at night. There were no lights, no neon signs, no traffic, but there were also no scream-ing kids, no burning bodies, no crumpled buildings. He heard people shouting, "What happened? Where's the fire?" Indone-sian and Balinese voices called out to one another. He didn't answer anyone.

They stumbled down the street and around another corner, where he found his car. It was covered in ashes, as if a volcano had erupted nearby. He unlocked it and pulled open the pas-senger door.

"I need to take care of this wound," he told her. She looked up at him, her eyes tight with pain.

He helped her into the car and then tilted her head toward him, removing the cloth over her forehead. The gash, at the side of her eye, bloomed red with blood. His stomach turned when he saw the raw, tender underbelly of her flesh. He found a T-shirt in the backseat and ripped it in thirds. With one part, he carefully wiped the blood away from her face; then he folded a fresh piece of cloth against the wound. She winced and bit into her lower lip.

"You're going to be all right," he said, his voice calm and measured.

He wrapped the last third of the T-shirt around her head, tying it in place over the wound. Her pale skin felt cool and clammy.

"What happened?" she asked.

"A bomb," Gabe told her. "At the club. Two clubs. We have to get you to the hospital."

"I'm going to sleep now," she said, like a child, and then she closed her eyes.

He arranged her sling on her chest and tucked her legs in so he could shut the door, then ran around to the other side of the car and got into the driver's seat.

He turned on the ignition. Breathe, he told himself. Focus. Where the hell is the hospital?

He was there once, when a dog had bitten him. Sanglah. Somewhere near Denpasar, at least twenty minutes away. There had to be something closer.

He pulled out into the street and did a U-turn—he knew that ahead all the roads would be blocked.

When he came to the first intersection—all the streetlights and traffic lights were out—he saw that both a left turn and right turn would lead him into another wall of stopped traffic. So he kept driving, in the opposite direction from where he wanted to go.

A few minutes later, he saw a group of young Balinese men gathered in front of a bar. He pulled up beside them and leaned out the window.

"Does anyone speak English?" he called out. His Indonesian was terrible, despite nearly three years in Bali.

"Little English," one man said, stepping forward.

"I need a clinic, a hospital," Gabe said.

"Sanglah," the man told him.

"Too far."

The man looked in the passenger seat. His face blanched. "What happened?" he asked.

"Is there a local clinic here?" Gabe asked. "I can't get through to the main streets."

The man turned and shouted to his friends. They all seemed to answer at once, many fingers pointing in the same direction.

"Not too far. Turn on Jalan Raya Kuta. Then Jalan Ngurah Rai. SOS Medika Klinik. Open all night."

Gabe had already pulled away from the curb when he said, "Thanks, man." He repeated the street names to himself like a mantra. Raya Kuta. Ngurah Rai.

As he drove, the sidewalks filled with people, doors opening, families spilling to the sidewalk to find out what happened. They were dressed in pajamas and bathrobes, the children huddling in doorways.

Next to him, he heard the woman's low moan, as if her pain was coming from far away.

"We're on the way to the hospital," he said.

When she didn't answer, he said the street names aloud. "Raya Kuta. Ngurah Rai." He turned the car onto Ngurah Rai and drove halfway down the block. A line of cars blocked the street. The doors to the clinic were thrown open, and injured bodies lined the sidewalk in front. They seemed almost piled on top of one another, crying out in pain. Blood pooled into the street.

How did they beat him here? He turned the car around and headed back in the opposite direction.

Down another road, he stopped in front of a couple of Western men crossing the street.

"Do you know a clinic nearby?" he shouted, his voice strained with worry.

"SOS Medika," one man said in an Australian accent.

"Too crowded. I need help right away."

"You in the bombing?" the man asked. Both men edged closer to the car.

"I've got a victim in here," Gabe said. "She needs help."

"What happened?" the second man asked.

"Tell me where to find another clinic!" Gabe yelled.

"Sanglah."

"Too far. And the streets are blocked."

"Try Artha Medika Klinik." And he spouted directions, the names of new streets filling Gabe's brain. Once again, he sped off.

Bodies lined the street of the next clinic, and keening sounds filled the air. People were shouting for doctors, for nurses, for anyone to help them. Gabe kept driving.

When he saw a sign for Sanur, he turned in that direction.

It was twenty minutes away—too far—but he knew a young doctor who lived there. He could go to his house and get help. He was wasting too much time driving in circles.

"Who are you?"

She had turned toward him, her eyes unfocused. The cloth wrapped around her wound was saturated with blood.

"My name's Gabe."

"You were at the club?"

"I was at a restaurant nearby."

"Thank you," she said, and her eyes closed again.

With a jolt, Gabe remembered a phone call from his wife, four years ago: "I'm taking Ethan to the hospital. I called Dr. Wilson. He said if the fever won't break, bring him in."

Gabe's breathing had started to slow at that moment, as if he needed to stop motion.

"Gabe? Are you there?" Heather barked into the phone.

"I'm leaving now," he said quietly, calmly. He was standing in front of city hall, waiting for an interview with the mayor. "What hospital?"

"Mount Auburn," Heather said, her voice choked. "He was shaking and now he's just limp. He's so sick. God, Gabe. I'm so scared."

Gabe turned away from city hall, his phone at his ear, even though Heather had already hung up. An odd thought flickered through his mind: The next step you take could change your life. Don't go. Turn back.

But he ran anyway: to his car, to his son, to the unholy rest of his life.

Now Gabe glanced at the woman in the passenger seat. He pulled out his cellphone, scrolling through his contacts, glancing up to make sure he stayed on the road.

Dr. Wayan Genep. He called the number.

The phone rang for a long time, and finally a woman's voice came on the line. "Who is this?" she asked in Indonesian.

"It's Gabe Winters. I'm sorry to wake you. There's been a bombing in Kuta. I need to talk to Wayan." Gabe had met Rai, Wayan's wife, a few times and knew that she spoke English.

She was Wayan's assistant at his clinic. Was she a nurse? He couldn't remember.

"A bombing?"

"At a couple of clubs."

"Wayan!"

Rai dropped the phone. Gabe heard their voices in the background, speaking in rapid-fire Balinese. And then Wayan came on the line.

"Gabe?"

"I've got a woman with me. She's hurt. She needs help."

"Where are you?"

"Headed your way. Should I come to your house or can you meet me in the clinic?"

"How bad is she?"

"Bad gash near her eye. Probably a broken arm. She fades in and out of consciousness."

"Meet me at the clinic. I'm on my way."

"Thanks, Wayan."

"Are there many others?"

"Hundreds," Gabe said, and then he hung up.

"Where are we?" the woman asked, startling him.

They were a few minutes from the exit to Sanur, speeding through empty streets. "We're going to a clinic. The doctor is a friend of mine."

"I keep falling asleep."

"You lost a lot of blood."

"My boyfriend. Miguel. He wouldn't have been there . . ." The woman's voice faded, as if talking took too much effort.

Had he done the wrong thing? Should he have taken her

away when she needed to stay with her boyfriend? But she needed medical help. Someone else would collect the bodies.

"I'm sorry," he said.

"At first I couldn't find him," she said, her voice weak. "And so many people needed help."

"Are you a doctor?" Gabe asked.

"No. Mountain guide. Wilderness EMT."

"What's your name?"

"Jamie. Jamie Hyde."

"There were too many. We couldn't save all of them."

Gabe thought about Ethan again. He couldn't do a damn thing when it mattered. He couldn't make Ethan's headache go away. He couldn't even make him smile. He remembered lying down next to him in the hospital bed, his boy curled into him. "I'm sorry, sir," the nurse said, walking quickly into the room as if he had set off alarms. "You're not allowed to do that." To hold my son? To whisper in his ear?

"Did you say it was a bomb?" Jamie asked. "I couldn't remember if I dreamed that."

"Yes," Gabe told her.

She was quiet for a moment.

"You live here?" he asked.

"No. Got here a few days ago."

"Are you in a lot of pain?"

"I think I'm going to rest now, if that's all right with you."

Gabe smiled. "I'll wake you when we get there," he said, but he knew that she was already sleeping.

Wayan came out to the car as soon as Gabe pulled up—he must have been waiting at the window. The streets of Sanur were empty at two-fifteen in the morning. They don't know, Gabe thought, looking up at the dark stores and houses and apartment buildings. When they wake up, the world will be different.

Wayan and Gabe helped Jamie from the seat and walked her slowly into the clinic. Rai met them in the waiting room, wiping her hands on her pants.

"I have the room ready," she said. She was wide awake and ready to work. She didn't even acknowledge Gabe.

"We'll bring her in," Wayan said.

Jamie moaned when they laid her on the table. Her eyes fluttered open and then closed again.

"Her name is Jamie," Gabe said. "American, I think."

"She is a friend?" Wayan asked.

"I don't know her."

"We'll take care of you, Jamie," Wayan said.

Gabe felt Rai's hand on his arm.

"Go sit in the waiting room," she said tenderly. "Get some rest."

"Can't I help?" Gabe asked. He felt unready to leave the woman. He needed to do something. "You have to leave," the doctor had told him when Ethan began to tremble uncontrollably. Gabe had wanted nothing more than to hold his son in his arms. "You have to leave *now*." Gabe had stumbled out of the room backward, holding Ethan's gaze as long as he could.

"We will work now," Wayan said. "I will tell you if you can do anything."

"You have done a lot already," Rai added.

Gabe pressed his hand on Jamie's bare foot. When did she lose her shoe? He curled his hand around her toes. He didn't want to let go.

"Be strong," he said quietly. He remembered her administering CPR in the wreckage of the club. She *was* strong. But strong enough?

He walked back into the waiting room, shutting the door behind him.

Gabe must have dozed—when the door squeaked open, he sat up, startled.

"Gabe," Wayan said gently.

"Is she alive?" he asked, his voice caught in his throat.

"She is alive. She's sleeping now. I gave her something for the pain."

"How bad . . . ?"

"I stitched up the gash on her face and put a cast on her arm. I do not know about internal injuries. We'll know more in the morning when I can run some tests."

"She'll be okay?"

"She will be okay. Tell me about the bomb."

"There were two, I think. Might have been more. Both in clubs in Kuta. Hundreds of people killed, hundreds injured. The place was an inferno."

"Were you hurt?"

"No, I was in a restaurant nearby. I found her at Paddy's. There were so many dead bodies."

"You need a shower and a bed," Wayan said. "Go back to our house. Rai and I will stay here with the girl. More people may be coming."

"No, I'll stay here."

"The girl will sleep for a while. Take a shower. Get some rest. And then you can help her when she wakes up."

"I left so many people," Gabe told him. "I couldn't help everyone. I stepped over them while they were screaming for help."

"You did what you could."

"No. I could have carried more of them out. The building was going to collapse."

Wayan put his hand on Gabe's shoulder, and Gabe bent over, releasing a sob that seemed to tear through his body. Wayan's hand remained there while he cried.

Gabe was deep in a dreamless sleep when his cellphone rang. He reached for it on his bedside table, but there was no bedside table. He bolted up.

His phone was on top of his jeans, which were on the floor at the side of the bed. An unfamiliar room—he was at Wayan's house. And then the memories flooded him: the bombs, the dead bodies, the woman in his arms. He looked at the light streaming through the window. It was mid-morning, he guessed. Why hadn't Wayan wakened him?

"Hello?" he said into the phone.

"Oh, my God, I was so worried."

"Molly."

"I'm in Singapore. My flight leaves in an hour. I just heard about the bombing. Are you in Ubud?"

"No, I was there. Nearby. I'm fine. But I saw it."

Molly burst into tears, and Gabe waited a moment while she cried. He looked around the room. His jeans were washed and neatly folded on the floor. A fresh shirt—Wayan's, he guessed—sat next to the jeans.

"Why?" Molly asked. "Why did they do it?"

"Who did it?" Gabe asked. "I don't know anything."

"Terrorists. I don't know, al-Qaeda, I guess. No one has claimed responsibility yet."

"Why would terrorists bomb clubs?"

Molly sobbed. "You saw it? You saw the clubs?"

"I went in one," Gabe said. "I tried to help."

He didn't say: I saved people. He felt a rush of emotions that he had buried the night before while he raced in and out of the club. Another bomb could have gone off. A firestorm could have rushed through every inch of space in the building. He had acted on pure instinct, never pausing to think about these possibilities. He remembered the line of the injured—his people—on the street in front of the club. Dozens more waited to be saved. He had failed them. He had quit. He took one last woman and fled as if there was no more that he could do.

"Wasn't it dangerous?" Molly asked.

"It was awful," Gabe said, surprised to find his voice. "The clubs were ravaged."

Once more, he saw the faces of young people begging him for help as he stepped over them, heading toward the street. He was crying now, pressing the phone against his ear, squeezing his eyes closed to stop the images in his mind.

"And you weren't hurt? You would tell me, right?"

"I wasn't hurt."

"Oh, God, Gabe. Come home. Meet me in Singapore and we'll fly home together. Don't stay there. It's dangerous. I'm sure it's dangerous."

"I'm not leaving, Molly. I need to be here. I need to help."

Gabe thought back to that day in Cambridge, waiting for the doctor down the hall from Ethan's hospital room. The lounge was painted in pastel colors, and still everything was too bright. Heather had sat in a child's chair at a child's table doing a child's puzzle. She'd create the picture of the house, the tree, the swing, the cartoon family, and then break up the pieces and start all over again.

"Sit down," she told him. "You're making me crazy."

He kept walking in circles around the room. Each time he passed the window, he'd look outside and think: It's a normal day. There are cars driving down the street. There's a woman pushing a stroller. Your son can't die on a day like this. If the day is normal, Ethan will live. If Heather puts the puzzle pieces together, the family is whole. If the doctor comes out of the room, he will say, "Ethan's waiting for you. He wants to tell you a secret."

The boy loved secrets.

"You can't help them," Molly insisted, pulling him out of his memory. Her voice was loud, and Gabe held the phone away from his ear. "This isn't your problem. This is their problem."

"This is my home now. It's my problem, too."

Gabe dressed and hurried out of the bedroom. Wayan's small and tidy house was empty, but there was a note on the kitchen table. *Call when you wake up. The news of the bombing is terrible.*

Next to the note was a bowl of fruit and a small cake. A glass of juice and a plate were set on the table for him.

He thought about the last time he ate. Lunch with Molly at a café in Ubud before the drive to the airport. The Balinese waitress had known him—she had a child at the school. She gave him a kiss and whispered in his ear, "Is she your girlfriend?" "My sister," he said, and he introduced the two. The waitress teased: "Why this man has no girlfriend?" When the waitress walked away, Molly had said to him, "It's time, Gabe. You could try again, you know. It's been more than three years since your divorce."

Had he answered her? He had been so singularly focused since he moved to Bali. Engage in life. Find meaningful work. Be a part of something. And yet he still felt as if he was watching his life from a distance. Love? He hadn't written that part for himself yet.

He knew that Molly hadn't dated since her boyfriend, Max, moved to Germany. Max hadn't wanted children—was that the reason he left her? Gabe never asked. Molly told him one night that she'd choose a child over a man at this point in her life. He was still hoping she'd have a chance at both.

"You can have another child," Molly said at the café.

"A replacement?" he asked.

"No, of course not. But don't give up on the possibility. You loved being a dad."

"I did. And so I teach."

"And then you go home alone."

"I don't know what will happen, Molly. I move a little more slowly these days. Maybe it's the heat. But it's easier to wake up in the morning now. I have something to look forward to."

Molly had reached out her hand across the café table. "I'm a pain-in-the-ass big sister," she said.

For the rest of lunch, they simply ate their sandwiches and talked about the Red Sox.

———

Now Gabe realized he was hungry. But he didn't want to take the time to eat—he wanted to find out about the woman. Jamie. In the car he had told her, "You're going to be all right." She had lost her boyfriend and she had almost died. How did *he* know she was going to be all right?

He pulled out his phone and then decided against calling Wayan. He didn't want to be told to stay away. He didn't want to hear Wayan's words: There's nothing you can do.

He drank the juice and took the cake with him to eat as he drove to the clinic.

The streets of Sanur were almost entirely deserted. Gabe loved Sanur—a beach town south of Denpasar, very different from the resort areas of Kuta and Seminyak. Sanur was not hip—the Seminyak set called it Snore. It was sleepy and quiet, without upscale boutiques and gourmet restaurants. Young people didn't vacation here, but families did: They loved the white-sand beaches, the calm sea, which was protected by a reef, and the low prices of the hotels and restaurants. The Balinese who lived in Sanur didn't seem to care that the big hoteliers ignored them and the European jet-setters who once flocked there had now moved on. Sanur was a good place to live.

Gabe had a friend with a weekend house here, and he often came down for a few days to swim in the warm sea or to take long walks on the beach. Billy had moved from Sanur to Ubud for a yearlong landscaping project, but he kept his beach cottage. Sanur was less than an hour from Ubud, so Billy rented a studio in Ubud and headed south as often as he could, usually with a carload of friends and beer.

As Gabe drove across town to Wayan's clinic, he noticed a small group of people gathered on the sidewalk, leaning in toward one another, the energy of their discussion animating all of them. On this tiny island, just a little larger than Delaware, news would spread very quickly. The bombing, he thought. That's all that matters now.

Gabe was surprised when he arrived at the clinic. Unlike the night before, tonight the place was packed, with injured people crowding the waiting room. They were mostly Balinese kids in their twenties, with bloodied clothing, burns and gashes, all of them standing around, dazed and in pain. When had they arrived? Who had brought them here?

Gabe rushed through to find Rai at the front desk. She looked calm and relaxed, as if she were not smack in the middle of a national disaster.

"Your friend is good," she said. "She is in the last room on the left. Go in to see her. I think she is awake now. But she must leave. We need the room."

Gabe didn't wait to ask questions. He sped down the hall and pushed the partially opened door to the last room.

Jamie was lying on a hospital cot, with her back to him. Her body was trembling under a thin blanket. Was she crying?

He waited a moment and then cleared his throat.

She turned toward him, wiping her face with the sheet. She offered him a smile, then pushed herself up in bed to a sitting position, wincing with pain as she moved.

"I didn't know if I'd see you to thank you," she said.

He nodded. "You look better this morning."

"I must look like hell."

"You do," he said, then smiled. "Last night you looked worse."

"Worse than hell," she said. "That's impressive." She grimaced and touched her face. "Don't make me smile."

"How bad is the pain?"

"I'm floating," she said. "I have no idea."

"What did Wayan tell you? About your injuries?"

"The doctor?"

"Yes. He's a friend of mine."

"Who are you? You probably told me. I'm sorry. I don't remember."

Gabe sat down in the chair next to the bed.

"I live here in Bali. I was in a restaurant near the club last night."

"And you saved me."

The woman watched him with wide eyes. Someone had washed the blood from her hair and cleaned her up. One side of her face was bandaged, and her arm, in a full cast, lay in a pale-blue sling against her torso.

"You saved a lot of people," he said. "I worked like hell to keep up with you. And then a part of the building fell on you."

"I remember all of that. Even the pain meds can't make the screams go away."

"Are there any internal injuries?"

She thought about it for a moment. "My mind's a mess," she said. "Does that count?"

Gabe smiled. "Yeah, I've got that kind of internal injury, as well."

"The doc said I'll survive. I guess I have to believe him."

"Can you walk?"

She looked down at her legs. "I think so. I must have made it to the bathroom at some point. I can't remember."

"They need the room."

"They're kicking me out?" Her face blanched.

"There are so many injured people."

"What happened?" she asked. "At the club."

"I haven't heard the reports yet this morning. My sister called a little while ago and said they think it was a terrorist attack."

Jamie adjusted her sling and fiddled with the edge of her cast.

"The man who died?" Gabe asked, his voice gentle. "He was your boyfriend?"

She nodded. She seemed lost in thought. Or maybe it was a wave of pain.

"Miguel," she finally said. "He asked me to marry him last night. And I said no."

"I'm so sorry," Gabe said.

"I have to get his body." Her breath came in short and choppy bursts. "I have to call his family."

"I'll help you with that," Gabe said. "I'll make some phone calls to find out about the victims."

"Thank you," she said.

"Is there anyone else here in Bali? Friends or family?"

She looked confused.

"Is there someone you should call?" he asked. "Someone who might be worried about you?"

She was quiet again for a long time. One question circled his brain. Will she leave? Of course she'll leave.

"Do they know about the bomb in the States?" she asked.

"Probably," Gabe told her. "I slept and then came right over. I didn't turn on the TV. But my sister knew in Singapore."

"I should call my mother," Jamie said. "And my boss. I lost my cellphone. I lost my purse and my shoes." She paused for a moment, her body trembling.

"Use my phone," he offered, standing and pulling his cellphone from his pocket.

"I can't call Miguel's family. I need to know if they can fly his body back—"

"You can do that later. After I get some information," Gabe said. "Call your mother. I'll wait outside."

"Stay," Jamie told him. "I won't make it long."

He walked over to the window. A Balinese woman sat in the middle of the lawn in front of the clinic. She was rocking back and forth, and, even through the closed window, he could hear her wails.

"Mom?" Jamie said behind him.

He didn't want to turn around. He wanted to give her privacy. But the scene on the lawn was too painful to watch; he could feel anxiety rising in his chest. He walked back to the chair beside the bed and sat down.

"I know," Jamie said. "I was there. I'm okay. Please listen. I'm really okay. I have a broken arm—that's all."

She glanced at Gabe and rolled her eyes like an impatient teenager. He smiled.

"I'm at a clinic. The doctor was fine."

After a pause, she said, "Yeah, sure. I'll get it checked out as soon as I get home."

She listened on the phone and then broke in. "Mom. Miguel—he died. He was buried under too much rubble when I found him—"

She lowered her head and cried, keeping the phone pressed to her ear.

Gabe felt chilled, as if a cold wind ran through his lungs. He had thought that maybe she was in shock, but, no, she was holding it all in. The pain of losing someone. He knew it too well.

He stood up again and walked to the doorway. In the hallway, Rai was helping a Balinese boy hobble to one of the rooms.

"I'll come home," Jamie said. "Yeah, I'm sure. I'll find out if there's a plane out tomorrow."

Gabe slumped against the doorway, suddenly exhausted.

"Today. Tomorrow. I don't know, Mom. I don't know anything." Her voice was rising. "I've never been in a terrorist attack, okay? I've never seen someone I know die before. I don't know what happens next." She stopped talking with a sharp intake of breath. Tears ran down her cheeks.

"I'm sure it's safe," she said, her voice quiet again. "I'll leave as soon as I can."

Gabe stood there, not sure of what he should do.

"I love you, too," she said, then hung up the phone.

She looked at Gabe, her face pale.

"I can take you to the airport," he said quietly.

"I'll go tomorrow," she said. "I have to find out about Miguel's body. I don't know what to do. I don't want to do anything right away." She adjusted the sling again and wiggled her fingers on her injured arm. "That doesn't make sense, does it?"

"It makes perfect sense," he told her.

Gabe stayed home for days after his son died, not able to leave the house. Heather held court in the living room, talking to the endless stream of visitors, all of them eager to share Ethan stories. Every surface of the house was filled with photos of him—baby Ethan in the tub, toddler Ethan in a carrier on Gabe's back, big boy Ethan at the beach. From his study upstairs, Gabe could hear the constant murmur of female voices: "He was so cute." "He was so sweet."

For Gabe, the world felt too difficult to navigate. He sat at his desk and filled a book of sudoku puzzles. He refused food; he refused comfort. He didn't want to reenter the world, because it would be a different world.

"Where were you staying?" he asked Jamie.

"At a hotel in Seminyak. I don't want to go back there."

They sat in silence for a few minutes. Jamie closed her eyes. She looked young—he couldn't guess her age. Thirty?

"I'll be right back," he told her.

"She has to leave," Wayan said impatiently. "I need the room."

Gabe had never known Wayan to speak harshly to anyone, much less a friend. But he looked as if he hadn't slept all night, and the crowd in the waiting room now spilled out the door. From the window in Wayan's office, Gabe could see a young man in a bloody T-shirt lying on the lawn in front of the clinic.

"I don't know what to do with her," Gabe said quietly.

"They are flying all the injured foreigners to Australia," Wayan said. "Take her to the airport."

"She's traumatized. She just wants to rest for one day."

"I can't help you, Gabe. She's only one person. There are hundreds. When I'm done here, I'm heading to Sanglah. They need doctors. They're doing surgeries in the hallways."

He walked out of the room, leaving the door open.

Gabe picked up the newspaper lying on Wayan's desk. He couldn't read the Indonesian words, but the photographs told a very grim story. One photo showed the nightclub destroyed, a fire raging. The other showed a ravaged street, with burned cars and bodies lying under sheets on the ground.

He threw the newspaper across the desk and walked back to Jamie's room.

"I've got a friend with a beach cottage here," he told Jamie. "I'll ask him if we can use it. I can take care of you until you feel ready to fly home."

"Why?"

"What do you mean?"

"Why are you doing this?"

Gabe leaned back against the wall. "I don't know." He looked down at his hands, then up at her. "I can't take care of everyone. But I can take care of you."

"It's yours, my friend," Billy said on the phone. "There's a key in the blue pot on the patio."

"Just for a day or two," Gabe told him.

He was standing outside the clinic, watching a Balinese woman wrap a young man's arm with gauze. Here all the injured were Balinese. The foreigners were taken care of first, Wayan had said, and Gabe began to understand his friend's anger. They turned the Indonesians away from Sanglah Hospital. Westerners were being flown to hospitals in Australia and Singapore, where they would get better treatment. There was no burn center at Sanglah. There weren't enough operating rooms; there weren't enough doctors. They had already run out of anesthesia.

Jamie waited in Gabe's car while he stood outside, making the call.

"Why isn't she flying out?" Billy asked.

Gabe had told him that he was taking care of an injured American. He was surprised that Billy assumed the American was a woman.

"She's pretty traumatized," Gabe said. "She wants to rest for a day or two until she feels stronger."

"Everyone else is fleeing this place," Billy told him. "Even the expats who were miles away from the blasts. They've all gone mad."

"Yeah. I can imagine." Gabe thought about his sister. *Come home. Come home.*

"I bet we'll find out the Americans did this," Billy said. "There's some American battleship nearby." Billy was British, and though he seemed to like Gabe, he hated most Americans.

"Why would Americans bomb nightclubs?" Gabe asked. I don't want to have this conversation, he thought.

"Everyone will blame al-Qaeda, and then the United States will get support for their war in Iraq."

"That doesn't make sense," Gabe said.

"I heard the U.S. embassy issued a warning to its citizens to avoid public places in Indonesia twelve hours before the bombing."

"That's insane."

"Yeah, well, you're American," Billy told him.

"Listen, Billy. I've got to run. Wayan needs help here."

Which was a lie. Wayan wouldn't allow him to do a thing. "Take the girl and give me the room," he had said. As if Gabe were to blame for what was happening at the hospitals in Bali.

"You saw the bombings?" Billy asked.

"Yeah, I saw them."

"Good lord," Billy said. "And you're still in one piece?"

"Hardly," Gabe told him.

———

"It's a short drive," Gabe said. "You comfortable?"

"Just keep me on these magic pills," Jamie said.

Wayan had given Gabe a bottle of painkillers as well as materials for Jamie's bandages. Rai walked him through the process of changing Jamie's face bandage before they left. Gabe saw the swollen line that ran from her eye to her jaw, now sewn together. Already the skin around it was changing color— purple, green, yellow.

He drove toward the center of Sanur. Jamie leaned her head back on the seat, her eyes closed. Maybe she didn't want to see the world, he thought. And then he knew it must be true, because he, too, wanted to be somewhere else. Not in the world. Protected from the world.

Wasn't Bali supposed to be that kind of paradise? Forget the troubles of the world and live in harmony with nature. That's what the brochures promised world travelers. So what happens when the troubles of the world descend on paradise?

Gabe turned down a lane and drove toward the beach. Despite the muggy heat, there were no cars in the usual spots for beach parking. And, sure enough, when they reached the end of the road, he saw that the beach was empty. It was Sunday, the day Balinese families often gathered seaside for picnics. Tourists usually swarmed the beaches, every day of the week. Now there was only one man, on a far pier, practicing tae kwon do, a lone figure in the distance.

What does one do after a terrorist attack? Gabe imagined that people were huddled around their TVs, watching the news. He had been living in Bali when the planes hit the World Trade Center—he remembered sitting in the living room of his joglo, watching CNN for hours on end. He had felt oddly numb, disconnected from the horror of it, and even days of television images didn't bring it closer to his heart.

Now he was too close.

He turned down a private lane and pulled up to the gate of Billy's cottage, then pressed a code onto the intercom and the gate swung open. Jamie kept her eyes closed.

"We're here," he said quietly.

He drove to the end of the lane and parked the car.

He'd always loved the privacy of Billy's cottage. It was tucked into a grove of bamboo trees, hidden from the road on all sides. Some hotel had offered Billy a lot of money to buy his property, but he turned it down. He was a successful landscape designer, and he didn't want to give up his slice of Balinese beach life.

Gabe opened the car door, then glanced back at Jamie. She hadn't budged.

"You okay?" he asked.

"I've never been scared like this before," she said quietly.

"You're safe here," he told her.

"How do you know?" she asked, looking at him.

Her eyes searched his. He noted her bandaged head, her plastered arm. Yesterday she was standing next to a wall of flames, impervious to her own fear, her own danger.

"I don't know," he admitted finally.

She nodded, then opened the door and slowly stepped out of the car.

They walked up the dirt path toward the cottage. Within seconds, they were swallowed by the forest. They could become Hansel and Gretel, he thought, wandering in the dark woods. But weren't Hansel and Gretel captured by a witch?

There is no paradise. There is no safety.

He heard hooting from above, and suddenly all of the birds began to squawk. The welcoming committee, Gabe thought.

The cottage appeared at the end of the path. The forest stopped abruptly and a stretch of newly mowed grass surrounded the house. Billy had hired a young boy to keep up the place while he was gone. The house was white shingled, with a red tile roof and a porch that wrapped around all sides. There were six French doors, and Gabe wanted to open all of them at once so that the house could throw open its arms to the outdoors.

Jamie stopped and gazed at the garden. Billy had done his best work here—he had used palms, tropical tree ferns, bamboo, and banyan trees to create a space that was somehow both contained and wild. Gabe always felt drawn in by the grace and beauty of this place. In the center of the lawn was a pond; long wispy fronds framed the edges. Flowers filled the garden beyond the pond—hibiscus, gardenias, frangipani. The air was thick with the smell of jasmine.

"It's as if nothing in the world should look like this," Jamie said quietly.

"What do you mean?"

"I keep expecting to see hell. Burning bodies. Fire. Now this kind of beauty doesn't make sense."

He reached out and touched the bandage on her face. He could see the spread of something dark under the gauze—more blood? "I need to change this already," he said. He didn't want to alarm her.

"Later," she said. "I want to walk in the garden."

"I'll open the house," he told her, and she nodded.

Gabe walked up to the cottage. A large blue pot containing

a lime tree sat at one edge of the front patio. The house key rested on top of the dirt.

He picked it up, wiped it off on his jeans, and went to the front door. His head brushed some chimes that rang too loudly in his ears. He reached up and quieted them, then unlocked the door and stepped inside.

It took a moment for his eyes to adjust to the darkness. When he could see the outlines of furniture, he moved toward the French doors, throwing them open. The house brightened. Billy had furnished the living room with two deep white couches, a wide teak table between them. A wooden Buddha sat in the middle of the table. The room was spare and clean and inviting.

Gabe felt his heart ease. They could rest here. He could take care of her. They could hide out for a while.

But of course that wouldn't happen. She would get on a plane tomorrow. And he would return to Ubud.

He walked through to the one bedroom in the house. He had never seen this room. Whenever he crashed here, he slept on a futon on the patio. Billy brought lovers but never friends into his bedroom. Gabe was a little unsure of what he'd find.

But the room was simple and serene. A large bed sat in the middle of the room, covered with a sea-green silk blanket. The walls and ceiling were covered with green grass cloth. There was nothing else in the room. Gabe smiled, imagining Billy's boyfriends as they crossed the threshold into his private world.

Well, now it would have to work to heal the wounded. Jamie would stay here, and he would sleep on the futon in the living room.

He pulled down the blanket—the sheets, also pale green, were clean—then walked into the bathroom. A white clawfoot tub sat at one end, next to a glass wall that looked out onto the side garden. Another Buddha, this one painted green, watched over the bathroom from his perch on the counter.

Jamie will be fine here, Gabe thought.

He walked back to the garden to find her.

But she was gone.

He ran down the lane toward the gate. When he got there, he stopped in the middle of the road. The gate was closed. Did she open and close it? Did she head in some other direction? There was only one other exit on the property—the door on the far side of the lawn, which opened onto the beach. Could she have headed out that way? Why had she run off?

He waved his hand across the sensor on the gate. It swung open slowly and he ran through the gap, glancing up and down the lane. No sight of her. Could she have made it to the beach? To the street? Too far in both directions.

He jogged back through the gate just as it began to close on its own. She must have headed through the door that led to the beach.

He ran, looking into the grove of bamboo trees on both sides. Could she have slipped into the woods? Why would she hide from him? Didn't she ask him to stay with her at the clinic?

He took off across the lawn toward the door at the rear of the garden.

Sure enough, the door was thrown open. It was huge and made of carved oak, painted red, with a steel bolt that jammed into the cement wall. He remembered arguing with Billy that the red drew too much attention to the hidden house, and Billy had laughed. "I don't even have to lock the damn thing," he joked. "It's too heavy to open."

Gabe stepped through the door and onto the path that ran along the beach for miles in both directions. He looked straight ahead, toward the sea. A horrible thought assaulted him: Would she drown herself?

But steps from the water's edge, Jamie sat, staring out to sea.

Gabe caught his breath and paused, watching her for a minute before crossing the beach to stand at her side.

"Jamie," he said.

She didn't respond. She kept her gaze on the water.

He sat in the sand beside her. "Are you okay?"

"I didn't want to marry him," she said. "He walked into the club to get away from me."

Gabe waited to see if she would say more. Finally he said, "It's not your fault."

"He wouldn't have been in there if I had said yes."

She glanced at Gabe, as if daring him. She looked fierce, her eyes angry.

He nodded.

"He should still be alive."

"You saved so many people. What you did was heroic."

"I couldn't save Miguel."

He reached for her and she smacked his hand away.

She turned from him. "I'm a fucking coward," she said, staring at the break of the waves on the beach.

"You're the bravest person I know."

She stood and walked back across the sand and through the red door.

———

Later, Gabe found some soup in the pantry and heated it up on the stove. He needed to eat.

He sat on the patio with his bowl and looked out toward the garden. A couple of birds flitted around the pond. The wind picked up and he smelled freshly cut grass; he heard the trickle of water from the fountain as it cascaded into the pond.

He could lock the gate and the red door and keep the world out. He could keep Jamie in.

But she would leave tomorrow.

What's wrong with me, he thought. She just lost her boyfriend and all I want is to keep her here with me.

His cellphone rang. He pulled it out of his pocket and answered it.

"This is Larson Willoughby," a gravelly voice said. "I got this number from Jamie's mother. I'm Jamie's boss. Her friend."

"I'm Gabe. Jamie's sleeping. Can I tell her to call you when she wakes up?"

"Is she okay?"

"She broke her arm. She needed some stitches for a cut on her face. And she's pretty shook up. But she'll be all right." He didn't know whether or not to mention the boyfriend.

"Who are you?" Larson asked.

"I live in Bali. I was nearby when the bombs went off."

"Is she heading home today?" he asked.

"Tomorrow," Gabe said. "She wants to rest today."

"Is she safe?"

"She's safe."

"Tell her—oh, God. I don't know. She's my best friend in the world. Tell her I'll fire her if she doesn't get her ass back right away." The man's voice broke.

"I'll tell her," Gabe said.

———

Gabe wanted quiet and then the house was too quiet. He wanted to be alone and then he found himself needing to hear the sound of her breath.

He carried a small wooden chair from the patio into Billy's bedroom, placing it next to the window, a few feet from where Jamie slept. Then he chose a book off one of Billy's shelves in the living room—a novel set in Hollywood. He took it with him back to the bedroom and settled into the chair.

Turning the book over, he looked at the cover. A kidney-shaped swimming pool. A woman in a bikini, resting in a lounge chair, a large pink hat on her head. A man sitting on the edge of the pool, a dog by his side. No one was smiling. The color had been washed out, as if it had sat in the sun for too long.

He remembered Ethan's fourth birthday party at his in-laws' house in Newton. Gabe sat with Heather on the deck, watching Ethan and his best friend play in the shallow end of the pool on a muggy August day. Heather had tried to plan a party for his entire nursery-school class—the school had strict rules about including everyone. But Ethan wanted only one friend at his party, and he stubbornly refused to have a party if more kids came.

Gabe and Heather had argued about it.

"I just don't want to get in trouble with the school," she said. "For not inviting everyone."

"You just wish he were a different kind of kid."

"What?"

"He's fine the way he is. He doesn't need a million friends."

"It's got nothing to do with that, Gabe."

But Gabe suspected that Heather kept hoping her son would be a golden boy, popular and charmed. She had led that kind of life; at her parties, the pool would have been filled with twenty screaming kids.

They sat in the hot sun, barely speaking. Heather's parents carried too many refreshments back and forth from the house to the deck. Her mother reapplied sunblock to the boys' skinny backs so many times that the surface of the pool gleamed with oil.

"I had a really good birthday," Ethan told them that night, surprising both of them. "Can I do that every year?"

Jamie stirred in her bed and Gabe turned toward her.

"Are you reading?" she asked, her voice breaking the silence of the room.

"No," he said quietly. "I've been on the same page for a half hour."

She sat up in bed and lodged a pillow under her cast.

"Are you thinking about last night?"

"I was thinking about my son," he said.

"You have a son?"

"He died," Gabe told her. "Four years ago."

"I'm so sorry." Jamie grimaced. When their eyes met, he saw a tenderness that surprised him. He had to look away.

He gazed out the window at Billy's perfect garden. A couple of finches gathered around a bird feeder. They pecked at the food, flitted away, then returned for more.

"The day that Ethan got sick, I was working on a story in South Boston. I used to be a journalist. My wife called me and told me that his fever had spiked. I told her to call the doctor. I said something awful about being in the middle of an important story, that I couldn't leave work every time he got sick."

He didn't say anything for a moment, remembering the way she'd yelled at him. "You don't have to be an asshole," she said. And for the hundredth time since his divorce, he wondered: How do people who love each other come to treat each other so badly?

Gabe had reimagined that day so many times—he would tell Heather that he'd meet them at the doctor's office. Poor kid, he'd say to her. Poor you.

When he got to the clinic, Ethan would already be feeling better, as if a mere change in Gabe's behavior could rewrite his story.

"What was wrong with him?" Jamie asked.

"It just started with a fever. By the middle of the next day he was in the hospital. Twenty-four hours later he was dead."

"My God."

"Spinal meningitis. But we didn't know that until it was all over."

They had gone to Legal Sea Foods for dinner the night before. "My head hurts," Ethan complained as soon as they ordered their food.

"Come here, sweetheart," Heather said.

Ethan climbed onto her lap, and Heather leaned over and pressed her lips to his forehead.

"He's warm."

"It's hot in here," Gabe said.

"He's really warm."

Ethan closed his eyes and curled up on his mother's lap.

"I'll take him home," Heather said. "Do you mind getting the food to go and meeting us there?" She was already lifting Ethan up and adjusting him in her arms.

By the time Gabe got home with three boxed dinners, Ethan

was asleep in his big-boy bed and Heather was lying beside him.

"I've got dinner," Gabe said to her, standing in the door-way.

"Sleeping," Heather murmured.

He ate alone that night; he slept alone.

"He was four," Gabe said to Jamie. "He was in a hospital bed that was too big for him. His skin was ghostly white. I said to my wife, 'Remember how tan he was after the week at the Cape? What happened to his summer tan?' "

Gabe waited a moment. Years later, and the memories were still too raw.

"My sister, Molly, stayed with us at the hospital all night. She was just here in Bali—I took her to the airport . . . yesterday? Was that only yesterday? Before the bombing."

He looked at Jamie, suddenly disoriented. She nodded.

"Molly told Ethan stories about a dog named Ethanopolis. The dog had superpowers, and whenever his owner was about to succumb to great danger, Ethanopolis would sweep in and save the day."

Jamie was smiling. Gabe thought: She's beautiful. Even now, with her face half covered in bandages, there's something allur-ing about her. He pushed the thought away.

"We could all use an Ethanopolis in our lives," she said.

"Molly was telling Ethan a story about a tornado in the small town where Ethanopolis and his boy lived, when Ethan started having a seizure. The nurses and doctors poured into the room and we were pushed out. This is crazy, but while we were sitting in the waiting room I kept imagining all the ways that Ethanopolis could save the day. Ethan was caught in the eye of the tornado, and while he was carried across Massachusetts, Ethanopolis raced along, barking in fury, until finally he swooped through the swirling mass of the storm, caught my boy in his front paws, and carried him to safety."

Gabe stopped talking. He heard the sound of a gecko—*uh-oh, uh-oh*, it seemed to say. He searched the ceiling and the walls, but he couldn't find it. *Uh-oh.*

"I bet he was a wonderful kid," Jamie said finally.

"He was," Gabe said. "Every day he told me a secret when he woke up in the morning. First he'd make me promise to never ever tell anyone. I would solemnly swear. Then he would whisper in my ear. 'I hate peanut butter,' he'd say. Or 'Miss Vera smells like poop.' "

"And you never told a soul."

He smiled. "I'm good with secrets."

"I'll remember that."

They both fell silent. Gabe put his book on the floor beside him.

"I could ask you how many people died last night, but I don't want to know," Jamie said. She ran her fingers along her cast.

"Can I get you something to eat?" he asked. "There's soup."

"No," she said. "Thank you."

"Your boss called. Larson. He said he'll fire you if you don't come home right away."

"That's Larson." She offered a half smile.

His phone rang in his pocket. He pulled it out and answered. "Hello?"

"This is Jamie's mom." He heard the woman's worry right away.

"Hold on," he said. "I'll put her on." He walked over to the bed and placed the phone in Jamie's hand.

"Mom," she said. She sounded exhausted.

The woman started to sob—Gabe could hear the sound reverberate through the room. Jamie closed her eyes.

"I'm okay," she said. "Really. Some cuts. A broken arm. Nothing—"

She shook her head and her face darkened. "Don't tell me about it. I don't want to know."

After another moment she said, "Stop. Mom. Please."

Pushing herself up in the bed, she rearranged the pillow under her arm.

"I'll find out about Miguel's body. Then I'll call his family."

Gabe walked toward the French door. He should have called already. He wasn't thinking clearly.

"Tomorrow," Jamie said behind him. "I'll get a plane out tomorrow. I'm not flying tonight."

Gabe walked to the edge of the patio, looking out toward the garden.

He could hear Jamie say, "I love you, too."

And then she was quiet. The next time he looked in, she was sleeping again, curled on her side, the blanket pushed to the end of the bed.

From the garden, Gabe called Wayan. He asked him to stop by at the end of the day and take a look at Jamie's cut. He was worried about infection.

"There is no end of my day," Wayan said.

"What have you learned?" Gabe asked. "About the bombing."

"Over two hundred dead," Wayan told him. "Many of them Australian. The hospitals can't cope. Hundreds seriously injured. We're shipping everyone out. It's a nightmare at San-glah."

"Has anyone claimed responsibility?"

"I don't know," Wayan said. "All I know is that we need doctors and supplies and we need a fucking burn unit. We don't even have enough IV saline to keep this many burn victims hydrated. We don't have the morphine to keep them from wailing with pain."

"You don't need to stop by," Gabe said. "Call in a prescription for antibiotics. I'll take care of her."

"Just send her home," Wayan insisted.

"She'll leave tomorrow," Gabe told him.

"There are flights out right now. They're putting medical personnel on the planes. They're getting victims to good hospitals."

"I'll tell her," Gabe said.

"Rai is going to a cleansing ceremony on the beach tonight," Wayan said, his voice softer. "Maybe you should go. It might be good for you."

"Thank you, Wayan. Good luck with all of it."

It was almost evening when Gabe heard Jamie cry out—a sharp scream and then a muffled cry. He ran from the edge of the patio, where he had been watching the colors of the garden change with the fading light.

"Are you all right?" he asked.

She was sitting in bed, cradling her arm.

"A nightmare," she said. "And pain."

He got a pain pill from the vial in the bathroom and poured water into a glass. He handed her both.

"In the nightmare," she said, "Miguel was alive. He was covered in blood. He tried to speak but blood spilled from his mouth."

Gabe sat at the edge of her bed.

"He was alive when I found him," she said, her voice shaky. "He was crushed by part of the wall, but his eyes were open and he could see me."

"Could he talk?"

Jamie shook her head. "He tried to say something, but nothing came out. I told him I was going to get him out of there. I told him he was going to make it."

She was trembling, and Gabe pulled the blanket up to her shoulders. He rested his hand on her arm.

"I don't even know if I loved him," Jamie said. "We only spent a few weeks together—whenever we could see each other between my trips to South America. I never met his family."

"I made some calls earlier," Gabe said gently. "The morgue identified his body."

"How?"

"He had his wallet. They were able to let his family know." Gabe had spent an hour on the phone with five different people at the makeshift morgue. Most of the bodies were so badly burned that the process of identifying them was very difficult, the woman told him. But they had already listed Miguel Avalos of Santiago, Chile.

"I have to call his parents," Jamie said. "What do I say? I invited your son to Bali for a fabulous vacation and now he's gone?"

Gabe straightened the blanket around her and let his hands drop onto his lap.

"You'll find the right words," he told her.

Jamie grimaced.

"Where's the pain?" he asked.

"Everywhere."

"Can I look at the cut?"

She turned her face toward him.

He carefully unwrapped the bandage. The wound was swollen, and he could see some weeping from the sutures.

"Wayan ordered antibiotics," Gabe told her. "I didn't want to go to the pharmacy while you were sleeping. In case you woke up and needed something."

"It's not infected," she said. "If it were, it would feel hot."

He placed his hand gently on the wound.

"It does feel hot," he said. "Wayan said they're flying the injured to hospitals in other countries. We can get you out tonight."

"Tomorrow," she insisted. "I'm staying until tomorrow."

"I'm going to walk into town. I'll just make a quick stop at the pharmacy."

Jamie didn't answer.

"You *will* get better," Gabe said. "This will end."

"I can't imagine," she whispered.

"When my son died," he said, "I couldn't imagine how to spend another day in this world."

"How'd you do it?"

"Every day was hell for a while, and then it got a little easier. About a year later, I noticed that I got through a whole day without thinking about him. At first I felt awful, as if I had betrayed him. And then I realized that maybe that's where I was headed. A life without him in my thoughts all the time."

"And now?"

"I think about him a lot. But not all the time."

She seemed to consider his words.

Gabe moved his hand to her shoulder. His fingers rested on the bare skin above the collar of her shirt. He thought of her boyfriend, touching her only a couple of nights ago. Lifting his hand away, he stood and walked to the chair by the window.

"I don't know anything about you," he said, sitting down.

"Nothing matters," she told him.

The day after Ethan died, he stood in the funeral parlor, looking at coffins. The undertaker asked him what he did for a living. He thought: What does it matter? My career, my wife, my beautifully restored Colonial house. Who gives a fuck? Yesterday he had a life. Today he had no life.

He chose a simple coffin, impossibly small.

He never wrote another article for the paper. His wife left him. His house sold for a fraction of what it was worth.

"Ethan had an imaginary friend," Gabe told Jamie.

She smiled, and he felt relieved to see it.

"His friend was named Fritz, and he was as tall as a tree but he could fold himself into tiny spaces. I pictured him as a kind of origami child. Ethan set a place for Fritz at the table at every meal. Fritz hated corn and tomatoes. He loved spaghetti. After dinner Ethan and Fritz would play in the backyard. He asked us not to come outside, though we were allowed to watch him from the kitchen window. If we came outside, Fritz ran away. He was very frightened of adults."

"I like this kid," Jamie said.

Gabe nodded. "I think he's not alone now. I don't believe in heaven, I don't believe in an afterlife, but I believe in Fritz."

"I believe in Fritz," Jamie murmured sleepily. She curled onto her side.

"The pharmacy is close by," Gabe said. "I'll be back very soon."

"Good night," she whispered.

When Gabe walked into town he was again surprised—the streets were empty, the cafés quiet. There was no music blasting from Sammy's Irish Pub, and only a couple of Westerners sat at an outside table, nursing beers. He heard chanting from the yoga studio in town; a kind of low breathy hum reverberated from the open windows. Prayers, he thought. The New Agers in Bali would have their yoga and chanting and prayer circles to turn to now. The Balinese had their religion. They would have rituals to help them through this crisis; they would have song and dance and their very strong belief in the afterlife to soothe their own pain. Whatever it takes to get you through.

He had nothing when Ethan died. His sister told him to talk to her rabbi in Cambridge. He sat with the surprisingly young woman for a strained hour, listening to her speak about God and his mysterious ways. He made a donation to the temple and never returned.

Heather had her wonderful friends, who swooped in and gathered her up, took her away. They fed her and walked with her in slow loops around Fresh Pond; they held her and cried with her. There were so many good women that there was no room for Gabe in the middle of it all. "Thank you," he kept saying to them all. "Thank you for taking such good care of her."

Six months later she was gone, swept away by the power of sisterhood. "You can't give me anything," she said to him the last night she spent in their house. "You can't even give me your grief to hold."

He couldn't argue. She went to live with one of her friends, and he heard through another friend that the two women had become lovers. He was surprised at first and then comforted by the fact that she was happy. She deserved love, Gabe thought. She deserved someone else.

He walked the city for a year. He sold the house and moved to a small apartment in the Back Bay. He quit his job. He had enough money to get by for a little while. "I'm okay," he told anyone who asked, and after a while they stopped asking. He woke up in the morning, put on his hiking boots, and walked the streets of Boston, stopping only to buy food when he was hungry. He walked in the rain and in the snow, and at the end of the year he had lost twenty pounds and all of his friends. He bought a one-way ticket to Bali because someone told him it was cheap and warm. He was tired of walking.

How odd, he thought, that he happened to land in the country of ritual, of prayer, of daily life devoted to community and family. Even now, three years later, with a job and a home on the edge of a mountain, he can imagine this: Walking away. Walking for hours, days, years. Walking alone.

But last night he didn't walk away from the bombs. And he didn't walk away from the screams. Now he has to buy medicine for Jamie.

The pharmacy was still open, and Gabe stepped through the door. He greeted the woman behind the counter with his few Indonesian words. She was pleased and began speaking to him much too fast, a long string of words that he didn't understand.

"I'm sorry," he said. "Do you speak English?"

"Yes," she said with a small smile.

"Dr. Wayan Genep called in a prescription for Jamie Hyde. I'm here to pick it up."

"Yes, yes," the woman said, and turned to find the pills.

Looking around the store, he realized he had no toothbrush or toothpaste—neither did Jamie. He grabbed a basket and walked through the aisles, choosing everything they might need. He found a short-sleeved shirt with buttons so Jamie could put it on over her cast. BALI BABY was stitched on the front, and a baby monkey graced the back. He picked out a teal-blue sarong and a pair of flip-flops for her, too, and then threw in a new T-shirt for himself. When he returned to the counter, the woman was waiting.

"It is awful," she said. "The bombing. All of those young people."

"Yes," he said, nodding as he unloaded his basket onto the counter.

"You have not left yet," she said. "I heard that all the Westerners are leaving our country."

"I live here," he said.

"You're staying?"

"Yes," he said simply.

"I am glad," she told him. "There will be a cleansing ceremony tonight. It begins soon. It will end on the beach. Everyone in town will go. It is important that we do this. For the community."

"Thank you," he said to the woman, handing her some cash.

"I am closing the pharmacy now so I can go to the ceremony. You come with me."

He smiled. "I can't. I have to bring my friend this medicine," he said as he turned to leave.

"You, too, must heal."

He looked at the woman questioningly.

"It is in your eyes," she said.

Jamie was in the bathroom when he returned.

"Are you okay?" he called out.

"I'm taking a washcloth bath!"

"I have fresh clothes for you," he told her. "Pharmacy special."

She opened the door, hiding behind it. "Really?"

He glimpsed her bare shoulder. Her skin was tanned and smooth. He looked away and held up the monkey shirt.

"I love it," she said.

He passed her the clothes and went back to the kitchen to wait for her. There was a bottle of scotch in Billy's cupboard, so he poured himself a drink and added some ice.

"That wasn't easy," Jamie said, and he turned around.

The new sarong was tightly wrapped around her waist, and Gabe found his eyes lingering on the curves of her body.

"You could ask for help," he said. "Or is it against your religion?"

"I may have to convert," she told him. "A one-handed bath is a bitch. Can I have one of those?"

He handed her his scotch and poured himself another.

"How long have you lived in Bali?" she asked.

"For three years now."

"Since your son died."

"Since a year after my son died."

"And your wife?"

"In Boston. We're divorced."

"Because of your son?"

"Grief has a way of ripping people apart."

She sipped her scotch. Then she asked, "Is this grief?"

"This? This is hell. Grief comes later."

"Oh, boy," she said, and he smiled.

"Sorry about the shirt. That was the best the pharmacy had to offer."

"I like my monkey," she said, spinning around and offering him a look. "Thanks."

She lifted her scotch and they clinked glasses.

"To hell," she said.

"To hell."

As they drank, Jamie caught his eyes, held them for a moment, and then gazed into her glass.

"I bought toothbrushes, too," Gabe told her. "Toothpaste."

"My clothes are at the hotel in Seminyak."

"We can get it all tomorrow," he said.

"I booked my flight for tomorrow. It's at four."

The word *tomorrow* settled like a stone in his ribs.

"We'll get your suitcase on the way to the airport."

"Miguel's things are there. I don't want to go back."

"I'll get it for you. I'll drive out first thing in the morning."

"Thanks. I have my passport and some cash stashed in one drawer."

"I'll find it," Gabe promised.

"Can you write down Miguel's parents' phone number when you're there? I think it's on the ID tag of his luggage. He lived with his parents when he wasn't working in the mountains."

"Of course."

Jamie pressed the cold glass of scotch against her forehead.

"I keep thinking of things to say to Miguel," she said. "I want to finish a conversation that we hadn't even started yet."

She sat on a stool at the kitchen counter, lifting her cast and placing it gently on the marble. She rubbed her shoulder under her sling.

"Would it help to talk about him?" Gabe asked.

She shook her head. Then she offered him a small smile.

"Are you always like this?"

"What do you mean?" he asked.

"Do you always charge into burning buildings?"

"No. I didn't give it much thought. I heard the screams and I couldn't run the other way."

"Good man."

"So why doesn't it feel good?"

He looked away from her gaze. Outside, the light of the moon reflected off the pond in the garden.

"Because there were still people left. People dying."

"I keep hearing screams," he said. "I hear someone shouting for help, and I turn my head and it's gone."

"I smell fire. All the time."

He met her eyes. "We're quite a pair," he said.

"Do you have a job? A girlfriend?"

Gabe stared into the bottom of his glass, then said, "There's a cleansing ceremony on the beach tonight. The Balinese believe they can free the spirits of the bombing victims."

She waited, her dark eyes on him. "You didn't answer me."

"I have a job. I don't have a girlfriend. But, truthfully, I don't know what I have. It feels like everything blew up in that explosion last night."

Jamie walked to the patio and gazed outside. She drank her scotch. Gabe watched her. For now, he thought, I have this.

"Can we go to the cleansing ceremony?" she asked.

"Yes," he told her.

He and Jamie made their way across the grass and pulled open the heavy red door at the back of the property. They stepped onto the paved beach path and closed the door behind them. The sky was filled with stars.

For a moment they could hear nothing. And then the sound of the gamelan seemed to surround them. First there were bells, then gongs, then chimes and flutes. The sounds chased one another through the air. A man's voice called out, and then many voices chanted together.

They walked out onto the beach and followed the edge of the surf toward the gathering. As they got closer, they could see that the crowd was large—a couple of hundred people. Everyone was dressed in traditional Balinese clothing: sarongs with bright belts on both the men and women, lace blouses—kebayas—for the women, head wraps for the men. Almost all the people were Balinese, but there were a few Westerners at the edge of the crowd. Many people held candles, the flames flickering in the dark.

"What are they doing?" Jamie asked.

"The Balinese believe in reincarnation," Gabe told her as they neared the crowd. "When a body dies, its soul is released so it can find the next life. If there is violence, then the soul has difficulty finding its way. The Balinese believe that this ceremony will help release those souls. And they're cleansing the island of evil spirits. At some point, the priest will sprinkle holy water over the people and the land."

"It's beautiful," Jamie said.

"When I first came here, I thought the Balinese Hindu religion would give me some peace. I studied a little, went to some ceremonies. But it's all about community. And I haven't made my way into a community."

"Why not?"

"I've always been a bit of a loner. Maybe that's why I like Bali. I'm allowed to be an outsider."

"When you were married, weren't you part of something?"

"Maybe for a while. When Ethan was alive, we were a family."

They stopped walking when they were close to the gathering. The light of the candles reflected off the water and seemed to glimmer in the night sky.

"And you?" Gabe asked. "Are you a solitary soul?"

"Sort of," Jamie said. "I'm an adventure-travel guide. My life is groups, lots of people, community love fests. But at the end of the day, I go home alone."

"No boyfriends before Miguel?" Gabe asked.

"An occasional boyfriend," Jamie said. "But I haven't been very successful with long-term relationships."

"Why is that?"

She looked at him and offered a sly smile. "Just because you saved my life doesn't mean I have to answer all your questions."

"Fair enough," he said.

They were quiet for a moment, listening to the chanting of the priest. Many people were openly crying, and one woman made a keening sound that seemed to echo the priest's song.

"When I travel," Jamie said, her voice soft in Gabe's ear, "I think: I love this country. I want to live here awhile. But then the next country lures me away. I keep moving on."

Gabe glanced at her. "You keep looking for something new."

"Something different, something better. I don't know. I do the same thing with men."

"Is your boss a boyfriend?"

"Most definitely not."

"And so he stays in the picture."

"Something like that." Jamie waited, then added, "I didn't have very good role models."

"Your parents divorced?"

"My father left us a long time ago. I'm not sure if I'm protecting myself from a man like him or if I'm becoming someone like him. Either way, it's pretty scary."

Gabe saw something in her then that he hadn't been able to identify. She was clearly tough—and yet there was something vulnerable about her, too. He felt some odd combination of awe at her strength and a deep desire to protect her.

The music stopped and one man began to sing. The voice carried out to sea; Gabe gazed toward the reflection of the moon on the water while he listened. It was full of yearning, this song. He couldn't understand the words, but he was surprised to find himself fighting back tears.

He'd had similar experiences throughout his time in Bali. The ceremonies always reached deep into his heart, tapping emotional reservoirs that he wasn't always aware of. And yet he always tugged right back, resisting that call.

A group of children—most of these seem to be the children of Westerners rather than the Balinese—ran to the edge of the surf. They released paper boats onto the water. Each boat, carrying a lit candle, glided over the gentle waves as it headed out to sea.

"I wish I believed that this might work," Jamie said, her eyes fixed on the shimmering light of the candles bobbing in the water. She turned to Gabe. "But the fire. And all those people buried under the rubble . . ." She looked up at him, her eyes filling with tears.

He pulled her into his arms and held her, running his hand over her back. He felt her lean her weight into him.

That night, Gabe set up the futon in the living room. He had thought about sleeping outside, under the stars. But he wanted to be able to hear Jamie if she cried out during the night.

The minute he lay down, his mind began to swim with images of the bombing. He could hear echoes of the screams, as if the people who were trapped in the burning club were just outside the walls of the beach cottage. He could still smell the awful biting odor of burning hair. He pulled the blanket up to his nose and inhaled musty closet smells, tangling himself in the cover, trying to find a way to settle down.

Finally, he sat up on the futon, his body soaked in sweat. The night loomed long, hours and hours long, all of them dark and filled with memory. He stood up, dropping the blanket onto the futon. Then he pulled on his jeans and walked outside.

The night air was warm and humid. He loved the heat. He let the air bathe his skin and slow the beating of his heart.

Gabe let his mind wander back to the night the doctor came out of Ethan's hospital room and walked toward them down the long corridor. Stupidly, he had thought of Ethanopolis, Molly's fantasy dog. Ethanopolis had failed his mission. But then he thought: It wasn't the dog's job. It was my job to save my son. It was my only job in the God damn world. He had glanced at Heather and Molly, standing beside him, numb and dazed. I failed all of them, he thought. The doctor mumbled words of consolation; Heather screamed, and Molly held her. But Gabe only stood there, his arms hanging at his sides, thinking: It was my only job.

The night was quiet. The moon reflected off the pond, and he could see something skitter across the lily pads and then splash into the water.

The terror is over, he told himself.

But as he waited for Jamie to cry out in her sleep, he knew that all over this island there were other people still shrieking in pain.

He awoke to screams.

He ran into the bedroom, and in his half-awake state, he thought: *Fire.* Get her out before the fire spreads.

He stopped when he saw her sitting in bed, her mouth open, as if gasping for breath. She was silent.

"Are you all right?" Gabe asked. He was now unsure if he had dreamed the whole thing.

She nodded, but she looked terrified.

"Let me get dressed," he said, suddenly aware that he was wearing only his boxer shorts. "I'll come back in a minute."

He waited until she nodded once more. She barely moved—she still looked stunned.

"I'll be right back," he repeated.

He tossed on his jeans, glancing outside—the sun was beginning to rise and brighten the sky. He felt disoriented and scared of something he couldn't name.

This time he knocked on her open door before stepping inside the bedroom. She was lying down again, the blanket pulled high. He couldn't tell if she was sleeping.

He stood there, unsure of what to do.

"I'm sorry," she said, her voice muffled.

"Can I get you anything?"

"No," she said. "I'll go back to sleep."

"I might drive out to get your suitcase," Gabe said. "If you're okay alone."

"Thank you."

"What's the name of the hotel?"

"The Swan," she said.

"I know where it is."

"Why did they bomb Bali?" she asked, her voice very small.

Gabe leaned against the door. "I don't know. Bali is part of Indonesia, but the rest of Indonesia is Muslim. The Balinese primarily practice Hinduism. So this island is a problem for Indonesia. It's also more popular on the tourist circuit. If it was Indonesian terrorists, it might have been about either of those factors."

She was quiet for a while and he thought maybe she had fallen back to sleep.

"I don't understand why they bombed a club," she said finally.

"They bombed two clubs," he told her.

"Don't tell me how many people died."

"I won't tell you."

"It's not numbers. It's Miguel. It's all those people dancing, drinking."

Gabe nodded. "Someone wanted to create fear, fear in Westerners." He put his head back against the wall. There was something comforting about speaking into the darkness of the room.

"I remember reading the *New York Times* articles after 9/11," Jamie said. "All those profiles of the people killed in the towers. I kept trying to imagine their lives and the lives of the people who knew them. I never got close to understanding what they went through."

"I was already here," Gabe said. "It felt very far away."

"Did you know anyone?"

"My sister had a friend on one of the planes that went into the tower."

Jamie nodded. "My mother knew someone who got out of the building before it went down."

A bird squawked, and both of them looked toward the window. A small bird with a yellow crest perched on the sill.

"What happens the next day?" Jamie asked. "And the day after that?"

Gabe didn't answer. He could remember that for a long time after Ethan died, he wore the same pants and shirt every single day, until they wore out. Was it lack of energy that kept him in the same clothes, or a desire to stop time?

"I'm scared to leave," Jamie said.

"You should go," Gabe told her, his stomach tightening. "You need to have that broken arm checked. And you probably want a plastic surgeon to look at the scar."

"I don't care," she said.

"You will care. Later."

She didn't answer, and then he could hear her breathing change and he knew she was sleeping.

Don't go, he thought.

—

On the way to Seminyak, Gabe called his boss, Lena.

"Where are you?" she asked as soon as she answered the phone.

"Sanur," he said. "I'm sorry. I should have called you."

"We canceled school. I left a message on your cell."

"I never checked my messages," he told her. "I'm helping out down here. I don't know when I'll get back."

"I might go down today," Lena said. "They need blood. They need volunteers to help organize some kind of tracking system for the people still missing. No one knows how many died."

"I was there," Gabe said.

"At the bombing?" Her voice changed. She paused and then said, "Were you hurt?"

"I got there right after it happened. I was having dinner at Santo's."

"Jesus," Lena said. "Gabe."

Gabe and Lena were lovers for a short time, a couple of years ago. When Gabe stepped in for a teacher who got sick and moved back to Australia, he stopped sleeping with Lena. They became friends then, real friends. And yet, in the past twenty-four hours, he hadn't even thought of calling her. In the cottage with Jamie, he felt somehow removed from both time and the world. It was only now, driving into the glare of the sun, that Gabe remembered that he should have been driving to work.

"Do you want me to come to you?" she asked.

"No," he said. "I have things I have to do."

Lena was Swedish, older than Gabe by five years or so, and

caretaker to the world. When she started a school in Ubud, every expat wanted his or her child to be under Lena's guidance. She was smart and nurturing and tough enough to train the parents as well as the children.

"Why are you in Sanur?" she asked.

"Helping out," he said. "Some of the bombing victims ended up here."

"Was it as bad as they say?"

"I don't know what's being said," he told her. "But it was unimaginably bad."

"Putu's brother hasn't come home," she said. Putu was one of the Balinese women who worked at the school. She was the cook and housekeeper, but she was training to be a teacher one day.

"Was he at one of the clubs?" Gabe asked.

"He worked at a hotel in Kuta," she told him. "He had left his shift twenty minutes before the bombs went off. He might have been driving past—"

He could hear Lena catch her breath. He didn't know Putu's brother, but she talked about him often. He drove his two sons up to Ubud on his motorcycle once to see the school. Putu had asked Lena if the children could attend the school next year. Her brother would drive them back and forth from Legian. He wanted them to get ahead in the world. He didn't want them to work as a security guard at a hotel, like he did.

"I'll see if I can find out anything," Gabe told her. "What's his name?"

"Ketut Taram," Lena said. "Two school families are leaving Bali. There will be others, too. I may lose the school."

"Don't worry about that now," he said.

"I know. I'm sorry. I don't know what to worry about. I feel so far away. Can I meet you down there?"

"I don't know where I'll be today. I'll call you along the way."

"You're okay, Gabe?"

"I'm trying as hard as I can."

The Swan was a high-end luxury resort on the beach in Seminyak, one of a half dozen that had opened in the past five years. Kuta kept its surfer image, its beer-and-bong atmosphere, but Seminyak went upscale, attracting tourists from New York, L.A., Paris.

Two marble swans graced the entrance to the hotel. Gabe drove along a manicured garden with a series of pools, one lapping into the next, all filled with floating candles. He stopped in front of the lobby and told the valet to keep his car near the entrance—he was only going to run in for a few minutes.

"That is what everyone is doing," the Balinese boy said. "Getting their suitcases and leaving the country."

Gabe turned back, surprised.

"No," he said. "I'm not leaving. I'm getting some things for a friend who was in the bombing."

"Sorry, boss," the boy said, looking at his feet.

"The place is emptying out?" Gabe asked.

"Everyplace is empty. Twenty-four hours and everyone's gone."

"Every tourist left?"

"The airlines had to add flights. Everyone is scared."

"Will the hotel stay open?"

"Our boss says that he will stay open. But he will not. He cannot. We all know it."

Gabe felt a wave of anger. Bali, this sweet island, was going to suffer greatly.

"You will stay?" the boy asked, hopeful.

"I live here," Gabe told him. "I'm not going anywhere."

"That is good." The boy smiled for the first time. "Tell all of your friends that."

"I will," Gabe said.

He headed into the grand lobby. It was beautifully designed, with teak floors and walls and billowing white fabric draped from the ceiling like clouds. A young man in formal costume played the gamelan from the center of the cavernous space. He was seated on a stone in the middle of a round basin, lily pads filling the water. How did he get to the stone?

"Can I help you, sir?" a woman asked. She was Balinese, dressed in a white blouse and a white sarong. She wasn't smiling—the Balinese are famous for their smiles. Balinese service, always with a smile. Not anymore.

She was the only person in the lobby except for the musician. Gabe couldn't find anything that looked like a desk or a counter.

"Where is the reception?"

"I can help you."

"I'm here to collect Jamie Hyde's belongings. She was hurt in the bombing and I'm taking care of her in Sanur."

"I am so sorry." The woman lowered her eyes.

"Can you take me to her room?"

"Of course."

The woman bowed and turned away. "Follow me."

They headed out the back door of the lobby and across a

long stretch of lawn. A few men bent over, cutting the grass with scythes. Gabe could see a deserted pool at the far end of the lawn.

The woman gestured for him to follow her down a long passage of stairs.

As they walked, Gabe listened to the click of her heels. There was no other noise.

She stopped in front of a white villa and pulled a key out of her pocket.

"We didn't know how to contact Miss Jamie. We didn't know if she was coming back."

She opened the door and light filled the room.

Gabe saw that the room had been cleaned by the maid—the bed beautifully arranged with pillows, some clothing piled neatly on one dresser. It was a large, airy space, and the fan moved silently overhead.

"Do you know where her suitcase might be?"

"Yes, sir," the woman said.

She slipped off her shoes; Gabe did the same.

He saw a jacket hanging over the back of a chair: Miguel's.

"She was with a young man who died in the bombing," he said.

The woman spun around and looked at him, her mouth open.

"I'll get you an address," Gabe said. "Maybe you can ship his things to his family in Chile."

"Yes, of course," the woman said.

"I'll gather them together," he told her.

The woman walked across the room and opened a closet door. Two small suitcases were set on a high shelf. A few dresses hung in the closet, along with a couple of men's dress shirts.

Gabe studied the dresses—one black and slinky, the other flowery and bright. Jamie would wear these, he thought. Before.

The woman reached for the suitcase.

"Let me get that," Gabe said.

He stepped up to her and pulled down the first bag.

"Can I help you pack, sir?"

"No," he said. "I can do it. Thank you for your help."

"There are phone messages for Miss Jamie. Will you give those to her?"

"Of course."

"I will have them ready for you when you leave."

The woman turned and left.

Gabe lifted the two dresses out of the closet and held them in front of him. Who are you, he thought? He pressed the black dress to his face—he could smell some kind of perfume, a little sweet, a little spicy. Adventure guide who tossed this on at the end of her day? He laid the dresses carefully on the bed.

He read the tag on the first suitcase: *Miguel Avalos.* An address and phone number in Santiago, Chile. Good. He wrote down the phone number. He found Miguel's clothing in a dresser on the other side of the large room. Jeans, shorts, T-shirts. Boy clothes, Gabe thought. A boy who went off on an adventure with a beautiful girl to Bali. A boy who wanted to marry that girl. Gabe packed his clothes quickly, his chest tight. Who would open this suitcase? His mother? His father?

He remembered packing Ethan's clothes in boxes to give away. Heather lay on the small bed in his room, staring at the plastic stars on the ceiling, humming the tunes to songs she once sang to him. Deep in the closet, Gabe found a baseball cap he had bought Ethan at the boy's first Red Sox game. He tucked it into his back pocket, unable to put it in the box. Then he opened a shoe box wedged in the corner of the closet.

"Heather," he said, his voice loud.

She stopped humming but didn't move from the bed.

He walked over to her, the box in his hands. He placed it on the side of the bed and she sat up to peer in.

"What is it?" she asked. Gabe had barely spoken to her in the days since Ethan had died. Molly had told him that he was pushing his wife away because she was so much a part of his life with Ethan. Without Ethan, he couldn't have Heather.

The box was filled with bugs, dozens of dead bugs. Both Heather and Gabe smiled at the collection as if they had found gold. Ethan would have known the name of every single one. Heather reached over and took Gabe's hand, and he lifted her hand to his lips. Don't leave me, he thought. But he couldn't bring himself to say a word.

The box now sat on the dresser in his joglo, next to the Red Sox cap and a photo of Ethan jumping into a swimming pool, a wide smile on his face.

He closed Miguel's suitcase and ran the zipper around the edges, then left it outside the door, on the patio.

He lifted the other suitcase from the closet and placed it on the end of the bed. The name tag read *Jamie Hyde*. He opened it. There was a photo of a dog in the empty case—an enormous hound that looked like a mix of Newfie and Saint Bernard. The long-haired dog gazed into the camera, pure love on its face. He turned the photo over—no caption to help him out. Jamie left a beloved dog at home while she traveled the world? No, the photo was old. This was a childhood pet, he guessed.

He slipped the photo into his shirt pocket; Jamie might want it with her.

Opening the top drawer of the large teak dresser, he discovered lacy things—bras, panties—and he felt as if he were doing something illicit. Quickly, he put the underwear in the suitcase. In the next drawer he saw shirts, shorts, a bikini, and he piled the clothing into the case. He found a passport with a couple of hundred-dollar bills tucked inside. The last drawer contained jeans, a sweater, a pair of silk pants.

In the bathroom he found another bikini, hanging on a hook. Midnight blue, covered with tiny stars. Very small. He wished he could find a picture of Jamie, something that would show him what she looked like before her face was cut, her body battered. She was once a girl who wore a bikini like this.

He gathered her toiletries into her red kit bag. She didn't wear much makeup, just a lipstick, eyeliner, mascara. She had a brush, some suntan lotion, face cream. He remembered how Heather traveled with two or three bags of toiletries and makeup. "We're going into the woods for a week," he would tell her. "Maybe I want to look like a sexy wood nymph," she'd say. But Gabe always thought sexy was simple, unadorned beauty. Hair falling out of a bun. Skin the color of a late-summer tan.

He looked up and saw himself in the mirror. He looked awful. His face was gaunt and his beard needed trimming. He hadn't run a comb through his hair in two days. He looked away.

On a shelf in the bathroom were two bottles: melatonin, birth-control pills. Again, he felt like a snoop. He quickly swiped the pill bottles into the kit and zipped it up.

When he was finished packing her suitcase, he took a quick

look around the room. There was a book by the bedside table. A memoir of a woman who explored the Arctic. I'm learning her, Gabe thought. Little by little. This is who Jamie is.

Or who she once was.

In the lobby, the Balinese woman walked up to him.

"I have the messages for Miss Jamie," she said.

"I'll take them to her."

She handed him two slips of paper. He held them in his open palm.

"Is there anything else I can do for you, sir?" she asked.

"No, thank you. I left the other suitcase outside the door of the villa. There's an address on the tag."

"We will ship the suitcase, sir."

"Thank you."

The woman stood there.

"I should pay for her room," Gabe said. "I'm sorry. Let me take care of that."

"There is no need," the woman said. "There is no charge right now for any of our guests."

Gabe nodded.

The woman turned and walked away.

He looked at the top message.

Report back, Legs. No answer on your damn cellphone. You better be fine. Get your ass out of Dodge. All expenses paid by Global Adventures. Larson.

The next one from her mother.

Please call me. I'm so scared. Please call me. I love you more than you could ever know.

Back in the car, Gabe's phone rang. He picked it up: His sister's name lit up the screen. He tossed the phone on the seat beside him. He didn't want to tell her again that he wasn't coming home.

When he turned his car onto the main road, he saw signs: KUTA. SANUR.

Without even giving himself time to decide, he turned toward Kuta.

The roads were clogged with cars and motorbikes. He heard some voice in his head say: *Get out of here. Go back to Jamie.*

The car inched forward. Another phone call. Lena this time. Again, he didn't answer.

Finally he cut across to a side road that would get him to the bomb site faster. He wove through traffic and hit a roadblock: NO ENTRY.

This was foolish. He should turn around. He should get himself back to Sanur.

Still, he pulled his car off to the side of the road—an illegal parking space, but the cops had far more important business right now. He got out of the car and headed to the bomb site on foot.

He could smell it before he could see it. Fire. The acrid smell of explosives and burned skin. Fire retardant. He covered his nose with his hand.

Indonesians and a few Westerners wandered aimlessly through the streets. This area was usually packed with tourists.

The shops along the street—souvenirs, leather, bikinis, T-shirts, straw bags—were all closed. One sign on the door of a store read: OUR HEARTS WITH VICTIMS. WE PRAY.

Gabe turned a corner and stopped. He saw burned buildings, collapsed buildings. That one was Sari Club, the other Paddy's Pub. In the middle of the road was an enormous crater. There were shells of cars, twisted metal, a melted sign for Coca-Cola. Just a few feet in front of him was a high-heeled shoe—emerald green—in perfect condition.

Gabe closed his eyes for a moment. He tried to breathe deeply, but the smell of fire and death filled his lungs.

None of it felt real in the little cottage by the sea. Even Jamie, with her wounds, seemed to have arrived from nowhere. But that night wasn't a nightmare. It was this very real, hideous carnage.

A man with crooked glasses stood on the street in front of the still-smoking rubble of Sari Club. He held a large framed photograph of a woman to his chest, as if he were pressing her into his heart. Gabe could see that the woman was pregnant, her small body stretched with a very round belly. She was smiling at the camera, a shy smile, as if she were telling secrets to the man taking the photo.

He lost her, Gabe thought. Unable to bear the expression on the man's face, he turned away.

A team of policemen with white gloves was busy combing the charred remains of the cars on the street. One of the cars was tilted on its side, burned to a skeleton.

Gabe saw flowers everywhere. Wreaths, bouquets, and single flowers lined the street, lying next to the blackened buildings. One young man—a Westerner—was placing a bouquet of flowers at the side of the street, in front of Sari Club. Tears poured from his eyes. Another man stood next to him, dazed, staring into the rubble. Two girls near Gabe kneeled in front of small prayer offerings, the kind that the Balinese used to maintain balance in their world. One of them chanted, "Laura, Laura, Laura." The other sobbed.

It started to rain. Gabe could feel the drops on his head and on his arms, and, though it was hot, he felt suddenly chilled. He stood there, stunned, unable to move. He tried to remember running into Paddy's, through the fire, toward the screams. It felt as if it happened to someone else. But this was real. This was a war zone.

"There was a snake in the road," an elderly Balinese woman said. She was standing beside Gabe; he hadn't even noticed her. "In the morning after the bombs. It was reaching toward heaven. It is an omen."

"What kind of omen?" Gabe asked.

"It was reaching to the gods. For help. We have done something wrong. We have angered someone."

"No," Gabe said, looking at her. He tried to keep his voice calm. "We have done nothing wrong. It is the terrorists who have done something evil."

"Because of our sins," the woman said. "Because of the dancing and drinking. We have lost our way."

Gabe thought of Jamie, lying in bed at the beach cottage.

"No," he told the woman gently. "These were good people. These were innocent people. They did nothing wrong."

Without another word, the woman turned and walked away.

Gabe watched a young man wandering through the devastation, holding a sign: TERI HUGHES. MISSING. On the sign was a picture of a woman with a beguiling smile. The boy, eyes swollen, mouth tight, walked in circles, his sign raised high above his head.

As soon as Gabe pulled onto the main road out of Kuta, he was snagged in a traffic jam, the cars barely moving, the heat of the day weighing on them. The rain had stopped, and steam rose from the sides of the highway. He drove a couple of yards, slowed, waited, then drove another yard. He could feel his heart racing.

Jamie's alone, he thought. I've been gone too long. How long did he stand and stare at the bomb site? He looked at his watch. They still had a few hours until they had to leave for the airport.

The traffic eased for a moment, and, as soon as Gabe sped up, a motorbike cut him off. He slammed on the brakes. The car behind him screeched to a stop.

He closed his eyes. In seconds, the air filled with the sound of blaring horns.

He looked up and thought: I can't do it. I can't go forward.

Again, the car horns blasted him.

He shook his head. He could taste bile in his throat.

Pulling to the side of the road, he put the car in park and rested his head on the steering wheel. His breath came in harsh gasps, as if he couldn't find air, and then he was sobbing, loud, racking sobs that came from deep inside his chest.

He let himself cry until he was done. Then he thought again of Jamie, waiting for him, and he pulled back onto the highway.

———

When the path opened up and the cottage appeared, Gabe saw someone sitting on the patio. The person was facing away from him, looking out toward the garden. Was it Billy, or one of Billy's friends, or a stranger he'd have to talk to? He felt a flash of anger, as if this were his home and no one else had the right to be here.

The person heard him approach and turned in his direction.

It was then that Gabe saw the bandage, the auburn hair, the pale-blue scarf that supported her cast. Jamie. He smiled, and then suddenly he couldn't stop smiling.

"Look at you," he said.

"I took a pain pill," she told him.

"Your arm?"

"My mind," she said. "These things work for psychic pain, too, it seems."

"Maybe I'll steal a couple," he told her.

"This is—" she started to say, then stopped and looked out at the garden. "Lovely," she said finally. "It's like I'm dreaming this."

He sat in the wicker chair next to her.

"My friend is a landscape designer. He's very good at what he does."

Gabe noticed a pad of paper on Jamie's lap, a pencil in her hand. She had sketched the garden, using quick lines and a delicate touch.

"You're an artist."

"Barely," she said. "I like to sketch while I travel. I found this pad in a kitchen drawer."

"Did you see much of Bali . . . before?" Gabe asked.

She shook her head. "I was only here three days. Now I don't want to see any of it. I want to sit right here."

"I'm sorry I was away so long," Gabe said. "Can I get you something to eat?"

"No," she said. "Sit here with me."

Gabe followed her gaze out into the garden. Lakshmi, a goddess holding two lotus flowers, sat at the center of the lawn, encircled by gardenias. There was a balé, a wooden pavilion, at the far end of the garden; Billy had found its original thatched roof in an antiques store in Seminyak. On the balé were a teak table and gracefully curved teak chairs. A red ceramic bowl sat in the middle of the table.

"I have messages for you," Gabe said.

He reached into his pocket and pulled out the two pieces of paper, which he passed to Jamie.

He watched her as she read them, her brow furrowed.

"The hotel will ship Miguel's things back to his family," he said.

She glanced at him and then quickly turned away.

"You should call his family, Jamie," he said gently.

She shook her head, her eyes on the garden.

Let her be, he told himself. You're done saving her.

"It's my fault that he died," Jamie said, her voice strained.

"It's not your fault."

"What do *you* know?" she said, with a sharp stab of anger. "If I had said yes to him—yes, I'll marry you, yes, I love you and want to spend the rest of my life with you—he'd be alive. We'd have stayed in that crappy little restaurant until we finished our meal. We would have taken a taxi back to our fancy hotel and spent the night making love instead of getting blown apart by a fucking bomb."

Gabe reached out and laid a hand on her arm. She stood up

abruptly, as if his touch had jolted her, and her chair clattered to the ground. She kept her back to Gabe.

"I was waiting for you to come home, and then suddenly I was angry. I've never waited for a man to take care of me. I can take care of myself. I don't even know who you are."

"We went through a lot together."

"I'll call a cab to take me to the airport."

"I want to take you."

She picked up her chair and sat back down in it. He could hear her release a deep breath.

"I stopped at the bomb site," Gabe said.

She turned to him, her anger gone in a quick moment. "Why?"

"It didn't feel real. Maybe it's this garden, this house. I needed to see the clubs in the daytime."

"I never want to see it," Jamie said.

Gabe thought of the Jamie he discovered in the hotel room. A girl in a bikini. Sweet perfume.

"I have this for you," he said. He pulled the photo of the dog out of his shirt pocket and handed it to her.

She looked at it and her face softened. He felt relieved to see her smile.

"Finn," she said. "My puppy."

"Big puppy."

"A hundred and twenty pounds of dog," Jamie told him, gazing at the photo. "She died the year before I started traveling with my job. I don't think I would have taken the job if she were still alive."

"What kind of dog was she?"

"A Leonberger," Jamie said. "A big teddy bear. She made me happy for a long time."

She touched the photo and ran her finger along the dog's back. "Miguel thought she looked mean. He didn't like dogs. I could never marry a man who didn't like dogs."

"Why didn't you want to marry him?" Gabe asked.

Jamie turned her gaze back to the garden. A large lizard slithered onto Lakshmi's head and sat there, staring at them.

"I'm a big kid. I'm thirty-one. And I don't know anything about love."

"I'm forty. Still trying to figure that one out myself."

"You loved your son," she said.

"I did. With all my heart."

"You know love, then."

Gabe watched the lizard skitter across the goddess's head and disappear down her back.

"We'll leave for the airport after lunch," he said.

Jamie nodded. She ran her hand through her hair, then rearranged the sling over her cast. Finally she said, "I'll call Miguel's parents."

Gabe pulled out his cellphone and the piece of paper with the phone number. He passed both to her.

"I'll leave you alone," he offered.

"No," she told him. "Please stay."

He nodded. She seemed to brace herself while tapping in the phone number. Her breath came in quick, choppy bursts.

When someone answered, she began to speak in an easy Spanish. Gabe was surprised by her fluency and then reminded himself: I barely know her.

He listened to the flow of words, not understanding them, but her voice was warm and compassionate. She talked for a long time.

When she was done, her face was wet with tears. She reached out her good hand to him, and he held it.

"They were glad to talk to me. They knew he was going to propose."

"What did you tell them?" he asked.

"I told them that he had. I told them that I said yes."

Gabe closed his eyes. *Yes.* She gave them a gift with that word.

He felt her hand slip out of his and he heard her walk away from him, back into the house. He let her go.

Gabe set out plates and bowls on the outdoor table. Earlier, he'd walked down to a restaurant on the beach to buy lunch. Now he pulled the food from the take-out bag and placed it on the center of the table.

From afar, he heard his cellphone ringing, and when he jogged toward the house, he found it on the wicker patio chair.

"Molly. I'm sorry. I haven't had a second to call you back."

"They're saying it might happen again. I want you to leave, Gabe. I'm watching the news around the clock. They think it's some Indonesian terrorist group that's worse than al-Qaeda. They're going to strike again."

"Don't watch the news, Molly."

"You don't answer my calls. I don't know how to find out what's going on."

"It's over. It's really over."

"What's over?"

"The killing. They don't need to kill more people. They did enough."

"You tell them that."

"Hold on," Gabe said as Jamie appeared in the doorway. He covered the phone with his hand. "Lunch is out in the balé. You can start if you want. I'll be there in a second."

She nodded and walked out across the lawn.

Gabe heard the sound of Molly's TV blasting in the background.

"Are you home?" he asked her. He couldn't remember how many days it had been since she left.

"Yes," she said. "I'm home. I just wish you were here with me."

"It's too cold back there," Gabe said.

"It's Indian summer. It's gorgeous."

On an Indian summer day, he had taken Ethan out for a long ride on their tandem bike. The leaves were gold and red, brilliant against a blue sky, and the weather was balmy, as if it were August. "I chase you, Daddy," Ethan had called from behind him. "Go faster!"

"Do you remember how Ethan loved that bike?" Gabe asked. Molly had bought it when she came to stay with them at the Cape that summer.

"What made you think of that?" Molly said, her voice quiet.

"Indian summer," Gabe told her.

"He wanted you to sit in the back on the little seat," Molly said. "He wanted the big seat."

Gabe smiled. Across the lawn, Jamie reached for an egg roll and popped it into her mouth. She's hungry, he thought. That's good.

"Heather called me to see if you were okay," Molly told him. "She's been watching the reports on CNN."

"How is she?"

"She had news," Molly said, her voice hesitant. "She and Hannah are going to adopt a baby from China."

Gabe turned away from Jamie, as if he didn't want her to witness his sense of loss. First Ethan, then Heather, and now the chance for a new child. No, he reminded himself. That's not the life that he chose for himself.

"Good for her," Gabe finally said.

"That doesn't make you sad?"

"No," he assured her. "She should be happy."

"*You* should be happy," Molly told him.

"I'm working on it," Gabe said.

"Delicious," Jamie said. "I couldn't wait." She was devouring another egg roll.

She seemed to have changed moods in an instant. She's scrappy, Gabe thought. She'll need that now.

He sat across from her at the table. "I'm glad."

"Who was that on the phone?" Jamie asked. "My turn to be nosy."

Gabe smiled. "My sister. She wants me to come home."

"Will you?"

"This is my home."

"Does it really feel like home?"

"Not yet. But I don't want to give up on Bali because of the bombing. This island will need a lot of love in the next months."

"This is what you did to start over?"

"Kind of drastic, huh?"

He reached for the bowl of pad thai and served himself a small portion. He thought of Heather and a new baby. I'll write to congratulate her, he thought. He imagined how pleased she would be.

Jamie tore a piece off the roti prata and bit into it. He watched her eat and felt the pull of desire.

"I forgot how good food tastes," she said.

"I bet you're not a woman who picks at her food and worries about her weight."

"Ya think?" she said, tearing at the buttery grilled bread.

"Were you always an athlete?" he asked.

"I hated team sports when I was a kid. I was a tomboy, but I couldn't get any charge out of girl games. Then my father took me camping in Utah. I was in heaven. The next year we hiked in Yosemite, and that's all I ever wanted to do for the rest of my life. Every year I waited for the next trip—just my dad and me and all that wilderness. Best times of my life."

She swiped the roti prata across her plate, soaking up all the juices from the different dishes, then filled her mouth with the rich bread. Gabe wanted to clear the spot of sauce at the side of her lips with his finger. He took another bite of his food, forcing his eyes away from her.

"When did you decide to make a career out of your love for the wilderness?"

"After college. Everyone else was heading to law school or business school—I wanted a higher mountain, a faster river. Some guy told me about a company in Berkeley that paid people like me to play on mountains all around the world. Being a guide isn't quite the same as going it alone. But it pays the bills."

"You're an adrenaline junkie." Gabe was smiling at her.

She looked away. "I was. I don't know what I am anymore."

"You're still that person."

She shook her head. "I woke up in the middle of the night and I thought I was buried alive. I pushed the blankets off me and still I couldn't get air."

"Last night was bad for me, too," he said.

She watched him. "I don't even know what you do here."

"I teach at a school in Ubud."

"Really?"

"You're surprised?"

"I would have guessed something more . . . I don't know . . . gutsier."

"You think facing a classroom of seven-year-olds isn't gutsy?"

"You didn't want to be a journalist anymore?"

"I couldn't."

Gabe remembered a meeting with his boss at the *Globe*, weeks after Ethan's death. "This is what you need," she told him, sitting across from him in her office, spreading her arms wide. How do you know what I need, he thought. She had a photo of her family on her desk, three smiling kids and a bean-pole of a husband. From what he had heard, she rarely saw her kids.

"I need a break," he had told her.

"If you throw yourself back into your work, you'll remember that you had a life before Ethan. You love what you do, Gabe. Don't give it up now."

But he didn't want anything to resemble his old life, with Ethan or before Ethan. He felt so unlike himself, so unfamiliar to himself, that he didn't want to fit this new dark being into old comfortable spaces.

"Can you pass the pad thai?" Jamie asked. "You're hogging it all."

He passed Jamie the bowl.

"Where did that come from?" Jamie asked, pointing to his arm. "I've been wondering."

"The tattoo?"

A small green and yellow bird spread its wings across his forearm.

"You don't seem like the type," she said.

"I got it the first day I moved to Ubud. I wanted a reminder."

"Of flight?"

"I'd been running away for a long time. I wanted to land somewhere."

"Did you?"

"Not yet," Gabe said.

Jamie reached out and touched his arm, tracing the bird's wing.

"I like it," she said, and then she took her hand away.

Jamie was quiet during the drive to the airport. She changed the radio station when news about the bombing came on and kept pushing buttons, trying to find a song she liked. Finally she turned it off.

"You packed your meds?" Gabe asked.

"Yes."

He'd left his own clothes at Billy's cottage—he would go back to Sanur after dropping her off and spend one last night there before returning to Ubud. He, too, felt unready for the real world.

He suddenly remembered Theo and their dinner at Santo's. He hadn't even called to find out if his friend was okay. Theo hadn't called him, either. No one knew the rules of behavior for post-terrorist bombing. Sympathy cards? Support groups?

He'd call Theo later.

"If you come to San Francisco—" Jamie said, and then stopped.

Gabe glanced at her, hopeful.

She shook her head. "I'll never see you again."

"You might."

"So strange," Jamie said. "I know you." She glanced at him. "And I don't know a thing about you."

"If you come back to Bali—"

"Not a chance," she said.

"Then I'll have to go to San Francisco. We'll have dinner and tell each other how we survived."

"What will you say?"

"I'll say that I love Bali more than ever. That I've finally made it my home. That it took a terrorist attack to get me out of my stupor and kick my ass back into life."

"I'm impressed. You've come far."

"One can dream."

He thought of another dream, one that included Jamie sitting with him on the deck of his joglo, drinking a glass of wine as they talked about their day. He pushed the thought away.

They passed a sign for the airport, and she looked down at her lap.

"And you?" Gabe asked. "What will you say?"

"Years from now? When we meet for dinner?"

"Yes."

She kept her head low. "I've become the poster child for survivors of terrorist attacks. I speak at international confer-

ences worldwide and tell people that we have to join together
to create a better world."

"Wow."

"Not likely, huh? I'm probably a barista in some stupid café
in Berkeley. I've become an expert at making those designs
with latte foam."

"At least you get out of bed every morning."

She looked at him with a flash of pride. "I'll get out of bed
every morning."

"I know you will."

Gabe pulled the car up to a barricade at the entrance to the
airport. While security guards ran a mirror under the chassis of
the car, Jamie kept her eyes closed.

"Do they always do this?" she asked through gritted teeth.

"I'm sure they're taking extra precaution," he assured her.

One guard asked for their identification. Gabe answered his
questions: Yes, she had a flight in an hour; she was heading to
the United States; yes, he would drop her off and leave. Yes, he
was a resident of Bali. He was an American citizen.

When the guard let them through, Gabe could hear Jamie
release her breath.

"It's good," he said. "We want tight security."

"Maybe there's been another threat," she said, her voice
trembling.

"No. If there were, they'd have closed down the airport."

"How do you know?" she asked.

"You'll be fine, Jamie. I won't drop you off. I'll walk you in.
As far as they'll let me."

"You don't have to do this," she said.

Gabe inched along in traffic, moving toward the front of the
airport.

"Breathe slowly," he told her.

She kept her head down.

"I'm going to turn in to the parking lot now," he said. "We'll walk in together."

He took the first parking space he could find, then switched off the engine and turned toward her.

"Jamie, you can do this," he said. "There's so much security here. Nothing's going to happen."

She looked toward the terminal, then back at Gabe, her eyes wide.

"Are you ready?" he asked.

She shook her head.

"Let me get your bag. Then I'll come around and get you."

She didn't say anything, so he got out of the car and pulled her suitcase out of the backseat. He came around to the passenger side and opened her door.

"Take my arm," he said.

She hesitated a moment. Then she stood, holding his arm with her good arm. He could feel her hand close around his biceps.

"Maybe they'll let me walk you all the way in," Gabe said. He kept his voice low and calm. "We can do this together."

He started moving toward the terminal, and Jamie kept pace beside him. He knew that she was watching the same thing that he saw: an enormous crowd of people, mostly Westerners, gathered together in front of the terminal. He felt her grip tighten on his arm.

They crossed the street and moved toward the door. A few photographers stood in front of the crowd. Gabe was shocked when a light flashed and a camera clicked.

"Stop!" he yelled at the young man with the camera.

"Were you in the bombing?" a woman at his side called out. She held a notebook and pen in her hands. "Will you answer a few questions?"

"Leave us alone," Gabe said as he snaked an arm around Jamie's waist, pulling her close to him. "Let's move fast," he murmured, hurrying her through the crowd.

Inside the airport, more lights flashed in their eyes.

"Stop!" Gabe shouted.

Jamie buried her face in his arm. He heard her grunt in pain—she must have pressed against her wound. He maneuvered her carefully through the crowd, knocking one photographer out of the way with his elbow.

Beyond the army of journalists was a crowd of travelers, almost all Westerners, and the room buzzed with noise. The chaos was electric—the crowd too tight, the energy too agitated. A loudspeaker barked announcements in Indonesian, and the sound was filled with static. Some people raised their voices over the din, and something crashed to the floor— a camera, perhaps—causing a few people to cry out.

Jamie pushed hard against Gabe and moaned. He let go for a quick second and felt her slip away. When he spun around to catch her, she was gone. He called her name, but the crowd closed in around him and noise filled up all the space in the room.

"Move!" he yelled, pushing through the crowd. He looked toward the doors but didn't see her. He scrambled toward the front wall, then stood on a chair to get a better view. There were people in every direction, cameras flashing, shouts and cries. Had she already made it out the door?

Then he saw her, farther down along the front wall, huddled on the floor. She looked like a child in hiding. Her good arm was wrapped around her knees, and her head was tucked into the angle of her cast.

He leapt from the chair and ran toward her.

"Jamie!"

She closed herself into a ball, her body rocking.

"We're going back," Gabe said, his hand on her shoulder.

She looked up. Her face was pale and she was shivering.

"To the cottage," he told her. "Please. Come with me."

She stood and leaned against him. He wrapped his arm around her, and they made their way to the front door and out of the terminal.

"Are you sleeping?" he whispered.

"No," she said.

"Can I come sit in here?"

"I'd like that."

Gabe walked into the bedroom. The room was dark, but he could see the silhouette of his chair by the window in the waxing moonlight. He sat down, barely able to make out the shape of Jamie's body under the blankets, her head on the pillow. Only the white bandage caught the light and seemed to glow.

"Did you sleep at all?" he asked.

"A little bit."

"I can't sleep," Gabe said.

"You said it would get easier," Jamie told him, her voice soft in the dark. "It's all getting harder."

"Maybe we're not ready yet."

"You, too?"

"Me, too."

They were quiet for a moment, and then Jamie whispered, "I'm sorry."

"Don't apologize," Gabe said. "It was awful. It was chaos in there."

"No. The chaos is in my mind. Not in the airport."

"It's in my mind, too."

In the quiet of the room, Gabe heard the rustle of a gecko scampering along a wall.

"Thank you," she finally said.

"For what?"

"You make me feel a little less crazy."

"Or we're both fucking nuts."

"Probably."

"Did you call your mother?"

"Yes. I told her I'll try again in a couple of days."

"Good."

"What will you do?" Jamie asked.

"When?"

"When you don't have me to worry about anymore."

"I'll go back to Ubud."

"It's all the same?"

"Nothing's the same."

"I like this."

"What?"

"Talking in the dark. I can barely see you sitting there."

"We need some stillness in our lives right now."

"When the camera flashes went off—"

"I know."

"There was an amazing light after the bombs exploded. Everything went white. And then it all changed to black."

She was quiet, and Gabe let the silence fill the room.

"I was walking toward the club when it happened. It was surreal: I didn't feel scared—maybe we watch too many violent movies—but for a weird moment or two it didn't seem dangerous. And then I saw people fleeing the building. They were torn apart, covered in blood. One guy was missing an arm." She paused, catching her breath. "I ran in there while everyone was running out. I had to find Miguel."

"The second bomb went off in the street," Gabe said. "Probably close to where you'd been standing. If you hadn't run in, you might have been killed."

Jamie didn't respond. Gabe fought an urge to move to the bed so he could rest a hand on her foot.

"Then all those people who ran out—" she said, and stopped.

"The second bomb was bigger," he told her.

"They wanted people to run into the street and get killed?"

"Maybe."

"Damn them," Jamie muttered. But she sounded more weary than angry.

Gabe waited.

"I was trying to find Miguel," she finally said, "but there were people dying everywhere. I couldn't leave them. I couldn't just run past them."

"You saved a lot of lives."

"Maybe if I got to him sooner—"

"You probably couldn't have saved him."

"He was twenty-seven years old. He was beautiful. He wanted to climb Kilimanjaro next year. He wanted—"

"He wanted you."

"He would have found someone else to love."

Gabe thought about Jamie's shoulder, tan and smooth. He

wanted to run his fingers over her skin. When he thought of Miguel, he hated himself for a moment.

"I'm sorry," he said.

"Until now Finn was the only one in my life who died."

"Your giant dog."

"Yes. I still miss her. One grandmother was dead before I was born. Everyone else is still alive. I don't know anything about death."

"And now you know too much."

"It doesn't make any sense. I have no right to be lying here in this pretty little room."

"You have every right—"

"Why? Who are you to say that? Why did you save me and not someone else? Someone else died because you ran toward my voice. If you hadn't carried me out of there and taken me away, you could have saved ten more lives. I'm alive and they're all dead."

"Jamie . . ."

Gabe sat for a long time in the dark. He listened to her breath ease, and soon she was sleeping. Still he sat there. When he looked out the window at one point, sometime in the middle of the night, he saw an animal perched on the table in the balé. Was it a cat? It had its nose in the bowl of leftover food from lunch, and it was happily feasting. Gabe imagined a dinner party of animals, filling the balé with their grunts and snorts. In the morning the food would be gone. The place would be a mess. And when Gabe and Jamie woke up, they would begin again.

"You are still here," the woman in the pharmacy said.

"I live here," Gabe told her again. "I'm not leaving."

"Is your friend better?" the woman asked.

"She's having a hard time," he said. "I need more gauze and tape for her."

The woman turned and walked into a back room. Gabe could see her reaching for a box on a nearly empty shelf.

"Our children are scared," the woman said when she returned. "I have a little girl who cries every night. A boy in her class lost his father in the bombing. She thinks I will not come home from work one day, that everyone will die from a bomb."

"My son," Gabe said, and the sound of the words reverberated in the air. "My son saw a car accident once, and a man was lying in the street. He was probably dead. My wife was in the car—I was at work. My son asked me every night for almost a year if I would die."

"What did you tell him?"

Gabe remembered the lemony smell of Ethan's hair as he bent over to kiss him good night. The memory jolted him; it was as real as if he had buried his nose in the tangle of his son's blond hair just moments before.

"I told him, 'I'm here. I'm with you. I'm alive.' "

"Did that work?"

"Until the next day."

"My husband thinks we are to blame for the terrorists' actions. I think we did nothing wrong."

"We didn't," he told her.

"So why do we suffer?"

Gabe pulled out his cash and handed some bills to her.

"I'm sorry," she said. "I talk too much."

"It's all right," he told her. "I used to be a very private man. Suddenly I feel the need to talk to everyone, too."

The woman smiled. Her smile revealed two dimples, and she looked like a shy schoolgirl.

"Come back and talk to me again sometime."

"I will."

Out on the street, Gabe gazed around. It was almost noon—Jamie had not yet come out of her room this morning. He would pick up food for lunch and then head back to the cottage. He would hope for an easier day.

He walked down the main street of Sanur and found a restaurant that was open. Tables were set up on the sidewalk, but they were all empty. He walked through the door and up to the bar.

"Can I order a couple of sandwiches to go?" he asked the bartender.

The young man with long blond dreads was downing a shot of something—tequila? He looked as if he'd been up all night and was nursing a hangover.

"We're closing. Nobody's here, man."

"I'm here."

"What are you doing here?" the kid asked, meeting Gabe's eyes for the first time.

"I'd like two sandwiches. Whatever you've got."

"I'm going back to a party I never should have left. Shit, man. This place is dead."

The kid pulled a bottle of tequila from under the bar. He poured a shot for Gabe and another for himself.

"Bottoms up, brother," he said, and pushed the shot glass across the bar to Gabe. Then he turned and walked unsteadily toward the kitchen.

Gabe surveyed the empty restaurant, then picked up the glass and drank the tequila in one quick swallow.

He felt a wave of fury at the bartender—for being drunk? For partying when the rest of Bali was suffering? He reached for the tequila bottle and poured another shot.

On the street, a Balinese woman walked by, her arms covered in sarongs. She must have given up on selling them at the beach. She walked slowly and heavily, her head low. Gabe imagined the hot sun beating on her back, the yards of fabric weighing her down.

"Groovy," the bartender said.

Gabe turned toward the bar. His eyes couldn't adjust to the darkness after staring into the light—he couldn't see the boy in front of him.

"What did you find?" he asked.

"Ham sandwiches. The cook said they're on the house. It's your lucky day."

"It's no one's lucky day," Gabe said. His eyes focused, and he could see the kid smirking in front of him.

"Bummer about that bombing thing, huh," the boy said.

Gabe took a deep breath. "Why are you in Bali?"

"To surf, dude. What else?"

"You going surfing today?"

"Hell, yes."

"You didn't know anyone caught in the bombing, did you?"

"Nah. My buddies don't hang at places like that. Skanks go there. Not the greatest loss to society, if you know what I mean."

Gabe punched him. He did it before he even thought about it. His fist connected with the guy's nose, and the kid stumbled back until he hit the wall. "What the fuck?"

Gabe walked out of the restaurant, leaving the sandwiches behind.

He found Jamie sitting on the patio. She looked at him, smiling, as he walked up the path.

"I made you a peace offering," she said, pointing to the table in front of her. She had spread out an array of crackers, tapenade, and cheese. "I raided your friend's pantry."

"Nice," Gabe said, smiling back at her.

"I even stole some wine," she said.

"It will go well with my tequila," he replied, sitting down in the wicker chair next to her.

"You had a morning tequila?"

"And then I punched a guy."

"The mild-mannered reporter from Boston?"

"I need some food to go with my alcohol breakfast," Gabe said as he dug in to the spread on the table. He could feel Jamie's eyes on him as he ate. She handed him a glass of rosé. He sipped it and sighed.

"A better way to start the day," he said.

"You accept my apology?"

"You have no reason to apologize."

"Why'd you punch the guy?"

"Because he was going surfing."

Jamie nodded. "I think I'm going to be careful what I say today."

"You're safe, I think," he told her.

"But you're not sure."

"I'm sure. I could never hit a woman with a broken arm."

They clinked glasses.

"You feel better today?" Gabe asked.

"I'm not going to the airport today. So I thought I'd save all my craziness for tomorrow. I booked my new flight."

Gabe nodded. They had today, then. A gift.

"I walked out on the beach," she said. "While you were gone."

Gabe felt an irrational fear rise up in his chest—but here she was, sitting beside him. She hadn't thrown herself into the sea. She hadn't walked for miles and never come back.

"I talked to a woman for a while," she said.

"A tourist?"

"No. A Balinese woman. She told me she swims in the sea every day for her exercise. She was old—I couldn't tell how old—and very strong. She lives in town and sells food at the market every morning. She babysits her three-year-old granddaughter while she works, until her son comes home from the night shift at a hotel in Kuta."

"Chatty woman," Gabe said.

"She was at the cleansing ceremony," Jamie said. "The one we went to. She said it was a tragedy but now all these young people will move on to the next life."

"She's lucky," he said, "that she believes in reincarnation." It would be so much easier, he thought, to imagine Ethan living the next good life somewhere. But when he thought about his son's death, he thought of it as the end of everything wonderful.

"I'm stuck in this life," Jamie said. "I don't get a chance to get reborn as a Balinese princess."

Gabe smiled. "You wouldn't really like the princess life."

"You don't think so?"

He shook his head. "You're gonna live this life."

Gabe thought of Jamie stretched out on her boss's couch in Berkeley. He imagined the boss as a rugged older guy, sitting across the room from her, a crooked grin on his face. He'd toss Jamie the new catalog of thrilling adventures in the world. Pick one, any one you want, he would tell her. Yes, she would say, pointing her finger at a page. This one.

In the early evening, Gabe was sitting on the patio reading his novel about love and lust in Hollywood, when Jamie walked outside and stood beside him.

She wore the silk pants he'd packed in her suitcase, and the soft material hugged her slim hips. A red scarf wrapped around her cast.

"You look great," he said.

"Except for the face part."

Gabe stood up. He touched her chin. "You'll look mysterious and sexy and a little dangerous with a scar on your face."

"I can't wait," Jamie said. She offered him a hint of a smile. And then she stepped away so that his hand floated for a moment, midair, before drifting back to his side.

"How's the pain?" Gabe asked.

"Okay for now," she said. "I'll take a pill when we get back."

"From where?"

"Dinner."

"Dinner?"

"I'm taking you to a restaurant."

"Really?"

"Is there one close by?" she asked.

"A short walk down the beach path."

"Let's go right now or I might change my mind."

Gabe offered her his elbow, and she slipped her good arm through his. They walked across the lawn to the red door; he liked the feel of her forearm resting on his.

He unlocked the door and pulled it open, letting Jamie pass through.

"Wow," she said. The sky was streaked with pink, as if a willful child had taken a marker and swiped it across the blue sky. It zigged and zagged before disappearing into the darker blue of the sea.

The white-sand beach stretched for miles in both directions. Farther down there were hotels with lounge chairs and restaurants and boats for rent, but here, in front of the cottage, there was just the smooth sand, a few palm trees, and the endless blue sea.

They stood there for a while, watching the gentle waves break along the beach. Gabe caught the spicy scent of her perfume, and he breathed in. The colors of the sky deepened; the sea grew dark.

"Which way?" Jamie finally said, breaking the spell.

He turned her toward the central area of Sanur Beach.

"Are you okay?" he asked when he heard Jamie catch her breath.

"Yeah," she said. "Walking seems to rattle my head a little."

"Maybe this is too ambitious," Gabe said.

"*Ambitious* used to mean bagging three peaks in one day. Now it means a slow crawl for fifty yards."

"You'll do the mountain summits next month."

"I doubt that," she said.

Gabe looked at her. "There's no reason you won't be able to do all of those things again."

"I don't think I'll want to do those things again."

"Why?" he asked.

"The world is a different place," she said simply.

"No," Gabe said, his voice louder than he had intended. "You have to head back out into the world."

"Like getting on a horse after you've fallen off?" There was a nasty edge to her voice.

"Otherwise the terrorists win," he said.

"They already won," she murmured.

"No, they didn't."

"You keep hoping for something better, don't you?" Jamie asked, looking at him.

"What else is there to do?" he replied.

He thought of those daily walks in Boston after Ethan died—a long loop that took him down one side of the Charles, across the river, and back up the other side—during which time he replayed every memory of his son's short life. But, at the end of the day, he was still alone. Memory didn't bring the kid home again. Then one day his boots wore out. On one, a tear appeared by his big toe; on the other, the sole wore thin. It was as simple as that. I can't walk in circles anymore, he thought. I have to move forward.

There had to be something like hope, or he and Jamie would never leave the house.

A young Balinese boy ran toward them on the path, making engine sounds, as if he were an airplane headed down the runway. Just before he zoomed past them, he stopped abruptly and stared at Jamie. Almost unconsciously, he reached up and touched his hand to his own face.

"Hello," Jamie said.

"Hello," the boy said.

And then he chanted, "Hello hello hello hello," and took off running again.

"I'm a freak," she said.

"You're alive," Gabe told her.

They walked a short way farther along the path until they came to La Taverna, a hotel with an open-air restaurant on the edge of the beach.

The restaurant looked festive, with lanterns strung on wires from tree to tree. A blue light glowed from the center of each one. There was a balé in one corner, with an ornate tapestry that hung from the back wall. A band played at the far side of the restaurant—Gabe could see three Indonesian men with guitars, but the music sounded more like Latin salsa.

"Would you like a table?" a Balinese man asked. He was staring at Jamie.

"Yes, please," Gabe told him. "Under the tree over there, if that's possible." He pointed to a table hidden in the corner.

"Of course," the man said.

He led them through the maze of empty tables to the one Gabe had chosen.

"I will be back with the menu and the wine list," the man said, after pulling out the chair for Jamie.

When he walked away, she said, "I'm scaring everyone. They know I was in the bombing."

"You're fine," Gabe said.

"No one will ask, will they?"

"No one will ask," he said quickly.

"I'll never know what Bali is really like," she said, looking at him.

"Years from now you might—"

She shook her head. "This is Bali. This restaurant on this beach with this man. I don't need more than this."

"Bali is a lot more than this."

"If I can keep my Bali this small, then I might not hate it so much."

"I hope you'll come back someday. Give it another chance."

The waiter appeared—a young Balinese man with a huge grin. "Welcome to La Taverna," he said, and then he saw Jamie's face and his smiled faded.

"Thank you," Gabe said.

The waiter hugged the menus to his chest, still staring at Jamie, who fixed her eyes on the table in front of her.

"Yes, yes," the waiter said, finally snapping out of it. He handed them menus and gave the wine list to Gabe. "I will return to take your order." He fled.

"Do you want to go back to the cottage?" Gabe asked gently.

"No," Jamie said, her voice soft. "I want to sit here and eat my dinner. I don't want to go away. I want the rest of the world to go away."

"Much of the world did go away. I've never seen Sanur so empty."

"Let's listen to the music," she said, her voice straining to be cheery. "Let's pretend that we're about to step onto the dance floor and kick up our heels."

"Elizabeth Taylor danced here," Gabe said.

"Really?"

"Sanur used to be a destination for the jet set. In the sixties. John Lennon and Yoko were here. So was John Wayne. This hotel was the popular gathering spot. Apparently, everyone slept with everyone else's spouse. It was a wild time. Or so they say."

"I can't imagine. It's so sleepy now."

"Kuta and Seminyak have grabbed the spotlight. But this was the happening place in its day. The owner told me that someone climbed through Sophia Loren's window and waited for her naked in bed."

"So I'm Audrey Hepburn. Who are you?"

"I must be Cary Grant."

"And we've left our lovers at home. I'm filming something in Australia and have hopped over to Bali for the weekend. I spent the day floating on my back in the sea. Then I slipped my little black dress on and I sashayed down to the restaurant."

"I was sitting here, drinking a Manhattan," Gabe said. "I looked up and thought to myself: That must be Audrey. I haven't seen her in ages. I've been filming in Nice, and I only came to Bali for a week to get away from my possessive girlfriend. I caught your eye and stood up. You walked over, with that sexy strut of yours, and you said—"

"Well, Cary. What a surprise. I had no idea you would be here."

"Please join me for dinner. Unless you're waiting for someone?"

"I must be waiting for you."

"That dazzling dress—I can't take my eyes off you."

Jamie caught his eyes, and her face changed. She opened her menu and studied the pages. Gabe reached out and touched her shoulder.

"I'm okay," she said quickly. "Really."

"What happened?"

"For a second I forgot everything. For a second I thought I

was just a girl at a beach restaurant having fun with an interesting guy."

The waiter cleared his throat and both of them glanced up, surprised.

"Your order?" he asked.

"I'll have the seared tuna," Jamie said. "And a martini."

"I'll have the same," Gabe told him.

"Very good." The waiter started to walk away and then turned back. "Are you guests at the hotel?"

"No," Gabe said. "We're just here for dinner."

"I was at a meditation meeting the night of the bombing," the waiter said, a bit shyly. "There were hundreds of us in the auditorium. All of us in silent meditation. Then we heard an explosion and the room shook. The leader looked up and said, 'Something terrible has happened.'"

"What did you do?" Gabe asked.

"He told us to return to our meditation. But I couldn't clear my mind. I didn't even know what terrible things could happen. And now I know."

"We all know," Gabe said.

The waiter glanced again at Jamie, but she kept silent.

"I'll get your drinks," he said, and walked away.

The band finished the pulsating rhythms of their Latin salsa, and the bandleader took the mike. "And now something different." They segued into a very bad rendition of Stevie Wonder's "You Are the Sunshine of My Life."

"Tell them to stop," Jamie said, and they both laughed.

"Audrey and Cary would be horrified."

"They'd leave the dance floor."

"They'd promise to fly in their own bands next time."

The bandleader crooned, his voice twangy and off-key.

"Audrey and Cary would have much better music playing for a dinner like this."

A quick bolt of lightning flashed, brightening the horizon. The sky rumbled with thunder.

"That's more like it," Gabe said.

And, in an instant, the skies opened and fat raindrops splashed down on them.

"Let's move to the balé!" Gabe shouted over the noise of the deluge.

He helped Jamie up and held her good arm as they ran to the table under the thatched roof. By the time they were under cover, they were both soaked.

"Wow," Jamie said. "That's some kind of rain."

They watched the downpour for a few minutes in silence; Jamie hugged her arms around herself. The curtain of rain was so thick that they could barely see the tables in front of them. Again a flash of light split open the sky, followed by the crack of thunder.

And then it all stopped, just as suddenly as it had started. Steam rose from the ground like wisps of smoke.

"Audrey would have liked that," Jamie said. "Very dramatic. Film worthy."

"Where did the band go? Was that like some kind of punishment for one lousy song?"

She laughed. "They're hiding at the bar."

"Look at me," Gabe said.

She turned toward him.

He touched the side of her face. "The bandage is wet. I'll change it when we get back."

She put her hand on his.

"Thank you," she said, then she dropped her hand and turned her face away from him.

Gabe found himself lifting her hair away from her neck. It was a gesture so simple and yet it felt as if he was undressing her. He saw a single mole in a sea of smooth tanned skin. Barely breathing, he traced the landscape of her neck. She didn't move away.

"Wet martinis," the waiter said, appearing in front of them. "And dry towels."

He gave them each a hand towel and placed the martinis on the table in front of them.

Gabe took his towel and reached toward Jamie's face.

"No," she said quietly. "I'll do it."

He put the towel back on the table.

"The last time I went out for dinner, I was with Miguel," Jamie said, her voice low. "It feels like a million years ago."

Gabe felt a stab of guilt. He wiped the towel quickly over his face. "Where did you go?"

"Some dive in Kuta. His last dinner. He deserved better."

Gabe nodded, waiting.

"He deserved a girlfriend who said yes," Jamie said.

They ate their dinner in the balé, though it didn't rain again. The band played Latin dance music, and even as Jamie and Gabe sat at the table, quiet and no longer hungry, Audrey and Cary spun around the dance floor, graceful and breathtakingly beautiful.

In the middle of the night, Gabe heard Jamie call out his name. He went to her doorway and waited, unsure if he had dreamed it. But again he heard his name, this time a whisper.

He opened the door and waited for his eyes to adjust to the dark.

"Can you sit with me for a minute?" she asked. Her voice sounded shaky—she must have had another nightmare.

"Of course," he said, moving to the chair by the window.

"No. Here," Jamie said, patting the side of her bed. "That's too far away."

He was wearing boxer shorts—he hadn't slipped his jeans on. But she was half asleep and the room was nearly dark, so he perched on the edge of the bed. She rolled onto her side to face him.

"Were you sleeping?" she asked, her voice soft.

"I'm not sure," he told her. "I kept pulling myself out of dreams. It already feels like it's been a long night."

"What time is it?"

"Two. Two-thirty, maybe."

"What were you dreaming about?"

"The sea," Gabe said. "I was falling into the sea from a great height. I had to wake up before I hit the water."

"I saved you," Jamie said.

He smiled. "Yes. You saved me."

They were quiet for a moment.

"I stopped taking the pain pills," she told him.

"Are you still in pain?"

"Yes."

"Then you should take one."

"On the flight home. Right now I don't want to be cloudy."

"Maybe that's why you can't sleep," he said. "You're in pain."

"No," Jamie said. "I can't sleep because of you."

Gabe looked toward the window. He could see the silhouette of a tree bending against the wind. Finally he turned back to her. She was lying on her side, the sheet pulled up to her waist. She wore the shirt that Gabe had bought for her in town: BALI BABY.

He reached over and brushed her hair away from her face, letting his fingers run along the line of her jaw. When he touched her neck, she closed her eyes.

He lay down on the bed, facing her.

She opened her eyes and looked at him. He could see so much in her eyes—her need, her guilt, her gratitude. He touched her lips as if to say: Don't speak. Just look at me.

She placed her hand over his and gently pressed his fingers against her lips. Then she moved her hand to his mouth and traced his lips with her finger.

His own hand ran along the outside of her shirt, over her breasts, her stomach, and when he lifted the shirt to touch her skin, she made a sound he had not heard before—some mix of desire and pain.

"Should I stop?" he asked.

"Get this shirt off me," she said breathlessly.

He smiled. He unbuttoned it and carefully worked it over her cast.

She rolled onto her back. His eyes had adjusted to the dark, and with the light of the moon, he could see that her breasts were full and round, so tan that he knew she had been sunbathing naked somewhere in the world. When he ran his fingers over them, she opened her lips and breathed deeply.

"Please," she said, her voice low and soft. "Touch me."

He leaned over and kissed each nipple and then reached up to kiss her face.

She winced, and he pulled away.

"I'm sorry," he said.

"It's worth it," she told him, smiling. But she put her hand over her bandage, and a furrow appeared between her brows.

"Are you sure?" he asked.

"Yes."

He kissed a line down her torso, and when he came to her belly he pulled back to read a tattoo that was inscribed well below her navel. *Take me higher,* it said in an elegant cursive.

"How old were you when you had that done?" he asked, grinning.

"My eighteenth birthday."

"Does it refer to drugs, sex, or mountains?"

"Yes, yes, and yes," she told him.

"Man, are you trouble," he said, and then he ran his tongue over the letters.

"It's working," she murmured.

He pulled down the sheet and gazed at her. Her legs were bruised. He had a flash of memory: pulling debris off her in the burning club. He rested his hand very gently on her thigh.

"I don't want to hurt you," he whispered.

"You won't. You make me feel—" She stopped.

He looked up at her.

"—everything," she finished.

He lay down again at her side.

"That is exactly what you do for me, too," he said, and then he took her in his arms.

They made love slowly, carefully, rearranging themselves

around her cumbersome cast. Gabe touched her as if discovering everything he didn't yet know about her. And when she reached for him, pulling him toward her, he said, "Slow. Take it slow."

"You're killing me," she said, but she was smiling.

Their bodies found rhythms that Gabe didn't try to control—he let himself move with her and ride her, and then she rode him, and when they came they didn't stop wrapping themselves around each other.

"Slow," Jamie said, teasing him as he hungrily pulled her to him.

"Every day has been so long," he said in her ear.

"Yes," Jamie whispered, and then she climbed on top of him again.

Gabe smiled as soon as he began to stir. His eyes still closed, he remembered a moment in the middle of the night. He had wakened and sat up in bed to gaze at Jamie. She slept with her broken arm resting over her head, as if the cast was no longer shielding her. She looked peaceful for the first time since the bombing. There were no lines between her eyes, no scream caught in her throat.

Gabe had watched her sleep, tracing the line of her hip with his finger.

He leaned over and kissed her hip bone. It was perfect. No bruise, no swelling, no cuts or scrapes. He let his lips rest there.

And then he curled around her and fell back to sleep.

Now his hand reached to the edge of the bed—no Jamie. He opened his eyes. The sun was up, filling the room with a soft green light.

"Jamie?"

He looked toward the bathroom. The door was closed. He rested his head back on the pillow. Soon he would take her to the airport. First he would make her breakfast and they would drink coffee, sitting in the balé. Maybe they would make love one more time. He would talk to her about breathing exercises he learned after Ethan's death, when panic attacks would pull him from sleep in the middle of the night. He wouldn't ask her to stay; she needed to get home. But he would visit her soon in San Francisco.

"Jamie?"

He sat up in bed. He didn't see a light under the door. Was she in the kitchen?

He walked to the bathroom door and rapped lightly with his knuckles. When there was no answer, he opened it and peered inside.

Empty.

It was then he noticed that her few toiletries were gone. The counter was wiped clean.

He looked back in the bedroom. The suitcase, which had been perched on a bench at the foot of the bed, was gone.

Racing to the living room, he called out, "Jamie!"

But the room was empty, the doors to the garden thrown open. He ran to the door and searched in all directions. She wasn't relaxing in her chair on the patio; she wasn't sitting in the balé with a cup of coffee, waiting for him.

His car, he thought. He'd drive the streets, searching for her.

He found his jeans and T-shirt and dressed in a mad rush, pulling the shirt on inside out. He searched for his car keys— they weren't in the pocket of his jeans. He glanced at the kitchen counter. They were sitting on top of a note.

He forced himself to pick it up.

Jamie had written on the bottom of her sketch of the garden.

Gabe. I'm so sorry. I woke up very early in the morning, thinking of Miguel. I should have been thinking of him when I called to you in the middle of the night. It was wrong to turn to you when I'm still mourning him.

I'm going to take a taxi to the airport. Miguel deserved better, and so do you.

Thank you for everything.

She didn't sign the note.

Gabe drove north to Ubud. He had cleaned up Billy's house, leaving the sheets in the washing machine, the towels on the floor beside it. He had written a note for Billy's cleaning woman, thanking her for finishing the work. He stashed some money with the note.

He had already called Lena to tell her that he would be at work in an hour. She had told him not to worry—so few kids were showing up that one teacher could take care of all of them—but he insisted.

"I need to work," he told her.

"I understand," she said.

What happens next? he wondered as he drove toward the mountains of Bali. He felt the weight of all that had happened that week descend on him.

The rain began, and he turned on the windshield wipers full speed. It soon became difficult to see through the torrent pummeling the car window. He pulled off to the side of the road and watched as the water drenched the rice paddies. A man on a bicycle rode along a path between the paddies, rain streaming from his hat.

You keep going, he thought.

And so, after a moment, he pulled back onto the road. And then he drove on, deeper into Bali.

Part Three

2003

"Don't walk away from me," Jamie says. "Please."

Gabe has not yet turned away, but she knows, somehow, that she will lose him. After one long year and so many miles, she can't let that happen. She, too, has an urge to flee—seeing him brings a surge of emotion that feels too big to contain. His green eyes recognize her immediately, and she's scared of what will happen if she matches his gaze.

Did I invent the story of that week? Jamie thinks. How much of love is invention?

"Give me a chance," she says. "Let me explain why I left."

Gabe lowers his eyes. "I know why you left," he says softly.

A motorbike drives toward them and then stops. As soon as Jamie looks up, the young man on the bike says, "Transport?" She shakes her head. She wants the rest of the world to go away. Except for Gabe. She needs him with a ferocity that astounds her.

"Can we take a walk?" she asks. Give me time, she wants to beg. Let me look at you awhile longer. I need to know you again.

"Jamie," Gabe says, his tone already telling her no. And then his expression changes—what might have been the shock of recognition turns to something like anger. His face darkens.

"I don't want to see you," he tells her. "I can't—" He stops abruptly and turns his face away from hers.

It's as if he can't bear to look at her. Is he scared that he'll soften if he gives her a chance? Then he has to give her a chance. Her mind fills with a storm of pleas, none of them strong enough to make him stay.

"Sorry," he mutters. And then he walks away.

She wants to run after him, to take his arm and stop him. She wants to pull him toward her and to press her body against his. Remember me.

But he does remember her. He remembers that he woke up in the morning and she was gone.

She leans against the tree, pushing her back into the hard bark. She curls her fist against the ache in her chest.

Turn around, she pleads silently. Come back to me.

But he continues to walk down the street, away from her. A man walks toward Gabe, who stops, and the two shake hands. They are too far away for Jamie to hear their words. She can't see the expression on Gabe's face, but his friend smiles broadly. Jamie feels desperate to see Gabe's smile, even if it's not directed toward her. She remembers how he smiled in his sleep as she slipped out of bed that last morning. He murmured her name as she silently lifted her suitcase from the bench and tiptoed from the room.

Now he pats his friend's shoulder, and then, without looking back, he turns the corner and disappears. Jamie leans her head against the tree and closes her eyes.

For the last year, she played out every scenario in her mind: He would listen to her, he would rage, he would cry, he would hate her or love her.

But he never walked away.

———

She finds Nyoman on the corner near his house, standing with another man. When she approaches, the two men turn toward her.

"Transport, miss?" the other man asks. "Nice car for you." Nyoman bows his head.

"No, thank you," she says to the man.

"This is Miss Jamie," Nyoman tells his friend. "She stays with me for the anniversary ceremony."

"Welcome, friend of Nyoman!" the man says with an eager smile.

"Nyoman," Jamie says, and she glances back and forth between the two men. "Can I ask you a question?"

He steps away from his friend to give her privacy, and she's grateful that he understands.

"Do you have a car today?" she asks. "Are you free right now?"

"Yes," he says. "When I do not have a job, I look for work on the street. I have the car if I need it."

"I'd like to go—" she says, and she stops.

"I can take you," Nyoman says. "My friend does not care. You are my guest."

"Have you been to the bomb site?" Jamie asks.

Nyoman's mouth opens but he doesn't say anything.

"If it is too hard for you—"

"I have been many times," he says.

"I want to go," she tells him. Her voice trembles even as she says it.

Nyoman shakes his head. "Maybe it will be too hard for you."

"I want to go," she repeats, her voice stronger.

"I will take you," he says.

"Can we go now? I don't want to change my mind."

Nyoman walks back to his friend. He speaks in Balinese and the man hands him a set of keys. He steps to the car in front of them and opens the passenger door, then pauses and looks back to Jamie.

"I am ready," Nyoman says.

The words ring in her ears. *I am ready.* And yet her feet do not move; her body stays stubbornly rigid.

She remembers that Gabe visited the bomb site only days after the attack. "I never want to see it," she had said. Somehow she knows that now she must see it.

She walks to the car and steps in.

"I met a man who also lost his wife in the bombing," Nyoman says as they drive.

Don't tell me stories to make me feel better, Jamie thinks.

"He married soon after. It is what I must do—I have waited too long. We must bring children into the world. I have no children. And so, even if I do not want a new wife, I must find one."

"That shouldn't be hard," Jamie says, offering him a small smile.

"It is hard because I miss my wife."

"Of course," Jamie says. She's surprised by his honesty. She glances at him, but he stares ahead, a thin smile on his face.

"Still. My parents need grandchildren. My nieces and nephews need cousins. I need a son."

"Or a daughter."

"A son," he repeats.

"What's so bad about a daughter?" she asks.

"A son inherits his father's land. I must have a son."

"Women can't inherit?"

"They do not need to," Nyoman explains. "They will live with their husbands on the husband's land."

Jamie doesn't have the energy to argue. She has already lost all arguments today, the moment Gabe walked away from her. Besides, why argue with one man when it's really a country, a religion, a thousand years of history that she's fighting?

They're driving through so much traffic that it seems as if they're crawling to the bomb site, inch by painful inch. The streets are full of evening commuters on motorbikes, and the air is thick with a coming storm. Jamie cradles her arm, which aches with phantom pain.

"The man you met?" Jamie asks.

Nyoman glances at her, his face blank.

"You were starting to tell me a story about a man—"

"Yes, yes. A man who lost his wife in the bombing. Like me. But this man, he married soon after. And last week a baby was born."

"A son?"

"A son."

Jamie looks out the window, past the stream of motorbikes, and sees a row of stores selling art. The paintings are crude, unsophisticated. One after another, the canvases stack up against the buildings, their bold, simple colors calling for attention. They're awful—only a half step beyond a velvet Elvis. There are images of birds and flowers and Balinese women with bare breasts. Clichés, all of them. Jamie feels a surge of anger toward the artists who think that tourists are so foolish. Who would buy these paintings?

"You are not listening," Nyoman says, like a patient teacher.

"I'm listening," Jamie tells him wearily.

"When a baby is born, the priest comes to make a blessing. The priest can tell the family where the soul of the baby lived in its past life. The priest knows these things."

Nyoman is smiling, happy in his belief.

"How does he know?" she asks.

"He knows. He speaks to the dead person's soul before a cremation and learns what the soul needs for its journey. And at a birth the priest knows the soul of the baby. The baby is new, but the soul is old."

"And your friend?"

"The priest who came for the blessing did not know my friend or the family of my friend—they had moved to a new village after a flood destroyed their old home—but he said that the soul of the baby came from a woman who died in a fire. She died very young."

Nyoman stops talking and looks at Jamie. "You see?"

"The baby has the soul of the first wife," Jamie says.

"Of course," Nyoman tells her.

He smiles and drives and smiles and drives. The traffic does not make him agitated or restless. The stories of his people do not confound him. The tragedy of his wife does not paralyze him.

"What's at the bomb site?" Jamie asks. It only now occurs to her that she doesn't know this.

"What do you mean?"

"Is there a memorial? Did they rebuild the clubs? Is it exactly the same?"

"You will see," Nyoman tells her. For once, he does not smile.

Nyoman parks the car and leads Jamie on foot from one street to the next. Nothing looks familiar. She sees rows of tourist shops, businesses, restaurants. Billboards blast brand names: Bintang beer, Coca-Cola. It's still daylight—she might not even recognize the area, since she was in Kuta that night after dark. But this looks so banal, so unthreatening. A bomb somewhere near here? Two bombs? Hundreds dead?

They turn a corner and suddenly Nyoman stops.

"We are here," he says.

Jamie looks around. An icy sweat coats her skin.

But there's nothing here.

On one street is an ice cream parlor, on another a bank and an office building.

"Where?" she says. The word barely escapes her mouth.

"This," Nyoman says, pointing behind them.

They are standing on a corner, and when Jamie turns, she sees a large sculpted design on a wall. Under the scowling face of a plaster god, there is a shiny black surface, about ten feet square. Etched in gold are names. Rows of names.

In front of the wall are bouquets of flowers, some fresh, some dried and crumbling. Someone has pasted photos on the wall—one shows a beautiful young blond woman, another a teenage boy, probably Balinese.

"Was the club—"

"This was Paddy's Pub," Nyoman says.

He points across the street. "Sari Club," he says. There's an empty space, the beginning of a construction site, between the two buildings.

"This is the memorial, then," Jamie says, pointing to the wall behind them.

"Yes."

Jamie walks up to a low fence that surrounds the corner, enclosing the wall of names. She is baffled: Why is there a fence here? Should she step over it? Is she not permitted to get closer so she can read the names?

Then she sees a small gate at one corner. She walks over, passes through the gate, and steps up to the wall.

She's the only person here. Nyoman stands on the corner, looking away from the wall. Has he traced his wife's name a hundred times? Or does he always stand this far away, too far to let that mass of letters turn itself into names, into one name.

Jamie steps close to the wall. She will look for one name.

They are divided by countries: Australia leads the list with column after column. Then Indonesia. United Kingdom. The United States has seven names. She stares at them. Of course, she doesn't recognize them. Sweden, Germany, Netherlands, France, Denmark. Guillaume, Daneta, Lise, Natalie, Emma. She scans the list of countries. Where's Chile?

And then her eyes find the word and the one name below it.

MIGUEL AVALOS.

She places her fingers on the wall, feeling the grooves of each letter, as if reading Braille. She remembers the way he kissed her behind the waterfall as they descended from Mount Batur; she remembers her thought: Can I love this man?

She remembers the sweetness in his eyes as he leaned forward across the table at the restaurant in Kuta and asked her to marry him.

I failed you, she thinks. I didn't love you enough to say yes. Days later, I loved another man. I cheated you of what should have been yours.

Her ribs feel tight in her chest. She leans forward and touches her lips to the cold marble. She feels each letter of his name.

After a moment, she straightens up. She walks back to the names of the Indonesians. Nyoman's wife. Ati. Elly. Tata. Widayati. Which one of you loved that good man?

She steps back and looks at the jumble of names, so many names. Who did I pull from the rubble, only to have you die in my arms? Who stood too close to the bar that went up in flames so quickly that no one had time to run? Who did I step over on the way out?

She drops to her knees. Her face is wet with tears.

Nyoman is suddenly beside her. His hand settles on her shoulder. They both stare at the list for a long time.

In the morning, Jamie wakes up, clear about what she has to do. She showers, dresses, eats breakfast, and tells Nyoman she'll be back in a couple of hours.

Outside the gates of the guest house, Bambang and TukTuk greet her as if she's been gone for weeks.

"You have job for Bambang?" the boy asks, and the dog circles them, as if tying them together.

"Sorry, kid," Jamie tells him, "I'm on my own today."

She starts to walk up the hill, away from town.

"You go to see Mr. Gabe at the school!" Bambang says proudly.

Jamie keeps walking.

"You fall in love with Mr. Gabe?" he asks, trotting after her.

"This is none of your business," she tells him lightly.

"You have no husband. You have no baby. Mr. Gabe will be baby daddy."

"No," Jamie says, laughing. "I'm not looking for a baby daddy."

"What are you looking for?"

"You're a nosy little bugger."

"I don't understand those words."

"Like hell you don't."

Bambang is smiling.

"Where are you from, Bambang?"

"Nowhere," he says, lowering his head and hiding his eyes.

"Where are your parents?"

They've reached the top of the hill. Jamie is happy to realize that, for the first time in days, she's not winded. She must be ready for what's ahead, she thinks.

"I am old enough," Bambang says. There's a crease between his eyes that she's never seen before. "Do not need parents."

"Where are they?"

"Too many questions, Miss Jamie. You told me not to ask too many questions."

"Do you sleep on the street?" she asks.

He looks away from her again.

"I find job in town," he tells her sadly. "You have no job for me."

Jamie leans down and rubs TukTuk behind his ear. The sweet dog leans into her leg and makes a whimpering sound.

"Don't get into trouble," she tells the dog.

Bambang turns and runs back down the street, whistling for TukTuk to follow him. The dog cocks his head, looking beseechingly at Jamie for one last moment.

"Oh, go on," she says, and he takes off after his master.

She turns the corner and stops in front of Gabe's school. She can hear the noise of children shouting and laughing—surely no one can study with all that commotion. At once, all of the sounds stop. There's an eerie stillness in the air, and then the voices burst into song.

Jamie reads the sign on the front door of the school: FULL MOON CELEBRATION ON FRIDAY. 10 A.M.—2 P.M. GAMES AND REFRESHMENTS.

Looks like I'm here for a party, Jamie thinks. She pushes her fear of crowds away. She has nothing to lose.

She walks through the door of the school and follows a corridor that leads past the empty classrooms and out to the back gardens. While she walks, the song—a beautiful Balinese melody—fills her heart and makes her feel brave.

"Welcome, miss," a teenage boy says at the back door. "Fifty thousand rupiah for raffle tickets. Fifty thousand rupiah for games. One hundred thousand rupiah for the food. All money goes to Ubud Community School."

He talks too quickly. Jamie hears an onslaught of noise now that the song has ended. And, from everywhere, kids race in all directions.

"You missed dance show. So sorry, miss. Now fair begins."

He sits at a table, a dusty field of tents and games and booths spreading behind him. The place is packed with kids and parents and teachers. I'll never find Gabe, Jamie thinks, her resolve melting in an instant.

"You are a parent? You have child here at school? My mother works in the kitchen. I am student here, too."

The boy doesn't stop talking. The sun beats down on them, and dust stings her eyes.

"How much to enter?" she asks.

"Free!" he exclaims. "But so many things to do."

Before he has a chance to rattle them off again, she hands him some rupiah and buys tickets for some kind of games. The boy is thrilled.

She wanders into the field. The great majority of kids are very young. She passes a makeup booth, where a woman paints a pouting clown's face on a little boy. There's a bottle toss and a dartboard—she could be at a county fair back in the States.

But on the next ramshackle stage, a group of kids play the gamelan—they're only ten or eleven years old, she guesses, and they're very good. Proud parents applaud them.

She passes a tall pole that has flags attached to the very top. A young boy is trying to shimmy up the pole so he can grab one of the flags, but he keeps slipping. The crowd cheers him on, but finally, about halfway up, he runs out of energy and slides down.

Jamie walks on. She passes long tables of food, mostly Indonesian specialties. She's not hungry—she has only one reason to be here. Where the hell is he?

A cheer rises up from the far side of the field. She sees a group of kids kicking a soccer ball and one man among them. Gabe. She takes off in his direction.

He looks up as she nears and he stops for a moment. All the light fades from his face when he sees her. His eyes narrow as if he's deep in thought. Then a ball hits his shin and a boy rams into him. He picks the kid up and tousles his hair. And just like that he's Gabe again, not some angry stranger. His face fills with warmth. But it's not for her—it's for these boys who keep smashing into him as if that's the goal of the game.

Stay here, she tells herself. Don't flee.

He plays with the boys, but she can tell he's distracted—the boys keep yelling at him when he misses the ball. Finally, he says something to the biggest boy and charges off the field, heading in her direction.

"I haven't changed my mind," he says, his voice cold.

He stands a few feet away from her, his arms crossed, as if ready to block a tackle.

"I came a long way," Jamie says.

"For the anniversary ceremony," Gabe says.

"For you," she tells him. She can no longer fool herself.

He shakes his head.

He steps toward her, and for a second she thinks that he'll fold her in his arms. But his head is down, his voice low. "I'll walk you out," he says.

He keeps walking, past her and toward the school. She turns and joins him at his side.

"It's not fair, Gabe," she tells him. "You know how hard it was for me last year."

"I'm not blaming you," he says. He doesn't look at her as he walks. "This has nothing to do with you."

"It has everything to do with me."

Again, he shakes his head. "I only mean that I'm taking care of myself this time. This is what's best for me."

"To turn me away?"

"Yes."

They hear a loud cheer and look up to see a crowd gathered around the pole. One skinny boy has made it to the top, where

he grabs one of the flags. The crowd whoops and whistles. The
boy's face glows with triumph; he slides down the pole like a
happy monkey.

"Mr. Gabe! He did it! He did it!" A redheaded girl flies at
Gabe and wraps her arms around his legs. Then she steps back
and gazes up at him, wide-eyed. "Only three boys. Everyone
tried. No girls, Mr. Gabe."

"Come on, Layla. You can do it."

"I tried two times. It's too hard for me. It's too hard for
girls, Mr. Gabe."

Jamie walks straight to the man who's collecting tickets at
the pole.

"Can I try?" she asks.

"Sure," the man says, pleased. "We haven't had any of the
parents try. You're very brave. I'd be mortified."

"I may feel that way in about five minutes," Jamie tells him.

He takes her ticket. She doesn't look back to see if Gabe is
watching. She hopes the little girl has her eyes on the pole.

Jamie grabs the pole high above her with both hands, then
pulls herself up and wraps her legs around. It's more slippery
than she would have thought. She wishes she had stopped to
rub her hands in the dusty earth, but it's too late for that. She
grips the pole tightly with her legs.

She reaches high above her again, grabs hold, and then pulls
with her arms while pushing with her legs. I can do this, she
thinks.

The first cheer goes up from the crowd.

"Who is she?" someone calls.

"Is she a mom?"

"Teacher, I think," someone else says.

"Mr. Gabe's friend!" a kid yells, and all the kids let out a whooping cheer.

Jamie shimmies up the pole with real energy, until she's two-thirds of the way up.

Then she needs a break; her arms are tiring too quickly. This last part's the toughest, and she needs her strength.

Is he watching? She won't look down to scan the crowd. He probably walked away. Anyway, she's not doing it for him. She's doing it for the girls. Hell, she could use a little success in her own life right now.

Her bad elbow aches, yet she pushes past the pain. This pure physical effort, the tangible goal of climbing a pole, feels so damn good.

She reaches again and grips more forcefully with her legs to make up for her tired arms. She's still too far away to grab the flag. She hears more cheers below; the crowd must be growing.

How silly, she thinks. If I fail now, what have I proved? That a grown-up should behave like a grown-up? That there are some things girls just can't do?

She stretches far above herself, grasps the pole, pulls and pushes, and hears the screams of the crowd. She's there. The flag dangles only a foot from her head. She'll be able to grab it. Her heart pounds against her ribs.

She glances below and sees the heads of so many people. They're all looking skyward, their mouths open as they shout and cheer. Gabe's there, his face turned toward her, as well. His mouth is closed, but the edges lift in a smile. She remembers his smile.

She reaches out her hand and captures the flag.

The crowd goes wild.

She tucks the flag into her back pocket and slides down the pole.

When her feet hit the dirt, she's bombarded by kids, who throw their arms around her. They're mostly little girls, but even some boys join the throng of admirers. Jamie is laughing, and the sound of her own laugh surprises her.

She hands the flag to the smallest girl. "The prize is yours," she tells her.

The girl shrieks and runs off, clutching the small rectangle of fabric.

Jamie looks for Gabe. He's standing at the back of the crowd, still smiling. She walks up to him.

"Pretty impressive," he tells her.

"You're surprised?"

He shakes his head. "I had forgotten," he says.

"Mr. Gabe! Mr. Gabe!" a young boy shouts. "Soccer game's starting!"

"Go on," Jamie tells him.

He holds her eyes for a moment, as if he has something to say. But then he turns and jogs back toward the field.

Jamie watches him for a while, but he never looks in her direction.

Maybe I can let him go after all, she thinks.

Early that evening, after dinner alone in town, Jamie walks back to the Paradise Guest House. When she arrives, the gate opens and Dewi, Nyoman's renegade niece, appears, scowling.

"I hate parents," she says.

Jamie nods. "I know what you mean."

"They say no party. I go swimming with girlfriends. No boys even. They no believe me."

"Is that where you're headed?"

"Yes. I go anyway. They too old to stop me."

Jamie remembers herself at that age—her mother was helpless in her meager attempts to curb Jamie's reckless behavior.

"Where are you going swimming?"

"Waterfall," Dewi tells her. Then her eyes brighten. "You come!"

"With your girlfriends?"

"Yes!" Dewi's face looks like a young girl's again, despite the rings of black kohl around her eyes.

"Why not?" Jamie says. "I'll get my bathing suit."

Minutes later, she's on the back of Dewi's motorbike, holding on for dear life. The girl maneuvers in and out of traffic, weaving around cars and pedestrians, then flying down the country roads. The noise of the bike makes conversation impossible; Jamie can only watch Ubud disappear behind them.

The sun sets over the rice paddies, turning the world velvet green. Jamie stops squeezing Dewi's bony hips and settles onto the back of the bike. The mountainsides are terraced with endless rice paddies—one field of green melts into the next.

Dewi turns the bike off the main road and down a path in the middle of the field. They bump along for a while and then the bike comes to a stop.

"We here," Dewi says.

"Where?" Jamie asks. She looks around.

"You follow," Dewi tells her.

They climb off the bike, and Dewi balances it next to two other motorbikes. Jamie follows the girl down the path.

Dewi cuts through a thicket of trees, holding back some branches to allow Jamie through. In another minute or two, they're swallowed by the jungle.

Jamie can hear the roar of a waterfall almost immediately. Dewi whistles loudly, and response whistles fill the air.

"Girlfriends," she says, and runs ahead.

Jamie takes off after her. She feels like a kid on an adventure—the thrill of this nighttime gathering, banned by the parental units, lifts her spirits. They pass through an opening of trees, and the waterfall appears in all its glory.

It's huge, sending an enormous screen of water crashing into a pond in front of her. Three girls' heads bob in the water— their jubilant faces all turn to Dewi, who strips off her clothes and dives into the water. She's wearing a bikini, and even in the twilight, Jamie can see a tattoo on the girl's back. Is it a guitar?

Jamie waves to the girls, who look at her suspiciously.

Dewi berates them in Indonesian, and then they meekly wave back.

"You swim!" Dewi orders from the middle of the basin.

But the cellphone in Jamie's pocket rings, startling her.

"In a minute!" she calls to the girls.

She flips open the phone and sees Larson's name. She takes the call and heads into the woods to find a quiet place so she can hear him.

"Larson!" she yells.

"Why are you screaming?" he asks. His voice sounds weak and scratchy.

"I'm at the edge of a waterfall. With a bunch of teenage Balinese bad girls. I've found my sisterhood!"

"I got you onto the New Zealand trip," he says. "You can leave as soon as you want."

Jamie finds a rock to sit on. It's almost dark now, and the forest muffles the sound of the waterfall.

"You were right," she says. "I'm not done here."

"Since when do you listen to a word I tell you?" Larson asks.

"You sound awful," she says. She can barely hear him.

"Not doing so well."

"Chemo?"

"Don't think so. It's the pain now. A lot of pain."

She hears a shout and looks back toward the waterfall. The girls are laughing riotously. She feels as if she's a million miles away. Larson's breath in her ear pulls her close to him.

"I'm coming home," she tells him.

"No."

"Don't say no."

"You love the New Zealand trip," Larson says.

"I've got more important things to do," she insists.

She will spend her time with him, in his old house in Berkeley, doing whatever she needs to do to help him. As hard as it might be—his last months or weeks—she will try to ease the way.

Larson doesn't say anything for a few moments. Jamie looks up and sees a sky suddenly full of stars.

"Will you go to the anniversary ceremony before you come home?" he asks.

He's not going to fight with her. Jamie feels a great relief. She also feels a deep sadness—it is so unlike him to let her take care of him.

"It's on Sunday," she tells him. "I'll go and then I'll fly home on Monday."

"Thank you, Legs," he says, his voice unbearably soft.

She closes the phone and tucks it into her pocket. She walks back to the waterfall. The full moon reflects off the water, and the girls' faces look almost electric.

"You swim!" Dewi shouts from the middle of the pond.

Jamie strips off her clothes. She stands in her bikini on a rock on the edge of the water. She listens to the roar of the waterfall, the shrieks of the girls, and Larson's voice in her head, which always whispers, *Dive in.*

Later, she stands outside her cottage. It's sometime after midnight and she's exhausted, but she can't sleep. She's been wrestling with the sheets for too long—she needs fresh air.

The light is on in Nyoman's cottage, too. We're both haunted, she thinks.

Now the door opens and Nyoman appears on the step, as if her thinking about him has called him forth. He looks at Jamie and nods, apparently unsurprised to see her there.

"Can a guest at this hotel get ginger tea in the middle of the night?" she calls out.

"It is very expensive," Nyoman says, smiling.

Jamie smiles, too. "Put it on my bill."

"I will bring it out in a moment," Nyoman says, stepping back into his house.

Jamie looks toward the other cottages in the compound. The windows are all dark—Nyoman's parents, grandmother, and his brother's family are all asleep.

She wanders over to the table under the banyan tree. The moonlight gives her enough light to make her way around the tree roots, and she sits at the end, in her usual breakfast spot. The air is surprisingly cool, though minutes before, in bed in her cottage, she had cursed the Balinese heat.

Nyoman steps outside again, with a teapot and two cups in his hands. As always, his smile lifts her spirits—she is glad to have his company.

"When I was in the bombing, there was an American man who saved me," she tells Nyoman when he sits down. "Yesterday I found him."

"He is still in Bali," he says.

"Yes. He teaches at a school in town."

He nods and sips his tea.

"Suddenly I'm not sure why I needed to find him," Jamie says.

"You needed to find something else in Bali," Nyoman tells her. "Not this man."

"What?" she asks.

"When my wife died—" he begins, and then stops. In the moonlight, she can see his face darken. "When my wife died, I lost my way in the world. Then I would look at my community and think: How can I be lost when everyone knows where I am? Grief is a very difficult thing. It weighs on one's heart and makes it hard to walk. Now I feel light again."

"Because of your community," Jamie says, trying to understand.

"You are not lost," Nyoman says, his voice strong. "You have friends who know where you are. Friends like me."

"Thank you," she tells him.

"Drink your tea and then you will sleep," he says, and she knows that it is true.

On Sunday morning, Jamie waits for a long time before getting out of bed. Today is the anniversary of the bombing. She doesn't want to participate in the ceremony. She has struggled enough on this journey; she just wants to go home.

But Nyoman would be very disappointed—she is his responsibility and this ceremony means a great deal to him. So she will haul her sorry ass out of bed and put on the ceremonial clothes that he has found for her. Tomorrow she can leave Bali.

Her cellphone rings. She reaches for it on her bedside table.

"Hi, Mom," she says. She lies down again, her phone tucked to her ear.

"Did I wake you?"

"No. I was about to get in the shower."

"It's today, isn't it?"

"Yeah. I leave soon."

"It will be hard."

"I know, Mom." Jamie pushes herself up in bed. Her ceremonial clothes are laid out on the bureau, waiting for her.

"What happened with your hero? Gabe. Did you find him?"

"I think it's time to move on," Jamie says.

"You all right?"

"Yeah, I'm all right."

"You sound sad."

"I had a dream about Gabe for a long year. Hard to let go of that."

"It might make you ready to find someone else," Rose tells her.

"You're lucky," Jamie says. "You've got Lou." To her surprise, she realizes she means it.

Her mother waits a moment before responding, and in the silence Jamie imagines Rose and Lou, drinking coffee at the kitchen table in Palo Alto, *The New York Times* spread before them. Lou leans across the table and kisses Rose's cheek.

She remembers sitting beside Gabe in the balé one morning, reaching for the milk. When he passed it, their hands touched. It was more intimate than Miguel's embrace, and she felt guilty for it. Now she yearns for that touch.

"Thanks," Rose says. "I *am* lucky."

Once they've hung up, Jamie gets out of bed. She's late for breakfast, but Nyoman hasn't banged on her door. She turns on the shower and steps in.

An hour later, Nyoman drives with her to Jimbaran, in the southern part of Bali. The ceremony will be held at a cultural park called GWK, named for an enormous sculpture that is being built there. The sculpture is of Wisnu, god of water, riding the back of the mythical bird Garuda.

They arrive at the park along with hundreds of other cars and motorbikes. Nyoman parks in the lot designated for special guests, and when they get out of the car they look toward the huge crowd ahead.

"You will be fine," Nyoman says.

Jamie steps close to him and swallows her fear. "Let's go," she says, and they walk toward the throng.

They're herded into a massive alley of limestone pillars called Lotus Pond. The giant head of Wisnu, made of copper and brass, towers over them. Nyoman explains that the rest of the sculpture is not yet finished. All the people file ahead as if they're a little awed by their surroundings. A solemn hush fills the air.

It takes a long time to organize the groups—families of victims, survivors, journalists, government officials, religious leaders, and the many hundreds of people, Balinese and Westerners, who have come to show their support.

Nyoman finds Dolly, the organizer of the survivors' and

widows' foundation, and asks her to take Jamie to her seat. Before they leave, Nyoman whispers in Jamie's ear, "I am with you."

She reaches up and straightens his glasses on his nose.

"This way," Dolly says impatiently, leading Jamie away.

The sun beats down on them as Jamie follows Dolly to the survivors' section, close to the stage, where she climbs the stairs and sits in the shade of a large canopy. The bleachers are full, and still more people spill into the enormous space. The crowd is so large that she can't see where it ends.

Jamie closes her eyes and begins to count. Larson once told her what to do when she awakened in the middle of the night after a nightmare: count backward from ten. Breathe deeply between each number. Start over when you hit one. Ten, breathe. Nine, breathe. But she can't get her breath to match the slow numbers; it's a force of its own.

Someone bumps her knee and she opens her eyes. A young Nordic-looking girl sits beside her on the hard bench. The girl is in her mid-twenties. Her face is a mess of scars—burn victim, Jamie thinks. The skin has been grafted and patched and mended. But the colors are wrong; the skin is mottled and bumpy.

"My name is Marit," the girl says. She smiles, and her face struggles with the change until it is complete—she is beautiful despite the damage.

"I'm Jamie."

"Are you from Australia?"

"No. The United States."

"I'm from Norway," Marit says. "But I live here in Bali. Thank you for coming. It means a great deal to us."

Jamie's breath slows. She feels her shoulders relax.

She thinks of Miguel's parents and wishes that they'd decided to come for this, too. She had spoken to them by phone a couple of times during the year, but they didn't want to see the country where their son had died.

A burst of music grabs everyone's attention, and the ceremony begins. There are speeches in Indonesian and in English. A children's choir sings a haunting Balinese song. The Australian prime minister speaks, and an eloquent British man tells the story about his son, a rugby player, who died in the bombing. Then a man takes the stand and begins haltingly.

"I was there that night," he says. He's tall and blond and very handsome—what a surprise to hear the trembling in his voice. Australian accent. Jamie sits forward, intrigued.

"I was eating dinner near the clubs on this night, one year ago. I had quit my career in journalism and had become an overage surf bum. I met up with a bloke for dinner—another expat—but, really, I was hoping to meet some sheilas at Sari Club later that night. I wasn't a very serious man a year ago."

His voice gets stronger as he speaks.

"The bombs shook our restaurant. Part of the balcony collapsed. Somehow I knew it was a bomb. I don't know why or how—I certainly wasn't paying any attention to the newspapers in those days, even though I once made my living writing for them. I then did a shameful thing. I walked away."

He stops speaking and waits to compose himself. The crowd is silent.

"I never slept that night. I listened to the sirens all night long. I listened to the echoes of the screams I heard before I walked away. And in the morning I became a journalist again. I went to the bomb site and to the hospital, and I talked to every person I could. I was driven by shame, the worst of reasons, but the more I learned, the more that changed. Soon I had to know, I had to understand. When I wrote my story for *Time* magazine, I felt a little bit of that shame slip away. I could tell the world what happened here in Bali. But still it wasn't enough. So I started a foundation for the injured and the widows. I raised money from almost every country in the world."

He pauses and gazes around. He's now standing tall and holding his head high.

"But I'm not a hero. I'm just a poor wanker who has tried every day to make up for what I failed to do on this day, one year ago."

He hangs his head for a moment, and the crowd waits.

"I'd like to call someone up here. He doesn't know I'm going to do this. But I'd like you to meet a real hero. I want you to meet a man who did the right thing that night."

He looks out into the crowd.

"Gabe Winters, please come up here."

Jamie leans forward in her seat, now alert. Her heart gallops in her chest—so much for the damn breathing exercises. He's here? Nervously, she runs her thumb over the scar on her face, as if rubbing it away. She scans the crowd, looking for movement. Suddenly he's standing next to the journalist on-stage, embraced in a bear hug. When the man releases Gabe, Jamie sees his face. He looks pale and unsure.

"I'd like to tell you about this man," the journalist says into the microphone. "That night, he ran into the burning buildings. He saved a dozen lives. The flames grew and he just kept charging back in, carrying people out to safety. Many of you—" The man stops and points to Jamie's section of the bleachers. Gabe turns and looks directly at Jamie. It doesn't take him a moment to find her—he knows where she is. He holds her gaze. "Many of you were saved by this man. He's the real hero."

The journalist steps aside and offers the microphone. Gabe averts his eyes from Jamie's and raises his hands as if to say: Do I have to do this?

"Come on, mate," the journalist says under his breath, but the mike catches it, and his encouraging words carry through the air.

Gabe reluctantly takes the microphone.

He looks at Jamie again, as if searching for something, and then out toward the crowd in front of him. He clears his throat and steps back, surprised by the noise as it reverberates through the sound system.

"I didn't expect this," he says quietly. "I'm more than a little surprised." He scans the crowd. When his eyes reach Jamie's, she sees that he's seeking courage. Something softens in his face. He's letting her in.

She nods. You can do this.

"Thank you, Theo. I don't agree with you, but I thank you. I think we all react in different ways. For that one night I might have been a hero, but you've done heroic things in the year since. We all thank you for that."

The crowd applauds for a long time. When the noise dies down, it appears as if Gabe is going to walk away from the mike, but he steps up to it again.

"I want to mention one other hero," he says, squinting out into the crowd. "When I ran into the building that night, there was already one young woman doing a hero's job. She went into the club to find a friend after the bomb went off, and even though that friend died, she kept going, pulling many people to safety. And even when part of the ceiling fell on her, injuring her, she didn't stop. She kept helping others. That's remarkable bravery." He looks directly at Jamie. "The woman never quits." He offers her a sly smile. "Jamie Hyde, will you please stand up."

Jamie's heart seems to stop. She can't stand—she'll pass out. Her legs aren't solid; her head spins. The young woman next to her reaches over and takes her hand. She takes a breath and then stands. Her knees wobble. She peers around at the kaleidoscope of faces and hears a roar of cheers. The sound fills her and makes her stand taller. She glances at Gabe, and now he nods, as if to say: I am with you.

Take it in, she tells herself. All of it. It feels bigger than anything she's ever experienced in her life. Somewhere out there, Nyoman is clapping his hands for her. She imagines Larson, her mother, Lou, her father in Connecticut—her own Balinese compound of family—holding her in this cheer. She imagines Miguel, and she can almost hear his voice in her ear. You did everything you could, he whispers to her.

She sits down and the young woman squeezes her hand.

"Thank you," Marit says.

The man in front of her turns around. "Thank you," he says.

Someone pats her shoulder from behind, then leans forward and whispers in her ear, "Thank you."

The gamelan plays and the crowd quiets. Jamie looks to the stage; Gabe is gone. A man plays a song that is so beautiful it brings tears to her eyes. The young woman next to her doesn't let go of her hand.

———

"I did not know," Nyoman says when he finds Jamie after the ceremony. "I thank you for what you did."

"I want to find Gabe," Jamie said. "Will you help me?"

"Of course," Nyoman says. "I just saw Mr. Theo talking to Dolly. We can ask him."

They work their way through the crowd. Halfway across the amphitheater, Jamie shouts, "I see him!"

It's the tall Australian she sees; his blond head towers over a group of Balinese women. They maneuver their way toward him.

When she gets closer, Jamie notices that the women are all aflutter—they're flirting with the handsome man. And he's flirting right back. Jamie has to call out to get his attention.

"Excuse me!" she says loudly.

He looks at her and his face lights up with recognition. He steps through the crowd of women and takes Jamie in his arms. She is swallowed by his enormous hug.

"Thank you," he says, stepping back to look at her. "I've heard stories about you from many of the survivors."

"Thank *you*," she tells him. "I know from Nyoman the huge impact of your foundation."

The man vigorously shakes hands with Nyoman.

"Wonderful ceremony, Mr. Theo," Nyoman says.

"Do you know where I can find Gabe?" Jamie asks.

Theo looks around. He's got the advantage of height—he scans the crowd in all directions. "If I know him, he sneaked off as soon as he could."

"Do you have his phone number? The one I have is disconnected."

Theo reaches into his pocket and pulls out his cellphone. He finds the number and gives it to Jamie, who writes it down.

"Thanks," she tells him. "For everything."

"Can I take you for a drink?" he asks. "Dinner?"

She smiles. "I'm leaving tomorrow."

"Tonight?"

"I'm sorry," she says.

"Will you come back?" he asks. "To Bali?"

"I may," she tells him. And for the first time, it is not a lie.

TukTuk sits across the street from the Paradise Guest House, alone. Jamie looks up and down the road, peering into the hazy morning light, searching for Bambang. She's never seen the dog without the boy, or the boy without the dog.

TukTuk trots over and stands next to her, leaning into her knee as if he can finally rest.

"Where's your pal?" Jamie asks.

The black dog simply pants.

"You lost him? Impossible."

Jamie scans the street again.

"Okay, hang with me for a little while. He'll show up."

She walks into town, the dog at her side. She needs to buy a few souvenirs, since she's leaving tonight. A necklace for her mom; bead bracelets for herself. Maybe she'll stop by Isabel's yoga studio and say goodbye.

She feels oddly content this morning. She doesn't have a mission anymore. White knight found and lost. She called Gabe's number many times last night, but he never answered his phone. He doesn't need to—she believes that he has forgiven her. She was a fool to let herself think that what happened during those days after the bombing had anything to do with love.

At least Bali loves her. She appreciates the lightness in her step, the eagerness to buy trinkets. She even enjoys the dog by her side. I'll get a dog, she thinks happily. I need a dog in my life again.

"Want to come home with me, TukTuk?" she asks.

The dog whimpers.

"Guess not. Why give up a life of crime?"

The word *crime* reverberates in her mind. Bambang must be in trouble, she suddenly realizes. With a quick chill, she imagines him beaten by someone he tried to con, left to die in a ditch at the side of the road. But the dog would never leave him.

"Where is he, TukTuk?"

The dog looks up at her. He tilts his head.

"You're going to make me figure this out, huh?"

She leans down and ruffles his fur; he makes a mournful sound, as if this is a poor replacement for what he really wants. He wants Bambang.

"You hungry?" she asks him.

He stares up at her, his soulful eyes pleading.

"We'll start with food."

They walk to the open market. Jamie enters one of the passageways, then makes her way along the stalls. TukTuk stays at her side.

"Where are the food stalls?" she asks. "Why don't I follow you, TukTuk? You must be able to smell all that good stuff."

But they take a few wrong turns, passing colorful sarongs and ceramic pots, straw baskets and beaded jewelry. Hawkers call out to her: "You want this? Good price! I give you best price!" Jamie ignores them all.

Then the crowded passageway opens to a courtyard and she

sees food stalls ahead. She wonders about their policy on dogs
near the food, but there are other strays combing the floor for
whatever someone has dropped.

She steps up to a stall and points to a meat and rice dish.
The old woman wraps the food in a waxed-paper cone and
passes it to her. Jamie pays. She won't feed the dog in the woman's
sight—she's sure that would infuriate all the watchful eyes.
So she leads TukTuk out of the market, and they stop in an
alleyway.

"Breakfast," she tells him.

The dog sits, waiting. She unwraps the paper cone and offers
it to him. He takes a delicate bite of meat and then grabs
the whole thing from her hand, scampers away, tosses it on the
ground, and devours it with his back to her. She smiles, watching
him.

"You needed that, didn't you?"

When he's done, he trots back to her side and, sure enough,
he's not whimpering anymore.

"My job's not done, sweet dog," Jamie tells him. "Where
the hell is your boy?"

They walk out to the main street and start wandering
through town. Jamie imagines that the dog will find Bambang
first. But why was he waiting outside her guest house? Had he
already given up his search?

She can't think of a soul to ask: Have you seen that young
boy who robs, steals, cheats?

Yoga lady! He talked about his yoga lady who helped him.
It wasn't Isabel, but that would be a good place to start.

"Let's go, TukTuk. We've got the first whiff of him."

They head to Isabel's yoga studio, a ten-minute walk down

the main street of town. When they get there, Jamie sees that class is getting ready to start.

"Wait here," she tells TukTuk.

She dashes inside and finds Isabel setting up her mat at the front of the room.

"Jamie! You're taking a class?" Isabel asks.

"I need help. Do you know a kid named Bambang?"

Just as Isabel shakes her head, two women call out at once: "I know Bambang."

Jamie turns toward the students. Most are arranging their mats and blankets and blocks and straps. One is in a headstand. But two young women, on either side of the room, walk toward her.

"His dog showed up at my place this morning," Jamie tells them.

"TukTuk," one woman says.

"Right. That dog is always with Bambang. I have a feeling something happened to him."

"Try the jail," the other woman says. "He's there once a month or so. They try to get him off the streets and they think that'll scare him. But nothing scares him."

"Has he ripped you guys off?" Jamie asks, suddenly curious.

Both women smile. "Who cares," one says. "He's a sweet kid."

"Where's the jail?" Jamie asks.

Isabel gives her directions, and by the time Jamie dashes out of there most of the women are sitting cross-legged on their mats, eyes closed, spines straight.

"Follow me," she tells TukTuk unnecessarily. The dog trots after her.

She finds the jail easily. TukTuk stands guard outside while she enters through the imposing front door. Inside, she's faced with a large open room with many desks, most of them empty.

Jamie finally finds a man who can answer her question. Yes, a boy named Bambang was arrested yesterday and charged with stealing the suitcase of a tourist at the Monkey Forest Hotel. Yes, he is still in jail. No, she cannot visit him.

The man—a scrawny cop too young to shave, it seems— eyes Jamie eagerly. He's waiting for a bribe, she thinks.

"Is there a bathroom I can use?" she asks.

He points toward a long dark hallway.

She uses the empty bathroom to pull a twenty from her wallet, then rolls the bill so it fits into the palm of her hand. Her heart is beating fast. She has no idea if this will work or if it will get her arrested for attempted bribery. She may get to visit Bambang by occupying the cell next to his. A lot of good that will do for TukTuk, she thinks. Besides, she has a plane to catch.

She heads back toward the cop, who is now leaning over a desk, talking to a pretty Balinese girl.

"Excuse me," Jamie says.

The cop turns toward her, unsurprised.

"I'd like you to give Bambang a message," she tells him. "Can you tell him that Jamie is taking care of TukTuk?"

The cop shrugs.

"I appreciate it," Jamie says, and puts out her hand.

The cop shakes her hand, and the money disappears into his palm. He turns and walks away.

Jamie waits a moment. She's not sure what she's waiting for: Her own arrest? Bambang's appearance? But nothing happens, and finally she walks out of the jailhouse and stands in the blinding light of the sun. It's still early morning and already oppressively hot. She thinks of her flight tonight yearningly.

TukTuk pushes his nose into her leg; she's been ignoring him.

"Sorry, buddy. I did my best."

But the dog lets out a long howl. And then he's flying into midair, landing in the arms of Bambang, who drops to his knees and wrestles with him. Both boy and dog make yipping sounds of delight.

Jamie laughs, watching their reunion, suddenly sure that the first thing she'll do when she arrives in California is find a Tuk-Tuk of her own. Larson loves dogs, and if she's taking care of him for a while, she might need a little moral support. Later she'll have to travel less, but maybe it's time she stuck around. She might try her hand at running the business end of things— the stuff that Larson does so well. She can find out if she likes that kind of work.

It's a lot to think about, but she'll take it slowly. Dog, Larson, home. A new life.

Bambang finally emerges from the tussle and bows to Jamie, his palms pressed together, thumbs to his chest.

"I thank you with my heart," he says solemnly.

"Stop stealing from tourists," she tells him.

"It was tourist with three suitcase," Bambang says. "I only took smallest of three."

Jamie shakes her head, but she can't ditch the smile. He's the unlikeliest of thieves, this scruffy kid who is disarmingly honest and sly at the same time.

"How did you find me?" he asks.

"Your yoga ladies take good care of you," she tells him.

He looks confused.

"And TukTuk told me you were missing," she adds.

Bambang scoots down for another love fest with his dog.

"I have to go pack," Jamie tells him. "I'm leaving today."

"I walk with you," he says. "I be protector from pickpockets."

"What a relief," she tells him with a smile.

They walk onto the main street, and TukTuk pushes his way between them. He bumps against their legs as he prances along.

"Why you leave?" Bambang asks. "Is too soon to go."

"I'm ready," Jamie says.

"I will miss you," he tells her very seriously.

Jamie glances at him. "Where are your parents?" she asks once again.

"Mother die," he tells her.

"I'm sorry," she says. She's not surprised. He's a kid in search of a mother. She has the feeling that all he really wants is someone to feed him a hot meal and run a bath for him.

"Where's your dad?" she asks.

They're walking past the Royal Palace; the buses line up and Japanese tourists wait patiently for their guide, umbrellas shielding them from the sun. Jamie's not sure if Bambang is ignoring her question or eyeing potential targets.

"Bambang?" she finally says.

"My father away."

"Away?"

"Yes."

"Where? Java?"

"Jail," he says quickly.

Maybe Bambang learned his craft at the feet of his father, in the good Indonesian tradition. Fathers train their sons to be farmers or sculptors or weavers or painters. Why not thieves?

"For a long time?" she asks.

"Long time," he says. "Maybe all time."

Not a thief, Jamie thinks. If I can buy this kid's release for a twenty, it would take some serious business to stay in prison for a lifetime.

"You have any family here in Bali?" she asks.

"No family," Bambang says.

They walk in silence for a few minutes; somehow their good spirits have vanished. I don't need to save this boy, Jamie tells herself. There will be other yoga ladies in his future.

But Bambang reaches out his hand to touch her shoulder.

"If I tell you story, you will hate Bambang," he says. His face is grim; she smells the jail on him now.

"I will not hate you," she tells him seriously. He seems to consider this for a while.

"Follow Bambang," he says, and he turns down a side street.

A con, she thinks. But she tosses the thought aside; there's no reason for him to trick her anymore.

They walk up a steep street. TukTuk runs ahead, then back, circling them, urging them on at a faster pace. Bambang is silent, his head bowed. Jamie waits for him to tell his story.

At the top of the hill is a path that heads into the woods. Jamie thinks for a moment: Is this safe? And then she abandons the thought. She's surprised to realize she trusts Bambang.

TukTuk prances in front of them as if welcoming them. Sure enough, it's home. Not very deep into the woods, Bambang has set up a wooden structure—not much more than a few boards nailed together. He painted one of the boards green, but it seems that he ran out of paint. There are the remnants of a campfire, and a blackened pot sits on the ground beside the ashes.

Jamie peers inside the opening to the shelter: A woven palm mat fills the entire space of the room.

"Nice," she says.

Bambang beams at her proudly.

"I never show house before," he tells her.

"I'm honored."

"You help me."

TukTuk pokes at her hand, so she ruffles the fur on his head.

"You drink tea?" Bambang offers.

"No. Thanks."

He points to a rock in front of the cabin.

"You sit here," he says.

Jamie climbs onto the rock and sits, cross-legged. Bambang sits beside her.

They're looking out over the rooftops of Ubud. There's shade from a mango tree, and the perch feels oddly lifted above the land, as if they're floating. I like it here, Jamie thinks. And then it's clear to her: I like Bali.

She can see the rice fields that surround the town in all directions. There's a mix of old buildings and new—a village in the process of becoming a city. She can smell frangipani from the garden below. She feels a kind of joy, even at this unlikely moment. Here she is with a street urchin, a baby con man.

"My father, he not a good man," Bambang says. He's staring out at the rooftops, his back as straight as those of the yoga ladies on their mats.

"What did he do?"

"My father angry man. He lose temper very easy, even for little thing."

He stops talking, and TukTuk comes to his side. Bambang rests his hand on the dog's head.

"One day, my mother and I sit in kitchen and play game with little sister. We are laughing—it is good time in our house. My father comes home and he is angry, always yelling at my mother. He tell her that there is no money and I can work, that I am too old to be spoiled mama's boy in school and at home. My mother says no, I am very smart and I will go to school. My father hits her, hard, and she falls and her head cracks against the stove. There is so much blood and she doesn't move. I take my little sister away so she cannot see."

The boy waits a few moments. When his hand stops stroking TukTuk's head, the dog pushes his nose into Bambang's leg. Jamie's body trembles as if she's suddenly very cold.

"The police come to my house. My father tell the police that my mother fainted and hit her head. I said, no, my father hit her. He killed her."

Bambang looks at Jamie. She can see his fear even now. She nods, unable to speak.

"My father go to jail. If it is not for all time, he will come to find me. He will kill me, too."

"My God," Jamie says quietly.

"Maybe I am bad man who put my father in jail."

"Bambang," she says. "You are not a bad man. You did the right thing."

"He is my father," Bambang insists.

"That's right. And he killed your mother."

Bambang lowers his head.

"The next day I want to go away from there. I have uncle—brother of my mother—who puts me on airplane to Bali. I do not want friend in Bali. I do not want to say, 'My father killed my mother. I put him in jail.'"

He stops talking. Jamie sees smoke rising from one of the fields on the far side of town. She's heard that the Balinese still burn their garbage, despite warnings from the government that it's harmful. But from a distance it's pretty, and the smoke curls in the sky, reaching toward the clouds.

She puts her arm around Bambang and he leans into her.

"You have done nothing wrong," she tells him.

Jamie packs the last item into her suitcase and closes it. She'll leave the straw hat for one of Nyoman's relatives; she perches it on the middle of her bed. She hears a rustle of noise and turns around.

Gabe appears in the doorway of her cottage.

"Your bags, miss?"

Jamie stares at him, bewildered. For a moment she's thrown back in time. It's the man she met a year ago. It's as if she knows him again, knows the gaze of his eyes, the lift of his smile. She knows the hand that is reaching for her suitcase.

"What are you doing here?"

"You ordered a taxi to take you to the airport?"

Jamie shakes her head. The man who walked away from her a few days ago was a stranger. He spoke to her in a voice that she had never heard before. This voice—it's familiar. She remembers listening to him tell a story in the dark of her room at the beach cottage and thinking: What would it be like to kiss this man?

"Taxi?" she asks. "What are you talking about?"

"This taxi comes with a guided tour. We leave now, see a little bit of Bali, then I take you to the airport."

"Who told you—"

"Shall I take this bag?" he asks, pointing to her suitcase.

"Yes. No! Why are you here?"

Gabe leans against the doorway. She remembers that tilt of his head. "I heard you were leaving." His voice is quieter. He pauses, looking at his feet. "I want to spend a little time with you before you go."

"I'm glad," Jamie says, taking a deep breath. She imagines reaching out to touch his lips.

"Let me drive you to the airport," he says.

"Gabe. Who told you I was leaving today?"

"An Indonesian boy. He found me at school."

Jamie smiles. "Troublemaker."

"Nice friends you make in Bali," Gabe says.

"The best kind."

"And the guy who runs this place—he cross-examined me as if he were your father."

Jamie's smile widens. "Another friend," she says.

"More like an armed guard."

"I like Bali this time around," Jamie tells him.

Gabe nods. "Will you let me take you?"

"Yes."

He lifts her suitcase and carries it out to his car. When he's gone, Jamie leans against the door frame, looking out into the garden. Nyoman appears in the window of his cottage, his head down. She feels a rush of too many emotions. It's as if she's saying goodbye and hello at the same time.

She hears a shout and sees Dewi waving madly from the door of her grandparents' cottage.

"Come on over!" Jamie calls out.

The girl runs toward her. Her hair sports streaks of vibrant blue. Today's T-shirt reads: SHUT UP AND KISS ME.

"Hey, you," Jamie says.

"I come with you," Dewi says, a devilish smile on her face.

"To the United States?"

"California. I will be California girl." The girl prances as if doing a go-go dance.

"You look a little more New York than California."

"New York!" Dewi shouts.

"One day," Jamie says. "You finish school and get your uncle to bring you for a visit."

"Really?"

"Will you email me?" Jamie asks.

"Yes!" Dewi races over to Nyoman's cottage. Jamie watches her, laughing. She runs back with a pad of paper and a pen. Jamie writes down her email address.

"You take picture of me?" Dewi asks.

Jamie pulls her camera out of her backpack. Dewi steps back and poses for the camera as if she's been trained in Hollywood. She juts one shoulder forward and tilts her head, lets a strand of blue hair fall into her eye. She offers a seductive smile.

"Look at you," Jamie says with a whistle.

Dewi jumps in the air. "Put picture on Internet. I get discovered by American movie director."

"No way," Jamie says. "Your uncle would kill me." She leans over and kisses the girl on the cheek.

Dewi runs to her grandparents' cottage. Before she disappears inside, she turns and waves at Jamie one last time.

"Who's that?" Gabe asks. He's walking up the path to her cottage.

"Another friend," she tells him.

"You've been busy."

"Very."

"Anything else I can carry?"

Jamie shakes her head.

"I have to say goodbye to my host. You better go wait in the car like a good cabdriver, or he might run you out of town."

Gabe salutes and turns back. Jamie looks inside her cottage one last time. She remembers her first night here. It was only six days ago, yet it feels like much longer. She's a little sad to leave.

When she turns around, Nyoman is standing in front of her.

"I was just coming to see—"

"You have a man here—"

"I know."

They stand awkwardly for a moment.

"I thank you—"

"You will—"

They both start speaking at once and stop again. Jamie laughs.

"My turn."

"Your turn," Nyoman says.

"Thank you."

"I say the same words," he tells her. "The words are not big enough."

"I know what you mean."

"The man is the one who saved you after the bomb."

"Yes," Jamie says. "He'll take me to the airport."

"I would take you—"

"I know. Thank you."

"You come back one day."

"I will come back one day."

Jamie puts her arms around Nyoman. He stands stiffly for a second, and then he wraps his arms around her.

When she steps back, she sees the sadness on his face.

"One photo," she says. "With a smile."

He stands very straight and offers his dazzling smile. Through the viewfinder she sees that his glasses are crooked. She snaps the photo.

"Where are we going?" Jamie asks.

Gabe drives along unfamiliar roads through the country-side. They cross a river, where a couple of women bathe their children under a small waterfall. The water glistens on their brown bodies.

"That depends on how much time we have," Gabe tells her. "When is your flight?"

"Nine P.M."

"We have time," he says.

"For?"

"You'll see."

"Thank you," she says.

"For what?"

"For what you did at the ceremony. I was very touched."

He shrugs. "I figured if I had to suffer through all that attention, then you should, too." He smiles.

"It wasn't easy," Jamie says. "I almost passed out, but I thought it wouldn't look very heroic."

"It was a good ceremony," Gabe says. "For a long time I didn't want to go. I thought it was too soon. But it was good for Bali."

"And for you?"

"Yes, for me." He smiles.

"You've hated me for a year now," Jamie says, her voice quiet.

He glances at her, his smile gone. "I was hurt by you," he says seriously. "I understood why you left. But I had opened my heart to you."

Jamie wants to reach out to him, but she keeps her hands folded in her lap. She won't say: I opened my heart to you, too. He's talking about the past, not the present.

Besides, she has a plane to catch.

Finally she says, "I'm sorry, Gabe."

He nods. She wants to run her finger along his jaw. She looks away.

The rice fields spread, like a lush carpet, over the hills. She thinks about her swim by the waterfall a couple of nights ago, the cool night air on her body as she and Dewi trekked back through the woods to find the motorbike, the hum of the girls' foreign voices as they gossiped with one another. I have always been a tourist, an outsider. What would happen if I belonged to a place? Now, driving through the Balinese countryside, she thinks about Berkeley, about a walk in the hills with her sketch pad. I've never drawn a picture of home, she thinks.

When she has been quiet for a long time, Gabe touches her knee. She watches his hand float beside her for a moment before he curls his fingers back around the steering wheel.

"Please," he says gently. "Tell me about you."

She nods. "I had a hard time. I was a complete disaster for a few weeks."

"Did you go back to your mother's?"

"Yes. But I hated having her take care of me. It's odd: I had such an easy time letting you take care of me."

"I think you didn't have a choice," Gabe offers with a wry smile. "If you could have, you would have bolted after the first day."

Jamie remembers lying in bed one morning after the bombing, listening to the silence of the beach cottage. He's gone, she thought. He went back to his mountain house, to his schoolkids, to a life of healthy people. And then she heard the front door open. Gabe walked into her room and he brought with him the smell of the ocean. I'll get through this, she had thought.

"You're wrong," she tells him now. "I may not have known very much about letting someone take care of me—I hadn't had much practice—but I wanted you there."

Gabe glances at her and his smile disappears. She tries to read his expression: He seems to be looking for something he can't find. I'm right here, she wants to say.

"Did you go back to your job?" he asks.

Jamie tells him about her mother's remarkable attention— the trips to the hospital and to doctors' offices to treat her wounds, the long nights when neither of them slept.

"I was scared that I'd never leave my mother's house," Jamie says. "After a month I knew I *had* to leave. I moved back to Berkeley and asked my boss for the first travel assignment he could find for me. I wasn't ready. But I needed to be busy."

Gabe reaches out his hand and tucks her hair behind her ear. It is a gesture so gentle, and yet she feels it deep inside her. Then he runs his finger along her scar.

"This healed well," he says. "You healed well."

"Not right away," she tells him. "I made myself believe I could do it. In the same way that someone talks herself into walking across a hanging bridge hundreds of feet above a raging river, I talked myself back into life. It worked. Some of the time."

She stops speaking for a while, exhausted by her torrent of words. They've been driving and driving, the countryside a continual stream of terraced rice paddies against a cloudless sky.

Jamie watches a young girl biking across the field. A boy chases her on his bike; she can hear the girl's triumphant shouts. Catch me, she thinks.

"Where are we going?" Jamie asks.

"We're almost there," Gabe tells her.

They drive into an unfamiliar town. Jamie thinks: He's wrong. I don't want to visit another town, another temple or tourist attraction.

But then she rolls down the window and she can smell the ocean.

"Is this where—"

"Yes," he tells her.

He pulls down a small street and drives to the end, where he parks the car. They both get out and walk toward the sound of the waves.

A path cuts between two stores, and then the sea is in front of them, calm and blue and enormous. They walk onto a small path that borders the beach; Jamie can see that it stretches in both directions.

"I remember this," she says.

"This way leads to town," Gabe says, pointing left, "and this way leads to the beach cottage where we stayed."

"Let's go to that restaurant—"

"La Taverna," Gabe says.

"Yes."

Jamie remembers every detail of the restaurant. She remembers running to the table in the balé in the rain—this time they take an umbrellaed table under clear skies. She remembers the waiter who talked about the meditation session interrupted by the bomb. She remembers their invention of Audrey and Cary, doppelgängers out for a spin on the dance floor. This time there is no band, only a recording of a popular Balinese song that makes Jamie think of waterfalls.

"And you?" she asks once they're seated. "What was it like to return to your life after the bombing?"

They're both drinking white wine. Their table faces the sea, and, since it's midday, they've got a view of the dozen or so tourists brave enough to come to Bali. It's different from the nearly empty beach in the days after the bombing. Now people swim in the shallow water; others sit in lounge chairs on the sand, reading or sleeping. A blond woman and her young son build an enormous mound in the sand, and, while Jamie watches, the mound becomes a turtle. There's a constant flow of people walking along the path between the restaurant and the beach—many of them young Balinese kids, in small groups and in pairs. One teenage couple holds hands and bumps shoulders as they walk.

"I fell in love with you," Gabe says, so suddenly that Jamie catches her breath. "At first I thought it was only the shared experience—no one else could understand what we went through. But, no, it was you. I knew that the last night, when we made love."

Jamie remembers the smile on his face while he slept.

"Then I ran away," she says quietly.

He nods. "I didn't know how to lose what I'd just found. Nothing in the world felt familiar except for you. And you were gone."

"Gabe, I'm so sorry." She wants to reach out and press her fingers to his lips. Don't say more. I understand.

The waiter brings a tuna carpaccio and a salad of oranges and mint. They wait until he refills their wineglasses and leaves.

"I went back to Ubud after you left," Gabe says. "I returned to my classroom. I lived my life more fully after that week. But when I saw you outside my school the other day, I was stunned. I had imagined that moment so many times, and in all my imaginings I reacted a little more like Cary Grant than Gabe Winters." He offers Jamie a smile. "Gabe Winters walked away."

"So this is Cary Grant sitting here?"

He shakes his head. "At the school fair a couple of days ago, I fell for the girl on top of the flagpole." His face brightens. "This is me."

She holds his eyes for a moment. She should know what to say. But maybe there have been too many words. She thinks of Dewi's T-shirt: SHUT UP AND KISS ME. Now she's got a goofy smile on her face, and she doesn't want to try to explain it. She looks out toward the water.

The boy has finished sculpting his sand turtle and climbs on top of it, as if ready to ride it out to sea. With a whoop of joy, he leaps up and then crashes down on the turtle's sand back. It crumbles, and the boy's face transforms. He bursts into tears.

Jamie looks back at Gabe. He's waiting for something.

"I've been imagining your life for a long time," she says.

"It's a quiet life," he tells her.

She takes a sip of her wine, then glances down at the food on their plates—it's beautifully presented, yet she can't imagine taking a bite.

"Have you been happy?" she asks.

"Some of the time. I love my job. And I love my joglo on the mountainside. It fits me like a good house should."

"Sounds nice."

The waiter appears at their table. "Is everything all right?"

"Yes," they both say, and then reach for their forks. Jamie takes a bite of the tuna; Gabe reaches for the orange salad. The waiter moves on to another table.

"We don't even know each other," she says, suddenly shy.

"We know a great deal," he tells her.

"I thought you might be living in Paris with a beautiful girl-friend."

"We knew what would happen if we sat together at a res-taurant."

"I need wine," Jamie says, reaching for her glass.

"I need food," Gabe says, laughing. "Can we share?"

She reaches for his orange salad and he reaches for her tuna—their forks collide.

"Sorry," they both say at once.

"I'll get this," Gabe says. "I was a waiter for about three months when I was a teenager. I should be able to handle it."

He switches the plates and they both eat in silence.

"Shall I switch them back?" he asks after a while.

"No," Jamie says. "You lose." She's devouring the oranges.

Gabe places his hand on top of hers.

"Why didn't you come find me after the ceremony?" she asks.

"I looked everywhere for you. I thought that maybe you left right away."

"I looked for you, too. And then I got your number from Theo. I called—"

"I know." Gabe looks down at his plate. "I didn't answer. I knew that I needed to show up. I didn't want a quick phone call."

The waiter arrives to clear their dishes. He refills their wine and leaves.

"It's one in the afternoon and I'm a little looped," Jamie whispers.

"I've never felt clearer," Gabe tells her.

"Shh. Let me breathe for a second."

She stands up and looks around, suddenly feeling the need to move.

"Do you mind . . . ?"

"The restrooms are behind the bar," he says, pointing.

"No, I need to put my feet in the sea," she tells him.

"We can walk on the beach after I pay the bill."

"I'll be right back," Jamie says. "Give me a few minutes."

She turns away from the table. There's a rush of noise—kids shouting from the swimming pool on the other side of the restaurant, a man yelling for someone to wait for him, the trill of birds, the swoosh of the waves hitting the sand. She had been so caught up in their intimate world that she hadn't heard any of it, and now it comes pouring in.

She kicks off her shoes and leaves them at the table.

"Can I help you, miss?" the waiter asks, appearing at her side.

"No," she says.

She starts walking toward the sea. She crosses the path, weaving through the small gatherings of people. She walks around the lounge chairs and the open beach towels and the smashed sand turtle. The sun is hot on her shoulders.

A couple of very young children play at the edge of the water. Their mother sits in the sand, the gentle surf running over her legs, then back out to sea.

Jamie walks past the children, lifting her skirt high. She's surprised by how warm the water is—my God, she hasn't been in the ocean once in a week in Bali. She loves the sea.

When the water wraps around her knees, she stops walking. She looks back. Gabe is sitting at the table in the restaurant, watching her. He looks worried. Does he think she'll keep walking and never come back?

She blows him a kiss.

Then she turns around and dives under the incoming wave.

The water embraces her, and in a quick moment she feels her heart expand. She would like to undress—her blouse and skirt wrap around her skin like seaweed. But it's Bali and she's no longer a teenager. She loves the impulse, loves the joy that propels her through the next wave and the next.

When she comes to calm water, she stands. She's shoulder deep, and she slowly spins around. One boy watches her curiously while treading water; she gives him a smile. He dives underwater. When she faces the beach, she sees that Gabe has walked to the water's edge.

"Come in!" she yells.

He's smiling.

"It's perfect," she calls to him.

He kicks off his shoes and tugs off his shirt. He pulls a wallet out of his pocket and tucks it in his shirt and places them on the beach. Then he races into the water and dives into the first wave.

When he emerges, at her side, his face is full of joy. He takes her in his arms. She kisses him and tastes the salt and the sun and the sweetness of his lips.

Jamie is startled to find the house exactly as she remembered it: the French doors, the white sofas, the cool dark-teak floors, the lazy ceiling fans. She's drawn to the bedroom; she needs to know if her memory is right. Yes, the bed is green; the walls are green. Her green cave. Yes, there is nothing but a bed and a small teak bench. The walls are bare. She did not strip it of all décor in her need to remember it simply. It's a simple green room. A room in which to heal.

They have put their wet clothes in Billy's dryer. Jamie has a suitcase of clothes, but Gabe has only his wet jeans. Now they're wearing large lemon-yellow towels wrapped around their bodies.

The decision to visit the house was never spoken. They finished their swim, dropped bills on the table of the restaurant, and sloshed their way down the path to Billy's cottage. Gabe had the key to open the red door. They walked barefoot across the garden, and Jamie had looked out in amazement at the abundance of water lilies in the pond. The goddess statue was surrounded by a field of morning glories. And bougainvillea draped over the thatched roof of the balé.

"Come in," Gabe had said. When she turned around, she saw that he had thrown open all of the French doors so that the small house looked like part of the garden.

Now they stand at the entrance to the bedroom, both trembling a little, neither of them ready to say, Come in.

"I love this cottage," Jamie says.

"You could stay for a few days. Billy—the owner—is in England for a month. I'm allowed to stay here as much as I'd like."

She shakes her head. "How much time do we have till we have to leave for my flight?"

"Two hours," he says.

"I thought I would be too scared to come back to this house," Jamie tells him. "I'm not scared at all."

"You were scared to leave," Gabe says. "This was a good place for us."

She turns toward him and they're kissing again, and this time the saltiness of the sea is gone.

"Come to bed," he says when the kiss ends.

"Yes," she tells him.

She drops the towel to the floor and lies on the green sheet. She's naked, and Gabe sits at the edge of the bed, looking at her.

"You're beautiful," he says.

"Scarred," she says, showing him her arm.

He leans over and traces a line near her elbow.

"The doctors had to reset the bone," Jamie explains.

"I was afraid of that."

"None of it mattered."

Gabe touches the scar on her face, then skims his lips over it. He finds a scar on her shoulder and presses his lips to that, too.

"I don't remember this."

"It's new. A neighborhood cat fell from a tree. She landed

on my shoulder. I had a five-minute nervous breakdown on the spot."

"Did the cat survive?"

"Yes. Larson barely survived. He was with me when it happened."

Jamie rolls onto her side and Gabe runs a line of kisses along her spine.

"You have a beautiful back. If the cat hadn't clawed you, it would be perfect."

"Apparently, perfection is not my thing."

He lies down next to her.

"You do imperfection remarkably well," he says.

"Kiss me," Jamie says.

Their bodies move together. Jamie's hand follows the contours of Gabe's arms, his back, his shoulders. She runs her fingers through his hair. She takes a deep breath and smells a mixture of ocean and sun and spice. She presses him closer to her. She tastes the salt on his skin when she runs her tongue along his chest. She likes the size of him, the weight of him as he rolls on top of her.

"Gabe," she murmurs.

"We begin again," he says, his voice as soft as a promise.

"My flight—"

"Shh."

They take a long time to learn each other's bodies again. They take a long time to taste and smell and play, and when they come together they take a longer time to fold themselves into each other, to press their skin together, to make all the space between them disappear.

They keep their eyes open, they watch each other, they whisper words to each other. Yes. Please. Now.

Later, it's Jamie who kisses Gabe on the forehead and slides out of his embrace. She walks quietly to the bathroom and closes the door behind her.

She showers for a long time, using Billy's lotions and sprays, then dresses in fresh clothes from her suitcase. When she comes out of the bathroom, Gabe is gone.

Her chest tightens. What a fool. He's getting his revenge.

Good, she thinks, though she knows it's a lie. I'll call a taxi. Easier not to say goodbye.

But he walks through the door to the bedroom, dressed in his jeans and shirt, his hair combed back.

"There's a shower in the garden," he says.

She takes him in her arms and holds him, though part of her is already saying goodbye.

"You could stay," he says.

"I can't stay."

They're driving to the airport. Gabe's hand rests on Jamie's thigh, her hand on top of his.

They drive past billboards advertising villas and condos and resorts. The street is lined with stores selling teak furniture and stone Buddhas and ceramic tiles. The sun is low in the sky, and the traffic crawls along. Jamie keeps looking at her watch.

"You have plenty of time," Gabe tells her.

This is ugly Bali, she thinks. The river is clogged with garbage, the streets are ruined by overdevelopment and everyone's need to cash in on it. A man with a wooden leg hobbles at the edge of the highway, begging for money. When their car stops near the man, Jamie can smell him, and it takes too many minutes for them to creep past.

It's hard to believe that within minutes of this mess there's the miracle of Bali's seaside cliffs, exotic jungles, emerald rice paddies.

"My sister, Molly, just had a baby," Gabe says. "She's forty-four years old. Right after the bombing she decided she didn't want to wait any longer for love to walk into her life. So she went to a sperm bank in Boston and chose a guy with good genes, and now she's got this incredible kid. He looks a little like Ethan."

Jamie glances over at Gabe, but his expression is joyful.

"It's a good thing," he says. "I love this baby. I love how happy Molly is."

"It's a little bit like reincarnation," Jamie says. "A chance at a second life. But she gets it without having to die."

"I guess that's the American version. We want a second chance in this life. Not the next one," Gabe says.

"I'm happy for your sister," she tells him.

"I visited for a couple of weeks last month. We rented a place on the Cape. I promised her I'd come back soon." He presses his palm on Jamie's thigh. "I can stop in San Francisco on my way."

Jamie thinks about home. Maybe she'll get a house of her own in Berkeley. She needs a home for the dog she'll find when she gets back. She has Larson to take care of, but soon—though it's impossible to imagine—he'll be gone. She'll need a place where she belongs.

And then a new vision fills her mind. She's standing in the doorway of her new house—a tiny cottage in the hills, which she can almost see now, as if it appears wholly realized in her imagination. Gabe walks toward her down a path that's bordered with wildflowers. There's only room for him on the path, parting the way through a mad profusion of color. Her dog—who looks suspiciously like TukTuk—races toward him, and Gabe bends down to ruffle the dog's fur. When he looks up at her, his face is full of light.

Welcome, she says. She adds one more word. *Home. Welcome home.*

"What are you thinking?" Gabe asks, glancing over at her.

She knows what she's supposed to say: *Come visit. Stay for a while.* But she can't find any words right now. She wants more of him; she wants all of him. And in a few minutes she'll lose him.

"Last year we missed the goodbye part," Jamie says. "This time I'm getting ready."

Finally he pulls in to the airport.

They get out of the car and stand beside it. People rush past them, nervously calling, "Goodbye!" "I'm late!" "Thank you for everything!" A woman stands at the curb, sniffling, while her daughter dashes into the airport. A garbled announcement blares from a loudspeaker. In the distance, thunder rumbles.

"I could leave the car here," Gabe says. "I could walk into the airport and buy a ticket to San Francisco right now."

He runs his hand through his hair and Jamie sees his tattoo, his bird looking to land somewhere.

"How do you feel about dogs?" she asks.

"I love them," he says with a smile.

She leans forward and presses her lips into his.

Acknowledgments

Many people helped me along the way as I researched and wrote *The Paradise Guest House*. First among them is my fabulous editor, Jen Smith. Jen worked tirelessly on this novel, guiding me from draft to draft. She does her fine work with intelligence and grace. I feel incredibly lucky to work with her.

My agent, Sally Wofford-Girand, performs miracles. She sells books, foreign rights, movie rights, and in her spare time offers her insight, comfort, and assurance. Sally, you're my rock.

Sometimes I feel like the happiest writer in publishing—because Ballantine has wrapped me in their arms and made me one of them. Jane Von Mehren, you're an all-star.

Thanks also to Gina Wachtel, Leigh Marchant, Cindy Murray, Susan Corcoran, Hannah Elnan, Maggie Oberrender, and my team of heroes at Ballantine and Random House.

Many people read early drafts of this novel and helped my characters and me find our way in the dark. I couldn't do it without you all. Thanks to Elizabeth Stark, Rosemary Graham, Nina Schuyler, Lalita Tademy, Antonya Nelson, Amanda Eyre Ward, Nick Taylor, Melissa Sarver, Boris Fishman, Kelli Fillingim, and Neal Rothman.

I spent a month in Bali doing research for *The Paradise*

Guest House (best research job a writer could dream up!). I met so many people who opened their doors and let me in. Many, many thanks to my new friends in Bali: Sarah Laight, Alice Dill, Wayan Suka, Carolyn Kenwrick, William Ingram, Andrea and Nyoman Phillips, Patrick and Jenny Scott, Janet De Neefe, Daniel Aaron, Patti Bollen, Rupert Skinner at La Taverna, Howard Klein at the lovely Desa Seni Resort, and the women of the Bali Book Club. Rucina Ballinger, who has lived in Bali for many years, read the novel and corrected inaccuracies about her country and people. Thanks so much for that, Rucina. If there are any mistakes about Bali, the culture, or the history, those are mine. At home, Mindy Goodman, at Mountain Travel Sobek, shared her intimate knowledge of Bali and its people with me.

I'd especially like to thank the Organization YKIP (Yayasan Kemanusiaan Ibu Pertiwi), which was established after the bombings of 2002 and has continued as a living tribute to the 222 dead and 446 injured victims of the two blasts. Sri Damayanti (Ida) accompanied me on visits to many victims and widows of the 2002 terrorist attacks. I feel greatly indebted to those remarkable survivors and widows who shared their stories with me.

I want to thank Lily Hamrick for the title and Vicky Mlyniec for Thursday café writing days.

Thanks to Foundation La Napoule for the gift of five weeks to write. I finished *The Paradise Guest House* while I was in residency at Chateau La Napoule.

Finally, I couldn't write a word without the daily infusion of love and support from Neal, Gillian, and Sophie.